Shadows and Sunshine

A Novel

A. Noelle Smith

To the younger me, who dared to dream, you did it! Now do it again.

To all those who pick up this book, thank you for giving my words a chance.

CONTENT WARNINGS

This novel contains sensitive subjects including themes of death, pregnancy loss, and grief. Please take care to protect your well-being while reading.

"She was all mine and she shone to blush the sun."

— Atticus

Table of Contents

Austin Watts glared at the clock on his nightstand, the white numbers piercing the darkness—four eighteen a.m. Another restless night, haunted by the familiar dream that waved from sweet to torturous. It didn't happen often, but occasionally his mind went there. He swung his legs over the side of bed and walked to the kitchen, the silence of the townhouse heightening the hollow ache inside him. It had been over a year since the accident, but the wound was still raw, a relentless reminder of how quickly things could change.

Pouring a glass of water, Austin tried to shake off the lingering shadows. He found solace in his carefully planned days, losing himself in the projects that filled his schedule. His business, The Honey-Do List Company, had become his lifeline, a way to regain the control that had slipped through his fingers. Each job was a puzzle to solve, each phone call a distraction from the constant hum of pain that lived just beneath his skin.

People and their emotions were messy and intrusive. Exhausting. He watched as friends and acquaintances drifted away, no longer demanding his presence or his pretense. It was a relief, if he were honest, but his isolation was both a shield and a prison.

Things hadn't always been this way, and somewhere deep down, he clung to the hope that they wouldn't always be. For now, he focused on maintaining himself and growing his business as he waited.

Deciding it was close enough to five o'clock to start his day, Austin headed to the bathroom to freshen up. He splashed cold water on his face, the shock of it a welcome jolt to his senses. He stared at his reflection for a moment, noting his tired eyes and overgrown beard. He grabbed his razor and trimmed his facial hair, hoping to bring some semblance of order back to his appearance.

It was time for his five-mile run. A ritual that grounded him and got his day started right. Pulling on his running gear, he stretched, feeling the familiar tension in his muscles before he stepped out into the cool air that would fill his lungs and invigorate him. The first few steps were always the hardest, but soon he found his stride, the steady rhythm of his footsteps finally settling the chaos the dream had caused.

As he neared the end of his run, Austin's thoughts drifted to his crew. Maybe he'd grab breakfast sandwiches for them on the way in this morning. They worked hard, and it was a small gesture, but one he knew they'd appreciate. He rounded the final corner and turned into his driveway, pressed the button on his watch, and slowed to a walk. He made note of his time—thirty-three minutes and thirty-one seconds—before dropping for his daily hundred push-ups.

Routine, after all, was what kept him going. It was the anchor that held him steady and kept him from unraveling. He thought of the day ahead, the projects waiting for him, the clients he would interact with. Each task was a small step forward. He knew there were no quick fixes, no shortcuts to healing. But time heals all wounds and with each day, each run, each job completed, he felt a little more like the man he used to be.

CHAPTER ONE

One year later

Lora-Beth stood in soaking wet socks in front of the dishwasher and admitted defeat. With all the things shutting down around her, she was convinced her house had decided to drive her crazy and her efforts to ward off the insanity had been for naught.

What had she been thinking about, buying this old house? Sure, it was charming, and she'd actually gasped when she set foot in the foyer of the little cottage, but that didn't mean she should have purchased it. But she had and it was a source of great pride for her, nabbing such a find in a city that had all but lost its charm to shiny, new, cookie cutter subdivisions.

Lora-Beth set about making it her own, leaning on her friends or YouTube University to help her out with projects of varying degrees. But the time had come to seek out the services of a professional. Someone she could call on for regular things and not have to feel guilty about being so needy.

She'd searched websites with local postings and hadn't quite found what she was looking for. Nearing the end of her patience, she'd even checked Craig's List before deciding, as much as she loved the house, it wasn't worth becoming any Craig's List Killer's next victim.

When Lydia, her divorced coworker, told her about The Honey-Do List Company she now used for many of the things her somewhat handy ex-husband used to do around the house, Lora-Beth had taken the number and promised to give them a call. Now, the Honey for Hire had arrived, and none too soon. She'd called about the ever-sticking bathroom door and what she suspected were the early signs of mold, but she needed him to address the standing water first.

He'd shut the water off, dried standing water, and moved the dishwasher out of its spot to get a better look at what could be causing the issue. He was pretty sure it was just a hose, but needed to get a better look.

"Can you tell what it is?" she asked. "I rarely use the thing. But I guess it's good I decided to use it today, at least you were already scheduled to come out and I didn't have to call in a panic."

"I'll probably have to run out to the hardware store to get a replacement hose, but this should be an easy fix."

"Except for all the towels I used to soak up the water."

"Except for that."

She was standing with her hip on the counter, folded over, watching him. Rather, she was watching him work. Her first impression of him had been *mmm*. Even in her hurry to get him inside to address the spewing water, she'd taken note of his smooth chocolate skin, broad shoulders, and chiseled jaw. He had one of those serious, expressionless faces that made women want to know what the man was thinking.

"So, there are a few other things I need you to look at. I understand if you don't have time or if I need to schedule another call since this issue came up."

"I'll take a look at what I came for. It's not a problem."

"For now, the guest bathroom is priority number one, but I'd like to get the deck updated, the windows weatherproofed, and wainscoting in the dining room and foyer, and eventually, I'd like to overhaul this entire kitchen."

"That's quite a list," Austin said, getting up from his position behind the dishwasher. She noticed the way his cargo pants sat on his lean legs. "The hose is dry-rotted. It's just age. I'm guessing it's been fifteen years or so since this dishwasher was installed. Like everything, parts wear out."

"Refer back to my previous statement about wanting to update the kitchen."

She couldn't be sure but she thought that was amusement on his handsome face. "The bathroom that's giving you trouble?" he hedged.

"Sure. This way." She led him to the guest room off the hall, telling him first about the door, then showing him the area she suspected showed the early signs of mold on the wall.

"I'll just be a minute." He effectively excused her.

Lora-Beth took the hint and left him to it. "If you need me, just give me a shout," she said and went back to the kitchen to focus on cleaning the floor a bit better.

Austin knew, moments later, it was just mildew. Luckily, she was observant and didn't let this linger. The mildew he noted could be cleaned with a product he'd also pick up on his run to the hardware store. The sticking door had more to do with the house settling over time. He'd try swapping the top and bottom hinges to see if that took care of it. He grabbed his drill, removed the screws from the hinges, swapped them, and screwed the door back into place. After testing and adjusting it a few times, he was satisfied.

He walked out of the bathroom, taking in the space around him. The house, like its owner, radiated charm. He could tell this woman took pride in her home. In the kitchen he found her on her hands and knees, wiping near the dishwasher. He stood and watched for a moment before he cleared his throat.

She jumped and raised a hand to her chest. "Ooh. You are a light stepper."

"Sorry. I didn't mean to startle you. I have good news and better news."

"Do handymen really say things like that?" she mused, plopping the towel she'd been using into the sink.

He didn't respond. "So, I've taken care of the door, you can go test it out. But I am going to have to get something to take care of the mildew in the bathroom."

"Mildew? So it's not mold? Are you sure?"

"Not mold."

"Awesome!"

"So, if you don't mind, I'll leave my stuff in the bathroom and run down to Lowe's to get what I need to address the mildew and see if I can get your dishwasher back up and running."

"Yeah, sure. Of course. And while you're gone, I'll get these towels in the wash."

He glanced over at the pile of towels. "No mop?"

"Yes, I have a mop, but I have many towels and there was *a lot* of water."

"Okay." He took her in as their eyes held for a breath. Gorgeous face, caramel skin, and full lips. "So, I'm going to run. I should be no more than forty-five minutes. If you want to get that list on paper, we can prioritize and come up with a game plan."

"Do you need me to give you any money for what you need from the store?"

"I'll bill you." He did smile then, she was sure of it.

Chapter Two

Austin had been working on projects at Lora-Beth's fixer upper for two and a half months. Since the first call, she'd dialed him several times, adding to his list and prioritizing with him on getting it all done. His workday done, he'd stopped by this evening to drop off the toilet and vanity he'd be installing in the torn apart guest bathroom later in the week.

There were moments in our lives where we knew, as they unfolded, that we weren't making the best choices. We knew this, yet we were helpless to stop ourselves from traveling down the path. Living in the moment. Not focusing on the outcome, we pushed forward and lived for today. Lora-Beth had this feeling as she watched him sip beer from the green bottle she'd handed him.

The way his lips parted to allow the liquid entry before closing his eyes on a swallow made her wonder what those lips would feel like on her skin. He was confident in his stride, moved swiftly and quietly. From the shadows in his eyes, she knew this man held secrets. Still, she was drawn to him. We all had our demons and she was finding it difficult to convince herself that the man standing before her in worn jeans, work boots, and a fitted Henley—rolled up, exposing tattooed forearms—hadn't slayed his.

Austin wasn't convinced. Warning her, in a moment that had grown electric in their closeness, that he wasn't a man she needed and getting involved with him was not what she wanted. And though he'd said the words earnestly, his eyes begged her to challenge them. The way he drank her in every time she opened the door to him. He wanted her to want him. Even if he doubted he was worth the fight.

Austin crossed the room, stepped out, and shut the patio door against the sound of the pouring rain. She watched the way his large body moved to the far end of the deck and took in the muscles in his back, imagining the feel of those muscles beneath her palms as he moved inside her. He was the most ruggedly handsome man she could remember ever seeing. His low cut beard was perfect. The faint scar at his hairline that reached his left eyebrow and nose that had obviously been broken didn't color him unattractive in the slightest. He drained his beer, moved to the other side of the deck, leaned over, and dropped the bottle in the receptacle. Austin lifted his face to the rain.

What was going through his mind? she wondered and wagered several guesses as he had made no attempt at explaining to her why he was warning her off.

Austin was thinking with something other than his brain. His heart raced and he felt warmth deep in his belly. He was loath to allow himself what he was feeling. His wasn't a normal life and he'd been fine with that, until recently. Being in Lora-Beth's presence made him wish things were different. She made him think things he shouldn't be thinking and feel things he'd forgotten what they felt like to feel. Austin had grown accustomed to not feeling like himself, so much that he'd forgotten what it felt like to just be him. Lora-Beth made him think about himself beyond the grief, the sorrow, and reminded him that he was a whole person.

Lora-Beth had come into his life in the most innocent of ways. She was a sultry voice on the other end of a service call that had been both soothing and exhilarating to his ears. He'd imagined the face behind the voice. Three minutes on the phone and he was picturing what her lips looked like forming the words she spoke. He shook his head, trying to clear the thoughts. He was torturing himself, making himself crazy. She had no pull on him, he'd simply been on pause too long. That was all that was happening. His body was reacting to having a woman's body present, not specifically to Lora-Beth.

Honey-Do List Company was doing well, and he took his fair share of phone calls, but he'd never taken a moment to think about the owner of the voice coming through the line before that day. He remembered looking forward to seeing the face of the woman who possessed the ability to speak to him on a level beyond the words coming out of her mouth. Something in him recognized something in her. It felt like an answer, only he wasn't sure of the question or who had asked it. It unsettled him.

Then he met her face to face. She'd opened the door, looked him in the eyes, and extended her hand. Her subtle citrus scent seeped into his nostrils and grabbed him. Her warm brown eyes, her smell, her touch, she'd overwhelmed him, and then she'd spoken. She greeted him in a way that suggested they weren't strangers, but in fact, familiar with each other.

"Hi, Austin! Perfect timing. Come in, please." She waved him in. "Let's start here with the dishwasher. I know it wasn't on the list but, as you will soon see, it decided that the water should go on the floor, rather than take its regular route down the drain."

Not wanting to be rude, he had replied warmly in return, inwardly amused. Her hair was wild and free, a crown atop her perfectly round face. She was flushed and her genuine, welcoming smile made him want to embrace her. She was beautiful and God help him, he wanted to reach out and touch her smooth, flustered face.

Austin shook off those thoughts of months ago and brought himself back to the present. He turned to head back inside. Through the glass, he saw Lora-Beth standing, leaning against the island, a towel draped over her shoulder and a curious expression on her face. She came to him and started soaking up the water from his head and shoulders. "Do you want to talk about what's on your mind?"

"Thanks for the towel. It's getting late. I better go."

Lora-Beth draped the towel over his shoulders and held onto the ends, pulling him into her space. "What is it, Austin? You can talk to me."

Instinctually, his hands rose to her waist and he lowered his head to inhale her scent before setting her away. Seriously, how was he supposed to clear his head with her only inches away as her scent filled his nostrils? He took a step back to put a bit more distance between them. "I'll be back with Trevor on Saturday to work on the bathroom."

She stepped back into his space, wrapping her arms around him this time and squeezing. He let himself enjoy the feeling of her embrace. When she leaned her head to rest on his chest, he closed his arms around her, closed his eyes, and buried his face in her hair. Wanting what he shouldn't. Enjoying what he had no right to enjoy.

"Saturday," he said when he let her go. Before she could protest, he was at the front door, tapping the bolt twice as a reminder for her to lock it behind him.

CHAPTER THREE

"Good morning, ma'am. I believe you're expecting us, The Honey-Do List Company. We've met, actually. I worked with Austin on removing your popcorn ceilings a few weeks ago and patching your roof a few weeks before that. I'm Trevor, this is Brock." The tall, lanky man she remembered reintroduced himself and his co-worker, who greeted Lora-Beth with a smile and nod.

Trevor and Brock had shown up at her door to work on her bathroom. She sized up the two men standing at her door, ready to get to work.

"Yes, but where's Austin?"

"Not sure, ma'am. When I pulled my list, you were my only call for today," Trevor answered.

The other, younger man, rocked foot to foot, then moved to secure his tool belt around his waist rather than holding it in his hands. "I believe your supplies are onsite. If it's okay, I can go on in and get started on the lights while Trev tries to get Austin on the line."

"Sure. Yeah. Of course. Come in. I'll show you where it is."

"Obliged."

Lora-Beth found Austin's number in her list of contacts and pressed the phone icon. After the two rings, his outgoing message started. He'd rejected her call. Lora-Beth held her phone in her hands and tapped anxiously at the keys.

LB: Austin, your guys are here. Where are you?

She held her phone in her hand and paced the length of her kitchen slowly, waiting. When she got no response, she kept herself busy, choosing now to rearrange the furniture and decor in her bedroom. The seasons were changing and she wanted a view of the window, rather than having her bed in front of it, so she could see the changing leaves. Two and a half hours later, she pulled her silent phone from the back pocket of her jeans and wrote another message to him.

LB: I hope you're okay.

She decided to go check on the guys, planning to offer them a glass of the iced tea with fresh lemons she made fresh this morning with Austin in mind. They'd been working diligently and she silently prayed it was going well.

Calling out, "Is it safe?" Lora-Beth stuck her head into the room and took in the progress. The new sub-floor was down, the wainscoting was up, and Brock was setting nails into the top rails as Trevor, speaking into his earpiece, laid the black and white hexagon tiles she and Austin had picked out last week at a discount tile yard on the outskirts of town. She'd wanted subway tiles, but Austin convinced her these would work perfectly in the space. So far, it looked like he was right.

"I came to see if you guys wanted to take a break, have a glass of tea or a bottle of water?" she asked when Trevor ended the call. They both walked toward her, accepting her offer of a break and a cold beverage.

"Was that Austin?" she asked, failing at her attempt at nonchalance.

"Third time. Boss man is on one this morning," Trevor said.

"He's called you three times?" She poured them each a glass and one for herself.

"Yep. Him twice. Me, once so far," Brock chimed in. "Guessing I'm up next. So I'm going to drink fast and get back to work. I don't want him to catch me on a break and lose his shit."

"I'm sure he'll understand you got thirsty."

Brock and Trevor shared a look. "Don't fuck this up," they said in unison and shared a laugh at their absent boss's expense.

"Though I wouldn't have put it quite that way, I would like it if you didn't screw it up either."

"Don't worry, ma'am, we won't."

"Hey, Trevor. Cool it with the ma'am, will ya? It's Lora-Beth."

"Yes, ma—. Tough habit to break, Lora-Beth. I'll do my best."

"Did your boss happen to mention where he's at this morning?"

"No, he didn't. But you don't have to worry Lora-Beth, you're in good hands. We wouldn't be here if he didn't think we could handle the job."

"Oh gosh no, Brock. I'm not worried about you guys or your work. I was just curious. This is the first project Austin hasn't worked on himself."

The guys exchanged another look.

"What's that look?"

Brock's boyish face curved into a knowing smile. "It's the first of your projects he hasn't worked himself, but we work on our own all the time."

"Well, if we're going to finish this up by four, we better get back at it."

"By four?"

"So you can make your five o'clock meeting," Trevor went on.

Lora-Beth tilted her head to the right and her eyes to the left, trying to find the meeting he was referencing in her memory. Drawing a blank, she picked up her phone as she asked, "My five o'clock meeting?"

Brock mimicked Austin's instructions from earlier.

"Be outta there by four, she has a five o'clock photography class that she doesn't want to miss."

"Right." She didn't find anything on her phone because she'd attended the last class in the series a week ago, but she thought it was sweet that Austin had thought of it.

"If we run into any delays, I'll let you know, but we should have plenty of time to set the floor. Austin will get with you on when we can come finish it. Best to let the floor set for a day or two before grouting."

"Yes, I remember him saying so."

Lora-Beth couldn't help but feel she'd been offered a conciliatory gesture of reassurance. It was unnecessary, but she appreciated it.

صـ

Austin walked into the room, set the flowers on the bedside table, and leaned over to kiss her forehead.

"Hi, Janet. It's me. I brought you some fresh flowers. Lilies this time." He moved to the sink, discarded last week's bouquet, and washed out the vase before placing the new flowers inside and setting it in the windowsill.

He moved to the bed and started his usual routine when he visited her. He ran his fingers through her hair, applying gentle, steady pressure to her scalp. "I brought you something else, but you're going to have to wait until I'm done before I tell you what it is. I know how much you love surprises." Austin took his time rubbing her neck and shoulders and down each of her arms, massaging her skin with oil.

"Your skin looks good. I can tell they're using the cream I brought you. I wasn't sure if they would." Finding her hands cold as he massaged them, he reached into the drawer and pulled out the cotton gloves he'd purchased some time ago for this very reason.

"Things are going well with the business. I have more clients than the team can handle and I'm thinking about bringing on one or two more guys soon. It keeps me busy and brings in good money."

Continuing his massage, he filled her in on his week, the highs, the lows, and things in between. When he finished her massage, he began his routine of physical therapy movements, working her arms and joints. "Your show is back this week. I've been watching it for you for so long, I wonder if deep down I'm interested in the staff at Grey Sloan Memorial Hospital." A chuckle rose deep from his throat. "Yeah, so, you're not going to like this, but…" He paused, thinking if he should give her the news about Alex's sudden departure, and decided better of it.

"You know what, I don't want to ruin it for you. You'll watch it soon. We'll have a marathon and catch up on all the seasons you've missed." His phone rang. "I bet this is Trevor. Give me a minute." He placed her foot down and reached into his pocket. Seeing that it was Lora-Beth calling, he pressed reject, silenced the ringer, and slipped the phone back in his pocket.

He closed his eyes and took a deep breath before returning to the task at hand. "What was I saying?"

"Austin."

He was surprised by the voice. He hadn't noticed Janet's mother standing in the doorway. "Joyce."

"It's good to see you." She moved closer and he rose to his full height to greet her with a hug. The two were comfortable and had grown to think of each other as family.

Joyce leaned down, took her daughter's hand, and brought it to her lips. "Hey, baby." She looked over her daughter and smiled. "I love what you've done with her hair," she joked, then went on. "It's good to see you, Austin. How are you? You're not usually here on Saturdays. Is everything okay?" Joyce moved to sit in the chair closest to the bed and Austin continued moving Janet's limbs.

"Yes, everything is good. And with you?"

"As good as can be expected, considering."

He nodded, agreeing with a sad smile. They fell into an awkward silence as she watched him take care of her daughter. Finishing up, he broke the silence. Feeling some kind of way under her silent scrutiny, he excused himself, saying, "I'm going to go check on my guys and give you some time alone with her."

"Oh Austin, you don't need to leave on my account. Please, stay."

"I'm just going to step out and check on work. I'm not going far."

Austin stepped into the hall, pulled his phone from his pocket, and read his text messages. Among them, was one from *her* and one from Trevor saying she had been expecting Austin and wasn't pleased to see him and Brock instead. Austin put the phone to his ear and dialed Trevor's cell, needing to check on the job they'd been assigned.

Not entirely satisfied, he dialed Brock when his call with Trevor ended. He knew the guys were capable, but this job was important and he needed to be sure they were on the same page.

When he reached the room, he heard Joyce's voice speaking animatedly. His eyes found her and he asked, "What are you doing?"

"I'm reading her this book. It was just sitting here. I hope that's okay." He moved quickly and took the book from her hands, miffed she'd been so presumptuous. That had been a surprise for Janet. An early release from one of her favorite authors, third in the series and prequel to a new journey. It'd been a year since the release of number two.

His tone was rough when he said, "That's personal." It was something they shared. Janet would often read scenes or chapters from her books to him. He didn't care about the subject matter; she enjoyed it and he indulged her because he loved her. Now, he read to her, hoping that even in her state she could hear and appreciate the stories being read in his voice.

"I'm sorry. I didn't mean to impose."

Austin leaned against the wall, his eyes trained on Janet's body in the bed. Her mother had sorted her hair while he'd stepped away and it was now in two braids, falling on either side of her neck. They stood in an uncomfortable silence, each lost in their thoughts about the woman in the bed. Their positions seemed to always oppose each other's this past year; where they'd once agreed and had contended with Janet's father.

"Austin."

A chill ran down his spine and his stomach lurched. Silently, he moved his eyes to hers, knowing what was coming. It was written all over her face. He'd seen it the moment he looked at her.

"It's time." Austin ran his hand over the lower portion of his face and sighed. No. It wasn't *time*. Who was she to say when it was time? Joyce went on, "We spoke with her doctors this week and they agreed. Her dad and I agree. We're going to allow a natural death."

"They don't always get it right," he said, speaking of the doctors who'd placed themselves on a board which allowed them to tell the families of patients when they should *let* their loved ones go. A bunch of God complexes walking around making these kinds of decisions.

"I know how she felt. She didn't want this."

"No one wanted this."

"You know what I mean, Austin. These weren't her wishes."

"So you're just going to give up on your daughter? Just like that? Some doctors want to play God and think just because they went to medical school they get to decide whether someone lives or dies? And when?" he snapped.

She flinched, but steeled herself. It broke her heart to hear him say these words, but she knew he didn't mean them.

"I know I'm not her husband. I know ultimately it's your call. And I know what the doctors have said. Still, none of that tells me it's time. You used to feel the same." Austin sat on the chair next to Joyce and buried his face in his hands. "Why wasn't I part of that conversation?"

Joyce dabbed at the corner of her eyes, wanting to catch the tears before they spilled. "I know how hard it is. You're not the only one who lost them." Tears stung his eyes as his temperature rose. He didn't need this shit today. Why had he come today instead of his usual Sunday? He knew why. He knew what he was avoiding.

"Do you think you'll ever get there, Austin? Do you think you'll ever be able to let her go?"

"I'm doing just fine."

"You can't live this way forever. You're allowed to move on. It's been nearly three years."

He linked his fingers and rested them on his forehead with a deep sigh. "Two years, ten months, three weeks, and five days. I know exactly how long it's been." He also knew why she was bringing it up. Three years. They said three years would be the timeframe. If she'd shown no signs of improvement in three years…

"I'm glad I ran into you. We were planning to reach out to you soon. It's been a tough decision, and we knew it would be, but we agreed. Her father and I have decid—"

Austin stood abruptly, cutting her off. "Sorry, I can't do this." He grabbed the book, leaned down quickly and kissed Janet's forehead, then walked out of the room, leaving a weeping Joyce calling out to him behind.

Austin's stomach churned and his heart raced in his chest. He hadn't agreed to anything. Sure, they'd talked with him and kept him in the loop, but her parents had made decisions for their daughter that he had no right to make. He banged on the steering wheel and screamed through his pain. "Fuck. Fuck. Fuuuck!"

After taking a few minutes to compose himself, he pulled out his phone, noticed the four missed calls from numbers he didn't recognize, and read the text from Lora-Beth hoping he was okay. He wasn't. He was definitely not okay.

Austin called Trevor who answered the call laughing. "Hello."

"Are you working or goofing off?"

"Lighten up, man, we're working."

"Do you have it under control or not?"

"Everything is going smoothly. I'm laying tile right now. We're on track. Relax, man."

"I need you to take your work seriously. Don't fuck this job up, Trev."

Austin heard her voice in the background. Speaking quickly to drown out the sound, he barked a few words at Trevor and hung up. It was just like her to interrupt their work being friendly and chatty.

Chapter Four

Lora-Beth looked up from her phone and listened closely. It sounded like someone was outside her back door. Quietly, and on her tiptoes, she moved in that direction. Noticing it was Austin, she ripped the door open. It was Sunday and he'd pulled a disappearing act. She hadn't heard from him since Thursday.

"What are you doing here?" she snapped.

Austin didn't look at her. He positioned his ladder against the house and started to climb. "Gutters."

She stared at him in shock. Gutters? Was he serious? Gutters were not on the list.

"These need to be cleared before the leaves start falling and cause problems."

She appreciated that. He really was thoughtful. Still she said, "Where were you yesterday?"

"Had shit to do." As soon as the words were out of his mouth, he regretted them. He busied himself clearing leaves and debris from the section of gutters in his reach.

She crossed her arms over her chest. "Right."

"Did the guys not do a good job?"

She narrowed her eyes. He knew they'd done a good job. She wasn't going to indulge his broodiness today. "I'm going inside."

"If it's alright, when I'm done here, I'll let myself in and take a look. Make sure everything is good."

"Whatever." He was not to be believed. Lora-Beth shook her head and before he could say anything else, she turned and walked into the house in a huff. Inside, she dialed her best friend, hoping she was free.

Austin swept the debris from the gutters and thought about adding gutter guards. She would benefit from them. Yesterday had been a particularly difficult day, and for some reason today, he felt like he needed to be working. Like he needed to be *here*. It wasn't that he was living in denial, it was that he'd decided he was okay to live his life like this until… until what? Until Janet woke up, until she took her last breath, until he took his? There was no answer to that, and as far as he was concerned, he hadn't needed one. He worked, worked out, kept up with sports and current events, and visited Janet twice a week. She was in a good facility and the medical bills were paid. What was so wrong with that?

Sure, there had been times when he'd drank too much, hadn't eaten or rested enough, but that was all in the past. That was when he was rife with grief and going through the stages in cyclical fashion. Though someone may look at him and think he was in denial, balancing on the edge of depression, he wasn't. He had balance. He'd accepted what happened and in no way was he unaware of Janet's eventual fate. Eventual. But he could be hit by a bus tomorrow, so there was more proof that no one could predict or should dictate these things.

Sure, some nights he still drank too much, but he never got behind the wheel of a car when he did. And yes, he was predictable, but that was how it went for adults, wasn't it? Adulthood was predictable. And he was fine. He was healthy, his business was doing well, and he had healthy-*ish* friendships.

He sighed. Who was he kidding? He was a man being pulled in two directions, constantly. Because of where Janet was, he didn't allow himself happiness anywhere else. He'd been suspended in time, merely existing, until a few months ago.

"Seriously?" Toni answered in a huff.

"What's wrong with you?"

"Oh, hi, LB. I thought you were Marcus. He's on my nerves. He's called three times already. I may as well have gone to the store myself."

Lora-Beth huffed. "It's going around. Would you believe who's outside my back door right now? After not showing up yesterday, he shows up today to work on my gutters? Argh."

"What am I missing?" Toni asked.

"Did you not hear me? He's outside working on my gutters. Now." She moved her laundry from the washer to the dryer with more force than necessary.

"Girl, you're going to have to fill me in. You're hot for Handyman and he's at your house. What's the problem?"

"I never said I was hot for him."

Toni sighed. "Why are you irked?"

Lora-Beth set the dryer, loaded the washer with darks, and started the cycle before answering the question. "I don't know. I just am."

"What did he say?"

"He said he 'had shit to do'." She mocked his voice for emphasis.

"Well, maybe the man had shit to do yesterday, LB. He's there now, on a Sunday. Doing something you didn't ask him to do. Cut him some slack."

"Why should I cut him slack?"

"You don't get to be pissy because your handyman sent someone from his team to do the work on your house. You hired him to get the work done. The work got done. He held up his end of the bargain. The businessman didn't do anything wrong."

She knew Toni was right, but still, it wasn't what he'd said. "He said *he* would see me on Saturday. He didn't say his men would be here."

"So, something came up."

"But he could've called, replied to my messages, something. He wasn't too busy to call the guys working here repeatedly, but my calls went unanswered."

"Okay. And?"

Lora-Beth groaned in frustration. Why wasn't Toni getting it?

She heard him clear his throat and turned to find Austin standing in the kitchen, an amused look on his face.

"I'll call you back." She hung up, not waiting for a response.

"About yesterday…" he started.

"You don't owe me an explanation."

"I had to be somewhere and my day was shot to shit when I left. I'd intended to be here before they finished for the day, but I couldn't make it. You're right. I could have texted to let you know. It was inconsiderate. I apologize."

Lora-Beth walked closer and stopped a foot away from where he leaned on the kitchen island, challenging him. "What came up?"

"I can't talk about it now." He held her gaze.

"Can't or won't?" she pressed.

Austin took in the way her nose flared at his silence. "Yes to both," he said, hoping she'd accept that he wasn't going to go into detail.

Lora-Beth searched his face and found no clue as to how he was feeling. "Tell me something."

"I just told you something."

"Can you at least tell me if you're okay?"

Austin looked down at his boots and took a deep breath before responding with a lie. "I'm okay."

At the look on his face when he finally met her eyes, Lora-Beth asked, "Why don't I believe you?" She moved closer and wrapped him in her arms. Austin gripped her tightly and tried to control his roiling emotions. "I can be a listening ear if that's what you need."

He ran his hand up and down her back as if it were she who needed comforting.

"Talk to me. What's going on?" she coaxed.

How could he share what he was dealing with? What would it even sound like coming from his lips? He took one last whiff of her, released his breath, and pulled away. "It's not your problem. I'm dealing with it. I shouldn't be here."

Austin wondered why he had come. Truth be told, he hadn't fully realized this was where he was heading when he'd gotten in the truck. He'd felt like driving and had done so for a while, then he looked up and registered where he was as he pulled into her driveway. As if by its own accord, his truck had brought him here, to her.

Lora-Beth grabbed his hand and led him to the living room. "Okay. You don't have to talk about it if you don't want to. But, just take a minute. I can see that you need something right now and I don't need to know your secrets for me to want to be here for you. If you need silence, okay, but your eyes tell me you don't want to be left alone so I'm going to sit here with you."

He let himself be led, trying not to notice the way her hand felt in his. She pulled him down to sit with her on the couch, where they sat in silence for a moment. Close enough for their thighs to touch.

"Can I show you the pictures I decided to frame for the bathroom? You've seen some of them, but I played with some filters and settings, and thanks to my phone, I've found something I love."

"Let's see."

Lora-Beth pulled out her phone and opened the folder of photos titled "Bathroom". She leaned closer and held the screen in his direction. Out of reflex, Austin raised his hand over the back of the couch and she leaned her back to his side. He looked at the shots, not really hearing her chatter that accompanied each new image she flipped to. His nostrils were filled with the soft citrus scent of her hair.

She put her phone aside, fitted herself closer into the crook of his arm, and shimmied until she found a comfortable spot. Tucking one foot under her butt, Lora-Beth talked as if she wasn't bothered that she was having a conversation with herself. The woman could talk for hours.

She was excited about her house, her projects, and life. He envied her in that way.

"Austin?"

"Yeah?"

"You're so quiet I thought maybe you'd fallen asleep."

"No. I'm listening. The sound of your voice, it's… familiar. I've never heard anything so fitting. I like it."

"My voice fits me? What does that mean?"

Austin tried to get the words right in his head before attempting to explain what he meant. After a moment, he spoke. "When I heard your voice the first time, I didn't just hear it. I felt it. I'm going to make a mess of explaining this, but it seemed as if something in me recognized the sound of it, as if it had always been there in the background, waiting to be heard. I tried to picture what you looked like. And when you opened the door that first day, in your wet socks, flushed and overwhelmed, talking to me like we'd known each other for years, it happened again, and I thought it was perfect. Your face, your personality, they're a perfect match to your voice."

Lora-Beth turned to see his face. On it, she found a sad smile. She gave him one in return. She got what he meant and thought he'd done a good job explaining.

"I get so much pleasure from being in your presence, simply being in the vicinity of someone with so much genuine joy in them." He shook his head. "I haven't had joy in my life in a long time. I want to talk to you freely, the way you talk to me, but the shit I'm dealing with isn't something you just talk about. It's impossibly hard. It's terrible and a constant reminder of how unfair life can be." He blew out a breath. "My life sucks. Trust me when I say you don't want to be a part of it."

"Austin, please." He brought her hand to his lips and kissed the fingertips.

"I don't want to give you that, what I carry around with me. You think you want to know, but you don't."

"You don't have to keep it bottled up."

"I've been selfish, taking what I need from you, giving you nothing in return."

"That's not true. You're a tremendous help to me."

She was being kind. He appreciated it, but he knew better. "You're sweet, but that's not what I meant."

Lora-Beth rested her head on his shoulder. "I know."

Austin rested his head on hers and sighed, absently playing with her fingers. "You're not crazy and I'm not oblivious. I feel the pull between us, but I can't give you what you need. I can't be what you need," he admitted.

"What do you think I need?"

"Someone who's able to be open and free, and give all of themselves, like you do. I can't do that."

"Why can't you? Whatever it is, you can tell me. It may help to get it off your chest."

"It won't. It'll change things, and the selfish bastard in me wants to keep this the way it is."

"Austin, what if I promise to listen and not judge? Whatever it is, tell me, and I won't let it change anything. Please, tell me what's eating at you."

He shook his head and didn't speak, trying to find a way to say what needed to be said. Once the words left his mouth, things would irrevocably change, and he didn't want that. He couldn't handle the thought of losing another person right now.

She took the hand closest to her and held it in both of hers. "Just say it. Whatever it is."

"I have a girlfriend. Had a girlfriend. Have. Jesus." He stumbled over the words. When her eyes bulged in shock and she pulled away, he held a finger in the air, asking her to give him a minute to finish his thought. "She has been in a coma for a while. Almost three years."

Tears sprang to Lora-Beth's eyes and she placed her hand over her heart. It ached for him, for what he must be going through.

"That's where I was yesterday. That's why I wasn't here when I said I would be." He pulled her back into the crook of his arm, wanting to speak without looking at her or having her look at him as he tried to get the words out. "It was a car accident. She was pregnant with our child when it happened."

"Oh, Austin." She raised her head to face him, but he pulled her close again, knowing he wouldn't get through the rest of it otherwise. He could feel the rapid beat of his heart in his chest.

"She was five months along. Our daughter didn't make it. Janet hasn't regained consciousness."

Lora-Beth's heart was breaking. She didn't know what to say, so she cried silent tears and listened.

"I was out of town for work at the time. We don't know exactly what happened, but from what the police could tell, there were no other cars involved. She was on her way home from her parents' house out in the country. The car skidded off the road somehow and hit a tree. It was late. Not sure how long it was before someone found her."

She sniveled and buried her wet face in his Henley. Austin held her to him and took what little comfort he could in her embrace. He cleared his throat and continued, "Her mother was there yesterday, and reminded me that…" He couldn't finish. He buried his face in her hair and breathed through his tears.

"It's okay. You don't have to say anything more. I'm sorry I made you talk about this. I'm sorry, so sorry, Austin."

After a moment, he cleared his throat, needing to say the words more for his benefit than hers. "Her parents, they're taking her off life support soon."

There were no words. Lora-Beth didn't try to stop the tears. She couldn't find any words to say after what Austin had shared. His body shook with his pain. Helpless to do anything else, she held him to her, and together, they cried.

Chapter Five

The hardest thing for Lora-Beth to do now was ignore her growing feelings for Austin. She could do that. She could put those feelings aside and be the support he needed. They hadn't crossed any lines. The genie wasn't out of the bottle so she didn't have to worry about getting it back in.

Lora-Beth called her best friend as she walked around the park on her lunch break.

Without a hello, Toni started talking as if they were mid-conversation. "So, what happened? I called you back twice yesterday."

By silent agreement, she and Austin hadn't said anything more about it during the evening. He'd stuck around and the two found comfort in the silence. It was now midday on Monday and Lora-Beth wanted to discuss it with Toni, but couldn't betray Austin's trust. She replied, "We talked. He had somewhere he had to be. That's all."

"So exactly what I said?"

"Yes, exactly."

"And you talked about it and now he's back on your good side? Still hot for handyman?"

"Seriously Toni, will you stop saying that? He's dealing with some heavy stuff and needs a friend right now, not someone falling over themselves at the sight of him."

"I was just messing around. Who peed in your Cheerios?"

"Well, it's not a laughing matter."

"LB, come on." When she got no response, Toni went on. "Lora-Beth. Hey, I'm sorry, okay. I didn't mean anything by it."

"I'm sorry. I don't mean to snap at you. He's going through a hard time. I guess I hadn't realized how much it was bothering me."

"Okay, girl. What is going on with him?"

"It's not my story to tell."

"Is he in danger? Is he sick? Is he a criminal? Is he in witness protection? Do I need to be worried about you?"

"No. It's nothing like that. My safety is in no way threatened."

"Then what is it? You can talk to me in confidence. You know that."

"Him confiding in me was very difficult. He's held onto this for a long time on his own. I can't betray his trust, not even to you. I hope you understand."

"I see," Toni acknowledged, though she didn't like it.

"What about you?" Lora-Beth asked, changing the subject. "Which of your sides is Marcus on today?"

"Don't get me started," Toni said and started her account of this episode of "Girl, Marcus Tried It." For all her complaining, she wouldn't trade her husband for anything in this world. She loved him, but she wouldn't be Toni if she didn't make mountains out of molehills.

Lora-Beth hung up with Toni and before crossing the street and heading back up the block, she sent a message to Austin telling him she hoped he managed to get some rest and was having a good day. Half an hour passed and she was back at her desk preparing for her next appointment by the time his reply came.

Austin: If it's okay, I'll be by at 6:30 to grout the tiles in the bathroom.

LB: You? Or one of the guys?

Austin: I'll be there.

Pork chops, smothered in gravy. Mashed potatoes and Brussels sprouts because something green was a must. That was the dinner she prepared while Austin worked in the bathroom. She hadn't asked him if he wanted dinner, she just assumed he would appreciate a home cooked meal. She hoped he would accept her offer when he was done. She leaned in the door, watching him work, thinking of something to say.

"I can feel you watching me."

"No you can't. You can see me."

His attention still on his work, he told her, "I knew you were there before I saw you. I looked because it's weird for you to be this quiet."

"I made dinner."

"Smells good."

"I hope you'll have some. There's plenty." When he didn't give a reply, she went on. "You were right about the tile. This looks really good. I sent the photos today, they should be ready for pickup on Friday. I went with canvas prints. Going to do the picture rail I showed you the other day. And once you get the vanity and mirror installed, we'll be done. I'm so excited!" As she talked, she sat on the floor just outside the door and leaned against the doorjamb.

"Done with this room."

She smiled. "Yes, done with this room." They were nearing the end of her list of projects for now. But she didn't think it was necessary to point that out. Sure, there were other, non-pressing things she wanted to do to the house, but that would come with time. She was nearing the end of her renovation budget and needed to be mindful of that. "I've decided to paint the guest room pink. Think I'll go down to the hardware store and look at paint samples this week. I have a shade in mind, but I need to swatch a few to see what works best."

"I can go any evening but Wednesday."

"Oh, no. I didn't mean to add to your list. I was just talking, I guess."

He looked at her over his shoulder. "I know." He dipped his sponge in the bucket of water and continued his work, wiping at the section of tiles he'd just grouted.

"This is going by fast," she said, noting his progress in the room. He was two-thirds of the way done.

"Yeah. Doesn't take very long. Has to cure before sealing though. I'll be back to do that on Thursday. If you can wait, it may be a good time to check out those paint samples."

"Thursday evening I have—"

"Pilates at six," Austin finished for her.

"Yeah."

"Stores are open until ten."

"Right. Yeah. That's plenty of time."

From his knees on the tile, he faced her and waited. Austin looked at her with no emotion.

"What? Why are you looking at me that way?"

He raised an eyebrow. "I'm working my way out the door." She looked at him, not understanding what he meant. "You're sitting in the doorway."

She stood in a hurry, flustered. "Oh. Sorry. I need to go check on the pork chops anyway."

"Pork chops? You're kidding me?"

"Not kidding. Smothered pork chops, actually."

"I hope it tastes half as good as it smells."

"I hope so too." Satisfied, Lora-Beth turned on her heels and checked on her dinner, leaving Austin to his work.

An hour later he was done with the grouting and cleanup and they'd finished dinner. "I haven't had someone cook for me in a long time. Don't know that I've had smothered pork chops since before I left home sixteen years ago." Austin's mind drifted as his line of thought trailed off. They were sitting on the couch in her living room, watching a drama-filled family show. He didn't care about the show, but he felt comfortable in the moment, so he went with it. "Thank you." He wasn't just thanking her for the dinner, which he'd found delicious and had told her as much. He was thanking her for everything.

"You're welcome. I'm happy you enjoyed it. And thank you for eating the Brussels sprouts even though I could tell you hated them."

He smirked. "I didn't hate them. They've just never been my favorite. My mother used to make them once a week. The meal reminded me so much of dinners growing up. You can say I ate them because I was trained to."

Lora-Beth felt a surge of pride in his words and didn't know how to respond, so she simply smiled and tried not to think too hard about it. She'd always heard the way to a man's heart was through his stomach. Not that she was trying to reach Austin's heart.

"Why does that embarrass you?"

"I'm not. It doesn't."

He ran the back of his fingers over her cheek and watched her close her eyes at his touch. "You're flushed. And your nose crinkles when you close your eyes and give that unsure, *I don't know what to say* smile."

"I, uh—" She looked in his eyes and found a warm and sweet sincerity in them. He paid attention to the intricacies of her face. He looked her in the eyes. She visualized him pressing his lips to hers.

Austin tipped his chin forward, breaking the moment. "Show's back."

Lora-Beth exhaled and turned her attention to the television, grateful for the distraction and frustrated that he tied her up in knots.

At the next commercial break he said, "It's getting late. I better get going. Early day tomorrow."

She stood and reached her hands out to pull him up. He took her hands and rose to his full height, hovering over her, in her personal space. "I'll walk you out. Do you want me to wrap up the leftovers for you? I don't mind."

He needed to get out of here. He wanted to kiss her. He'd wanted to kiss her for weeks and this sweetness she gave him constantly wasn't helping. He wanted to shrink her, tuck her into his pocket, and take her with him everywhere.

"You don't have to do that. I appreciate it, but enjoying the dinner you made was more than enough. Thank you." He released her, walked quickly toward the door, and stepped into his boots.

"It's no problem, really," she said, walking to the kitchen.

"Lora-Beth." She stilled at the sound of her name. It was a whisper. A plea. She went to him and as soon as she was within reach, he pulled her into his arms. He was overwhelmed. Conflicted. She made him feel cherished by simply being herself. She was pure and giving and he was selfish for indulging in her. He felt happy in her space, and at the same time, guilty for feeling happy in another woman's presence.

Austin pulled away, stepped to the open door, tapped the bolt twice, and left without another word.

CHAPTER SIX

Lora-Beth sat at her desk glaring at her phone. Two days of radio silence. He'd left in a rush, and even if she'd come out the next morning to see that he'd thought to pull her garbage can out to the curb before leaving, that was the last she'd seen or heard from him. Principal Brand Strategist by day. Girl Who Waits for the Guy to Call by night. That was what she was turning into. It wasn't even like he said he'd call or that he should have.

She turned in her desk chair and stared out at the blue, cloudless sky. She was being ridiculous and she knew it. But she was worried about him. She cared. She was curious and wondered about his days, his nights, if he was eating, if he was sleeping. Nearly three years he'd lived this way. Closed off. Shut down. Denying himself pieces of his life he'd meant to be living with her. She searched the depth of her imagination and couldn't bring forth what that must feel like. If she felt this way, Lora-Beth could not fathom the difficulty he must be having trying to reconcile all that was going on in Austin's world.

Her phone hummed in her lap, pulling her from her thoughts. A text from Toni, confirming their happy hour plans at Kalo for Tapas and 'Tinis. After confirming their plans, she got back to work. She had to be across town for a client prep meeting in an hour and a half. She didn't have time for daydreaming.

ص

"Alright LB, let's get into it. And I'm not buying the 'I can't talk about it' crap you've been giving me. What's up with Mr. Fix-It?"

Lora-Beth sipped her salted caramel apple martini. She wished she could spill. Just mind dump on her best friend and get it all out of her head; to have someone to share it with. But, of course, she wouldn't do that. "Can you call him Austin?"

Toni waved her hand dismissively. "No can do, girlie. Until I meet him, and you introduce him to me as Austin, he's your hot handyman and I don't need to concern myself with his name."

Lora-Beth laughed. "Why are you like this?"

"You love me."

She was right. Lora-Beth loved her friend and cherished their relationship. The two could gab for days about everything and nothing. "We're fixing up my house and getting to know each other," she started, by way of explanation. "He has a lot going on and I'm trying to be there for him," she went on.

"So, no chemistry?"

"Oh there's plenty of chemistry. But the timing isn't right." Toni eyed her curiously, but Lora-Beth didn't fold.

"He's dealing with something, Toni. And he's struggling with it. Instead of focusing on it, I'm ignoring my growing feelings for him and putting my attention on being the safe space he needs."

Silence fell over the table as the waiter delivered their first two tapas plates, farm bread topped with tomatoes and Manchego cheese and garlic shrimp. Kalo, the tapas fusion spot, nailed the mix of rustic charm and modern sophistication in both their ambiance and menu.

"You really like him, huh?" Toni asked, unfolding her napkin over her lap. Lora-Beth mirrored her movements, looked her in the eyes, but didn't respond. She didn't need to. The question was rhetorical.

Dropping one of the shrimp atop the farm bread, Toni closed her eyes and savored the flavor of the bite and moaned. "So good. Hurry and try this, girl. The shrimp, the cheese, this delicious soft bread, it's a great combination. They should combine the two and make it a menu item."

Lora-Beth took a bite and agreed it was delicious. She was looking forward to the rest of their small plates. "How are the Marcuses?"

"MJ is perfect. Of course, I'm biased, but never have I seen a better-behaved, smarter, more caring three year old. The boy is just so yummy," she gushed. "Even though I give him a hard time, Marcus is also good. I know I have a good man. Sometimes I wonder how he puts up with me."

"The man's a saint."

"Hush it." They shared a laugh. Lora-Beth was happy she'd managed to change the course of the conversation.

"And work?" she asked Toni.

"Work is work. Sometimes I wonder what I was thinking about going into finance. I love what I do. I just don't love where I have to do it. Some days I hate that I'm stuck in an office all day, every day."

"I can see that. I appreciate that I'm not tethered to my desk forty hours a week, but those times when work goes long and I'm still on the job at seven or eight, or have to start my day before seven a.m. Thankfully, I haven't had many of those days lately."

"It's exciting though, isn't it? That your work isn't the same every day. I think your job is perfect for you."

"It can be exciting. I like what I do, but it's not always easy."

Toni waved her off again. "As if you'd want easy. Easy is boring."

Their waiter appeared again with two more of their small plates, wasabi shumai and basil fried rice, and two fresh martinis. Their tuna tostadas and corn fritters were out before they had a chance to taste the others.

"I seriously love this place. Why don't we come here more often?" Lora-Beth asked, eyeing the food.

"Because it's not smart to spend this much on dinner often. I love this place too, but it ain't cheap. So once a month or so is sensible."

"Of course, you're right. And this is why finance is the perfect job for you."

After several minutes of eating silently, enjoying the delectable fused flavors, Lora-Beth looked up from her plate and noticed Toni watching her, smiling.

"What?"

"What are you thinking about?"

"Nothing, I'm thinking about the food. It's delicious." She lifted her napkin to dab at her mouth and looked at her phone she'd set on her lap.

"I'm usually the one quiet and shoveling food into my mouth. You're usually talking, even when you're eating. You're thinking about him."

She was thinking about him. She'd been thinking about little else in the last few days. Like the way he looked at her sometimes and the look in his eyes after they'd shared a moment.

"I'm worried about him," she admitted. "But, there's not much I can do, so I'm doing what he allows."

"What does that mean?"

"It means…" She sighed. "I'm not sure what it means, actually. He doesn't say much, but he's letting me in, slowly. I'm trying not to pry, or push, so I wait until he's ready to come to me."

"You don't have to wait for him to come to you to let him know you're there. If you want him to know you're thinking about him, just send him a message. Friends do that, ya know?"

"I know." Lora-Beth took another bite of shrimp.

"Just text him. Don't make it a big deal."

This was funny coming from her. Toni was notorious for making things big deals. "Fine." She picked up her phone and started her message.

Toni laughed from her gut. "Seriously? Your phone has been in your lap this whole time?"

LB: Hoping you had a good day. Tomorrow still good for paint shopping?

Finishing her brief text, Lora-Beth laughed and said, "Gimme a break, just this one time."

They lingered longer than usual after finishing their meal. Toni didn't mention him again but she noted Lora-Beth had not received a response to the message she'd sent.

46

Austin settled into the chair and picked up the book, now ready to read to Janet after his usual attempts at seeing to her comfort. He wasn't sure why it had irked him that Joyce had picked up the book and started reading from it the other day, but it had. These days, it seemed everything irked him. He was constantly on edge, except for… Austin shook his head, cleared his throat, and started reading aloud. *"It was the warmest day of the season thus far and Sinet appreciated the familiarity. Even in this realm, the sun sat perched directly overhead, responsible for the day's mid-eighty degree temperature, looming, acting as Big Brother, illuminating her every more, ensuring she saw things in the best light possible; figuratively and literally, of course. Aklavia, a universe much like the one you know…"*

Midway through chapter two, his phone vibrated and he paused at the end of the sentence to check it. It was a text from Lora-Beth. Setting the phone and book aside, he took Janet's hands in his and drew in a breath. "There's something I want to talk to you about. I don't know if the doctors are right. I don't know if you can hear me or if you're still here with me." Austin brought her hand to his lips and pressed it there for a long moment.

"It's happening. Your parents are going to take you off the machines and let you go be with our daughter."

He gazed at her, the calm on her face giving him the courage to speak the words he's rehearsed silently for days, preparing to say them to her.

"I'm having a hard time getting there, to the point where I feel any comfort in letting you go. If you could send me a sign, I'd really appreciate it. Throw me a bone. Flick the lights, send a draft down my spine, something." Austin smiled at his teasing words. Janet had always loved the idea of the supernatural. *Ghost Whisperer* had been one of her all-time favorite shows, but he'd never bought into that sort of thing.

He reached up and touched her face, then her hair, attempting to smooth the fly-aways he'd created with his massage. "You'd hate what we've done to your hair." He smiled. "Remember when you came to Charlotte when I was working on the Orchid project? That soul food spot we found tucked away in that alley. You said those were the best pork chops and the best cornbread you'd ever had. Well, I had a pork chop the other day, and even though I didn't try them that day in Charlotte, I'd bet these were better."

What was he doing? Austin paused and thought carefully about his next words. "There's something else I wanted to talk to you about. I don't know how to say it so I'm just going to say it. I've met someone. I mean, I've met many people, obviously I've met people, but there's someone who's different." He closed his eyes and pictured her face.

"Her name is Lora-Beth. Yes, she has two first names." He chuckled and after a moment's hesitation, he went on.

"I've been doing some work on her house, she bought this fixer upper cottage, and I can't explain it, but I'm drawn to her." He paused for a beat to center himself. "I know this is fucked up, talking to you about this, but I feel like I need you to know before…" His voice trailed off and he brought her hand to lips again and pressed a kiss there. "I just want you to know."

He was losing it. Was he asking for her approval? Here he was telling the woman he'd loved for four and a half years that he was having feelings for another woman. "I guess I just want you to know that I'm starting to feel okay again."

Austin felt a tap on his shoulder. He hadn't realized he'd fallen asleep. He tried to focus his eyes on the person dressed in scrubs leaning next to him. "I'm sorry, Mr. Watts, but it's eleven o'clock. Visiting hours are over."

He cleared his throat and wiped his big hand over his face. "Yeah, okay. Thanks."

Austin crawled into bed and stared into the darkness. He was exhausted, but the nap he had in Janet's room had thrown him off. He grabbed his phone and dialed Lora-Beth, as if it was something normal for him to do.

The ringing phone woke her. She'd just found sleep or at least that was the way it felt. She reached for her phone and read the clock, twelve twenty-seven a.m. Austin's name was on the screen.

"Hello?" When she didn't get a response, she tried again. "Austin? Are you there?"

"Tomorrow is still good."

She wasn't following. Sitting up in bed, she rubbed her eyes. "What?"

"The paint. I'll be there."

"Okay. Good. I'm looking forward to it." She could hear him breathing, but he didn't say anything.

"Austin?"

"I'm here."

Realizing he wasn't going to say more, Lora-Beth started talking. "So I was thinking, and hear me out before you decide I'm crazy, I would love, love, love, a skylight in the kitchen."

Austin groaned.

"Just think about all that natural light. Wouldn't it look great shining down on buttery yellow walls?"

Austin put the phone on speaker, rested it on his chest, and listened as her voice filled the room. She rambled on about natural light, white cabinets, tiles, and better moods. How was it that without having to tell her, she knew he just wanted to sit and listen to her? He thought of her face, lit up with excitement, and said a silent thanks that she'd answered his late night call.

"Let's put the skylight on the back burner for now," he tried.

"Why? What's on the front burner?"

Austin felt himself smiling. "Pink walls apparently."

"Well, yeah, but that's minor. I'm talking about big changes. After the bathroom, what other big projects do we have?"

"I believe there's a matter of your budget you're forgetting."

"You sound like Toni."

"How so?" He knew who Toni was. He'd heard her name, and stories of her, many times over the past several months.

"She reminded me tonight of the importance of my budget." He laughed at the many things he did around her house that she wasn't paying for nor had she asked him to do. If he noticed something needed to be done, he got it done. Without noticing, he'd assumed responsibility of her house as if she were his.

"Maybe we can put it on the list for next year."

"That's probably a smart move." Lora-Beth waited a beat before asking, "Do you want to talk about whatever has you up so late?"

He didn't. He just wanted to end his day on a lighter note. "I visited with Janet this evening. I try to visit Wednesdays and Sundays," he said anyway. Though he wasn't sure what would come out of his mouth these days, he found it easy to talk to her.

"Oh." Lora-Beth wasn't sure what to say. She had questions, dozens of questions, but it was none of her business. He'd share what he was willing to share and she wouldn't push.

"I dozed off earlier while I was there, and now I'm having a hard time finding sleep. I apologize for calling so late. I won't keep you. I just..." He let that hang in the air.

"You just what?" she asked.

"I wanted to hear your voice," he confessed, but the whole truth was that he wanted to see her. Looking into her smiling face and shining eyes had a way of making him feel like everything would be okay.

"I don't mind."

He let them rest on that for a few seconds then asked, "Where did you learn to cook?"

"My Gram taught me. She was a wonderful cook, and I don't just mean in the way that everyone thinks their grandmothers are good cooks. That woman was amazing in the kitchen. She could teach Julia Child, Ina Garten, and Paula Deen a lesson or two about putting together a meal."

Austin listened, and before long, he found sleep. Lora-Beth listened to him breathing for a while, happy she'd been able to help him find rest after what she was sure had been a tough day. An earnest smile unfurled across her face when his even breathing turned into quiet snores. "Rest well, sweet man," she said, then hung up, rolled over, and fell into slumber.

CHAPTER EIGHT

They were working on the driveway and entry for a stately home in a gated community. The client had called Austin and presented him with an intricate design. After a few tweaks, he agreed it would match perfectly with the style of the home, keep in tune with the neighborhood standards, and at the same time uniquely represent the owner's personal style. It was day three of the project and Austin felt in his element as he lay the stones, three different colors, in the pattern and saw it come together. Chris, his employee whom he leaned on heavily for brick masonry, was working nearby on the stones on the gate, training Brock on the skill.

Austin joined their ongoing conversation, discussing college football and the merits of the much talked about freshman quarterback on the local team. Chris felt strongly that the team could make an appearance in one of the bowls for the first time in more than eight years. Brock cosigned this, agreeing that with the maturing defensive line and the new addition of the quarterback and kicker, they stood a chance. Austin wasn't so quick to jump on the bandwagon. "He has a great release but it doesn't look like he throws a very good ball with much velocity. And don't get me started on him running the ball. He needs to tighten up on that. Gotta protect the ball. He may be good but there are plenty of good QBs all over the country. He needs to work on his weak points, then we can talk about putting the team on his shoulders. Until then, I'm not calling him the next Russell Wilson."

Chris and Brock looked at each other. "That may be the most words I've ever heard you speak at once that weren't directly related to a job, Boss Man. You're in a good mood," Brock said.

Chris made a gesture for Brock to knock it off. He wished he hadn't said anything and just let it pass as if it were normal for Austin to shoot the shit with them on the jobsite.

"Work is steady. The weather is holding up. That's cause for a good mood."

"Work has been steady, and save for a few quick rain showers, the weather has been pretty good. So that ain't it," Brock mentioned, earning a shrug from Austin.

"If you say so." Austin stood, admiring his job and went to bring over more stones. The intricate work was nearly done, and he was pleased with the progress.

"Are you smiling? Oh shit. Brock, I think he just smiled. Okay man, what gives? I've been working with you for two years, and until this moment, I didn't think you knew how to smile."

Austin shook his head. They were ridiculous. "So because I don't walk around with a smile plastered on my face I don't know how?"

Both men nodded, now smiling themselves. "Well, whatever has caused it, I hope it sticks around," Brock said finally.

He shrugged off their ribbing. "When I'm done here, I have to leave you guys. I'll be back later, but I need to get across town to the Knights. That ramp needs to be finished today."

"I thought Trevor had that covered?" Chris asked. "I'm sure they got it under control."

"I'm sure. But I need to put my eyes on it."

"Another one of his," Brock said absentmindedly and matter-of-factly, still stacking stones.

"One of mine? They're all mine," Austin said.

"They are, but some more so than others. You have pet projects."

"I don't. I care about every job, every client."

The guys shared another look, but let that hang in the air. They knew better. Even if Austin hadn't, they'd realized some time ago that Miss Haines' cottage was Austin's project.

A less than twenty-minute drive across town and Austin felt as if he was in a different world from the one he'd left. The home he'd left was full of luxury and more than five thousand square feet. The home he'd just pulled up in front of was less than fourteen hundred square feet and belonged to a family of six who'd soon be welcoming their recently wheelchair-bound father home from the rehab center. Walking up, he found the guys had built the railings and were nearly done laying the concrete. He had nothing to worry about. He had a great team. The four guys he employed took their work seriously and he appreciated it so much. Still, he was a bit of a workaholic and a bit of a control freak when it came to his company's work product. He wouldn't apologize for it.

ص

"Barely Blush. Plaster Pink. Pale Shadow. Gentle Butterfly." Lora-Beth read the paint samples for the four colors she'd chosen as they stood at the register waiting to check out. There was so little difference in the four shades, Austin was starting to think he may, in fact, be colorblind. He knew better though, he'd persuaded her that the Pepto Bismol shade she held up was a definite no and the mauve tone made him think of old people. That had been enough for her. He'd managed to steer her into the range of pinks that were soft enough to be neutral. Beyond that, well… they were all the same to him. He was standing close enough that he could smell her perfume and feel her body heat, but they weren't touching. Several times, he placed his hand at the small of her back or walked up behind her and peered over her shoulder.

Outside, he opened the passenger door for her to climb into his truck. Once she was inside, he reached over to secure her seatbelt as if it were the most natural thing. Climbing in on the other side, he asked, "What do you say we stop at Homestead Tavern? Let me buy you a burger and a beer. Payback for the meal the other night."

"I say yes to a burger and beer, but not because you need to pay me back for anything. More like, because we got a late start then you kept me in the paint section forty minutes too long and now I'm starving."

Austin looked at her and took in her attempt at a serious expression. "Is that what happened?"

"You were there. You know how it went down."

"Huh. The way I remember it—"

"Okay, fine. I was delayed. I'll take that one. But the paint aisle delay is all you. I would've picked up the first five I liked and been out of there in five minutes, but you my friend, are a colorist. Without you, I might be living in a house with bubblegum pink walls with mauve trim and hot pink bedding, straight out of a crazy person's Barbie dream book."

Austin laughed and Lora-Beth thought it seemed easy, natural. She turned and caught a glimpse of his face and instantly loved the look of it wearing a smile and the sound of his laughter in her ears. "You have a great laugh."

Austin enjoyed this easy banter between them. He ran his hand over his hair and let his mirth wane naturally. The guys had been right. He was in a better mood and Lora-Beth was the reason for it.

"Tell me about your day," Austin said after their beers, from the pub's brewery, had arrived.

"Today was a typical day. Most of it went smoothly, but I have one client who's being particularly difficult. They've refused our second pitch at the new layout and logo for a product and it's pushing an already too tight schedule."

"Is that why you were there later than usual?"

"Yes, the pitch was at four. And afterward, we needed to put in some time on it. We lost two team members right at five two a sponsorship party, so that left Lydia and me working on it together. We're not quite there yet."

He nodded his understanding. "What's the product?"

"Can't say specifically because of the confidentiality agreement, but imagine if your smartphone could be trained to know you."

Austin quirked an eyebrow, and she rushed on, trying to better explain. "Okay, I shouldn't be saying, but, what the heck." She took a sip of her beer and swallowed before beginning her explanation. "Think of all the information we plug into our phones. It goes everywhere we go and we consult it for practically everything—directions, research, random questions. You know how your internet browser saves cookies and your streaming services recommend TV shows you might like and your text messages suggest what you mean as you type?"

"I'm following."

"Well, with an existing product already in their line, my client has created something that allows your smartphone to get to know you better, on a deeper level, and be a virtual life coach, for lack of a simpler way of explaining it."

"Artificial intelligence accessible to everyone." Lora-Beth looked at him and smiled. He got it and had managed to sum it up in a single sentence.

"Yes. I'd say that's a good way to put it."

"Sounds like a conspiracy theorist from the early aughts' worst fears come true."

"Honestly, there were bits of feedback that resembled that in focus groups, but it's the world we live in. We can't avoid it. If my client doesn't, someone will. Someone probably is already doing it. We're just trying to help our clients beat them to market."

"You like your job." Their food arrived before she could respond.

"I do. Very much."

"What's that look, then?"

"There've been mumblings about a promotion. No one has said anything to me directly though."

"Why does it sound like a bad thing?"

"Well, because I really like my job now. A promotion would mean more desk time, more people management, and it's not where I want to be at this point. I've done the grunt work. Late nights, three or four nights a week, proving myself, and in the last year and half, in this position, I've only now started to understand what work/life balance is all about. I don't want to give that up."

He understood. He'd been a workaholic trying to figure out how to balance it all at once.

Not wanting to let the conversation wane, Lora-Beth went on. "Enough about me. I want to know something about you. What did you do before?"

"Before?"

Lora-Beth chose her words carefully. "Before you owned Honey-Do List. You mentioned being out of town for work the other day."

Austin dabbed the corner of his mouth with a napkin and answered the question. "Structural engineering. I have a Civil Engineering degree from U of Tennessee Knoxville and was offered a job through my internship. Went to work right away."

"Did you work on any projects I might recognize?"

"Well, if you've ever driven through Clarksville, then I'd say so. I worked on the roadway redesign, the bypass. I worked on that project during my internship and my first eighteen months on the job."

"I'll make a special trip," she vowed.

"I worked on a revamping project for midtown Nashville. Upscale shopping center with overpriced luxury condos above the shops. And uh, several projects in Charlotte."

He lit up talking about his projects. Lora-Beth was getting a glimpse of Austin outside of the grief and she lapped it up. He was slowly peeling away his layers, revealing the real him to her and she liked every new bit he uncovered. "You miss it."

"Sometimes I miss it. But I'm not sorry I'm doing this now."

"I'm grateful you're doing this now too. You've been an amazing help to me. I may never be able to say enough how much I appreciate you."

Austin finished the last of his burger, stalling. "You're easy to be around. I never mind doing anything for you."

"Do you have any siblings?" she asked, giving him a break and steering the question back to lighter topics.

"Yes. A half-brother and sister. My dad remarried while I was in college. They're teenagers now. I don't really know them."

"How old are you?"

"I'm thirty-four. And now I feel like I'm at a disadvantage. Tell me about your family."

"I was an only. Paul divorced us when I was seven. My momma remarried when I was nine and that marriage gave me a stepsister who, at twenty-nine, is only two years younger."

"College?"

"I went to Western Carolina University because I grew up in Asheville, got my BS in Marketing, then came here for grad school at UNC Chapel Hill and got a communications degree and liked the area so much, I made it home."

"Have you always known this was what you wanted to do?"

"When I was young I thought I'd be a kindergarten teacher, then for a while a lawyer. I stumbled into this career. I fell in love with the versatility of it. There's such a wide range of what a PR person does. In this position, the lines of

PR and marketing have been blurred and I've fallen into this hybrid of the two which I absolutely love."

Austin admired the passionate way Lora-Beth talked about things. He really could listen to her talk for hours. Now, he stared at her expressive face as she talked and wondered if she ever got in a bad mood.

"Austin? Are you listening?"

"I'm sorry, I got lost in my thoughts. Did you ask me something?"

"I asked you what you were smiling about."

"I didn't realize I was." He ran his hand over his hair and said, "It's hard not to smile around you. I love how happy you always are. It's refreshing."

Lora-Beth didn't press by asking him what he meant or tell him she wasn't *always* happy. She could admit she was rarely in a bad mood, but they happened. For now, she'd let Austin go on thinking the way he was. If her happiness gave him a break from his sadness, then she counted herself lucky to be that for him. He could borrow her happiness until he found his own. She was okay with that.

"Is this where we say goodnight?" They had just pulled up at her house and Austin hadn't shut off the ignition.

He thought about saying it was. He shouldn't go in. He would prefer to relax with Lora-Beth and just be, but there was a niggling feeling in the pit of his stomach. Besides, it had been a long day. A shower wouldn't hurt.

She unfastened her seat belt and made a decision. "Come on. What else do you have to do tonight? Sleep? You can make it with an hour less sleep. I'm not tired yet, come inside and chill."

Austin looked straight ahead. "I probably shouldn't, not tonight."

Lora-Beth sighed. She understood his hesitance. She had no sense of how it would feel to be in his position. She couldn't imagine the depth of his pain.

He could feel it happening. In his periphery, Austin watched her face grow sad. It was a look he recognized. Not because he'd seen it on her face, but because he'd seen it directed at him many times before: from the nurses, from his friends before he'd stopped hanging out, and most recently, from Joyce. Resigned, he switched off the ignition. "Come on, Lora-Beth. You're right. Let's go inside."

She gave him a small smile, not exactly because she'd gotten her way, more because he'd decided that for tonight, it was okay for him to enjoy hanging out.

There it was. That beautiful smile. This may have been the first of her smiles he'd worked for. She gave them so freely. It pleased him that she was happy to be in his presence because he got so much from being in hers.

Inside she asked, "Do you mind hanging out here? I want to get this chicken cooked. It's been sitting in this marinade since last night and I want to have it for lunch tomorrow."

"Not at all, but if you don't mind, can I use your bathroom?"

She looked at him and tilted her head to the side. "Did you really just ask me that? Please, Austin, you probably know this house as well as I do. By all means, make yourself at home."

"I'll try to keep that in mind."

Lora-Beth watched him walk away and admired the lines of his back and the way his worn jeans fit just right on his waist and long legs. The dark gray Henley fit just so and showcased his lean waist and defined arms. There was little bulk to him, but the planes of his body fell just right. And when he smiled, they were rare, but man, when he gave her one… she swooned. She shook her head of the thoughts and chastised herself for thinking them. She'd told herself she was going to focus on being his *friend*. She wasn't supposed to be thinking these thoughts.

After checking something on her phone, she decided that chicken quesadillas and Spanish rice was the way to go. She started the rice then busied herself chopping the peppers and onions.

Austin took a seat at the island and took her in. The tune she hummed was one he couldn't place, but it was soothing to his ears. He listened for a moment before asking, "Can I help with anything?"

"Yes, you can help by keeping me company. This will be quick. I promise." Done with the veggies, she tapped something into her phone again before starting on the chicken.

"Toni?" he asked, referring to who she was texting.

"No, I'm not texting. It's the app I mentioned. I've been using it, letting it get to know me."

"You mean training it to spy on you?" he teased.

"Whether we want to believe it or not, Big Brother is always watching."

He paused, as if remembering something. Big Brother. He'd heard that lately, hadn't he? "You got me there."

When the chicken was browned, she tossed in the veggies, gave them a stir, and rinsed her hands.

She picked up the device and rounded the island to where Austin sat. "Here, take a look." She stood next to the stool, showing him the screen. "Here I've keyed in my demographics and basic preferences. It's connected to my calendar, music, and vision board, to name a few. I get an alert when there's a concert or event it thinks I'd be interested in. I key in my food choices and it's connected to my heart rate monitor when I exercise and the fancy scale in my bathroom. It sends me an alert when my weight fluctuates more than five pounds, which helps because I need to keep an eye on things."

Austin pulled her between his legs and touched his palm to her face. When she leaned into his touch, he pressed his forehead to hers. "You're beautiful."

Lora-Beth placed her hands on either side of his head and tilted it to look into his eyes. "So are you."

"I appreciate you. Your company means more than you know."

Ignored desire simmered just beneath the surface anytime he and Lora-Beth shared space. Their heads made decisions at odds with their bodies. He respected it, even if he hated it.

Chapter Nine

It was six-thirty on Friday morning and Lora-Beth was just waking up for work. Her phone went off with an early morning call with her mom.

"Hey, Mommy." Lora-Beth answered the phone with a smile in her voice.

"Good morning, honey."

"How blessed are you this morning?" She followed her usual greeting for their calls.

"Blessed enough to know that when I love what I have, I have all that I need," her mother answered with her usual confidence.

"Okay, Mommy!"

"That's the second Mommy, Lora-Beth. I stopped being Mommy and became Momma or Mom, except for when you need me, a long time ago. One, I could let go, but two in a minute's time tells me it's serious? Before we get into it, tell me if it's work or personal."

"Personal. It's a guy." She stretched out on the bed and sighed.

"There's a guy? Well, this is a first to me. Tell me all about him."

"Oh, Mama!" she whimpered but didn't go on. Lora-Beth felt the tears spring to her eyes and let them flow. She needed to talk to someone and she needed some advice. She couldn't talk to Toni about what was going on with Austin, but she could talk to her mother. Her mother was her confidant. She was wise and would listen without judging.

"Oh, honey. If you need to cry, you cry. Feel what you feel, let it out, and I'll be right here when you're ready to talk."

Lora-Beth did as her mother said and let the emotions she was feeling leave her. When she no longer felt overwhelmed, she started. "I've been getting to know this guy, he's a good guy, but he's in a very difficult spot."

"Difficult how?"

"Listen before you pass judgment, Mama." Lora-Beth gave a reminder she wasn't expecting to issue.

"It is not my place to judge any man, or woman for that matter. I'm listening, baby."

"He's still in love with his girlfriend who has been in a coma for nearly three years." When her mother didn't respond one way or another, she went on. "He's struggling with her parents' decision to take her off life support. There's chemistry between us, but neither of us have acted on it. It twists him in knots, what he feels for me. He hasn't said this to me, but I can see it on his face. He enjoys spending time with me but feels guilty."

"I see."

"Mommy, please, I need some advice. What am I supposed to do in this situation?"

"I think you're doing what you're supposed to. Stop worrying about things that are out of your control. The doctors, her parents, they can say what they want and decide what they want, but it's the Good Lord who decides when it's time to call someone home. That child's body could still be there and her soul could be resting with Jesus."

"That's not what I meant."

"My sweet girl, he found you for a reason. And unless you're telling me you can't handle it, I would tell you to continue to support him. If it's as you say, he's going to need you. The rest, if it's supposed to happen, will happen."

"It breaks my heart to know he's so sad. When he opens up and lets me in…" she trailed off. "It's wonderful."

"You're in love with him."

"I'm not in love with him, Mama. I don't doubt it could grow to love, but right now, I just want to see him okay. I want him to find peace."

"I don't think you needed answers at all, child. I think you just needed to talk about it. It sounds like you've got a hold on things."

"Except I don't. Part of me feels terrible. Like, I'm waiting for—"

"Don't even think it, Lora-Beth Haines. Don't poison your heart with those thoughts. What you feel is pure. Give him that. If you're feeling guilty about something beyond anyone's control, it may push him away. You care about him. You know he needs you to be there for him. If you're who he leans on, he's going to need you when that time comes."

She knew her mother was right. She needed to say the things she'd said. They needed to be out of her head. And not that she was seeking validation, but it felt good to have her mother speak with such positivity and understanding.

"What you're feeling, that's what it feels like to love someone, Lora-Beth. You may have thought you'd loved before, but I'm guessing this feels different."

"I love you, Mommy."

"I love you, sweet girl."

ص

LB: Launch party starting @ 8. Should be fun.

She pressed send on her phone and waited for a reply from Austin. She wanted him to know she had a work obligation this evening. Not that they had plans or anything, she just wanted him to know she wasn't going to be at home. They'd kept a steady stream of texts today. Talking about nothing specific, just the happenings of their day.

Austin: Been a long week. I'm beat. The guys have been giving me a hard time all day.

LB: About what?

Austin: According to them I'm in a better mood and smiling and you're the cause.

LB: Me? {Blushing Emoji}

Austin: You.

LB: They know we're hanging out?

Austin: They think they know.

Before she responded, another text came through.

Austin: They're not wrong.

What was she supposed to say to that? *Thank you?* Opting for basic honesty, she wrote back.

LB: I wish I could see more of it.

Austin: Me too.

Eleven eighteen p.m. Austin was sitting on his couch, staring at the muted kung fu movie on the screen.

Austin: How did it go?

He turned on his music and started doing pushups as a distraction after sending the message to Lora-Beth. When he reached one hundred and still hadn't received a response to his question, he sent another.

Austin: Still @ the party I guess. Have fun. Be safe.

He reached for the pull up bar in the doorway and reached twenty-five, then walked to the shower to wash away the day. When his shower was over, it was nearing midnight and he hadn't heard from Lora-Beth. He admitted to himself that he was worried and dialed her number. When he got her voicemail, a chill ran down his spine and he began to pace. Moments later, the phone, still in his hands, started ringing.

"Lora-Beth, where are you? Are you okay?"

"Hey, yes, what's wrong?"

"I sent you a couple of messages. When I didn't hear anything, I started to worry."

She recognized the anxiety in his voice. "My phone died in the Uber. I'm home now and I was about to grab a shower but when I got my phone on the charger, I saw that you'd messaged. I apologize for worrying you." She heard his exaggerated sigh.

He'd gone mad. He was sure of it. He was losing his mind. "I'm overreacting. I just needed to know you were home safe and not in a di… I needed to know you were safe before I could fall asleep."

"Listen to me. Hear my voice. I'm okay. I'm home. The doors are locked. I'm safe."

"Yeah. I know. I'm glad."

She knew where his mind had gone and her heart longed to pull him back from there. But, how? How could she? "I want to hear your voice as I wind down, but I want to take a quick shower first. Can I call you back in a few minutes?"

"You don't have to call me back. I know you're tired. I'm tired. We both need some rest."

"I'm calling you back in fifteen minutes." When he didn't reply, she added, "When I call you back, you better be awake and alert. I want to talk to you, but I don't want to lay down dirty. Let me get comfortable, and then we'll talk."

"I'll be waiting." Austin disconnected the call and expelled a large breath. He'd feared the worst. In just a few minutes, he'd gone from calm and winding down to exceptionally nervous back to calm again. Of course, he wanted to talk to her. He wanted to do little other than talk to her or be in her presence. This woman was sending him on an emotional rollercoaster and he wasn't prepared.

He should be getting some rest. They had projects lined up starting at seven sharp and would likely be working well after the sun had set. But he went to the fridge, grabbed a beer, popped the top on the edge of the counter, and waited for her call. He could catch up on rest tomorrow night.

Chapter Ten

The homeowner's name was Lucinda, but she insisted he call her Cin. He was consulting with her again, before demolition began on the kitchen of her and her husband's second property. Cin's words were full of innuendo. Austin wondered briefly if she'd given herself that nickname because of her actions or if she'd been given the name and made a point of living up to its promise.

"Maybe I'll stick around a while and watch you boys sling your sledgehammers. I can't tell you when I've seen men in action, tearing things up and letting out their aggression. Hell, maybe I ought to join in."

Austin let that hang in the air while Chris spoke up. "Sure, we can get you some safety goggles and let you take the first swing if you want. It's not unusual for the homeowners to want to get a few swings in."

She waved him off. "Oh gosh no, I wouldn't know what to do with that thing. Austin, if you'll walk me out, I have some marble samples in the trunk of my car from my designer and I'd like to get your opinion on them."

"Sure, if you're ready." He gestured to the door, hoping to get her out so they could get to work. He had more to do today than feed her fantasies.

Cin showed him the three small pieces of marble. They were too small to give an idea as to what a full slab would look like and he told her as much.

"I'm supposed to look at marble samples again tomorrow. It's by appointment only on Sunday and my designer doesn't work on Sunday. Won't you come with me? I'd love your input, you have a great eye."

"It just so happens I don't work on Sundays either. I can ask Chris. He may be open to it. He'll be able to help you find what you're looking for."

"Oh, I have something in mind. I'm looking for a piece with thick veins running through it. I'll know it when I see it. I don't doubt Chris knows his way around countertops, but I was hoping for your input." She leaned close and ran her finger down his chest. He stepped away.

He didn't want to offend her, but this was ridiculous. He was here for a job. Nothing more. "I hope you're able to find what you're looking for."

"Oh loosen up. You don't have to be so serious. Live a little."

"I'll take that under consideration."

"No need to ask Chris about tomorrow, I can manage without him." She stepped into her car and he closed the door, hoping he didn't have to endure much more of this over the next few weeks. Walking back to the house, he picked up the phone to send a text to Lora-Beth and saw she'd already messaged him, wishing him a good morning. Austin remembered that she had to work a half-day. Her difficult client had finally accepted their ideas and they were putting the final touches on the project.

Austin: Off to a good start. Don't work too hard today.

Austin walked into the kitchen through the back door and noted the guys standing around, not working. "What are you waiting on to get started?"

Brock left Chris to answer. "We started removing this countertop but decided waiting to see if we still had a job to do here today once you shot her down was a smarter plan." Then, the two of them shared a laugh. Austin grabbed a pair of goggles and walked toward the row of upper cabinets over a small alcove, not giving them the satisfaction of his reply.

"This job is never boring, that's for sure," Brock chimed in.

"No, never boring. I have to agree with you there. Well, let's do this. This kitchen isn't going to demo itself," Austin said before taking the first swing of his sledgehammer.

They worked and shot the shit and within the hour, had the cabinets out. Well, they were down. To say they were out was a bit of a stretch.

"I see your golden boy had a decent quarter the other night." Austin broached the subject, referring to the quarterback the guys had been talking up for weeks.

"Man, I told you. Watch this kid. Mark my words. He's the one."

"And I told you, it's too soon to be making those calls. Are you going to pretend Barrett out of Ohio State isn't doing big things? Or Watson out of Clemson? Boykins out of TCU? Come on, man, your boy has too much competition to be considered great."

"You make a good point, but I'm telling you, don't sleep on Jarod Hickson. Doing so would be a mistake," Brock chimed in.

Austin reached for his pocket and retrieved his phone that had sounded with a text message. He read Lora-Beth's words and a sound of amusement left his throat. After typing a quick reply, he looked up to find both guys watching him. He looked from one to the other and back again.

"Finally, you're getting laid," Brock said.

The kid was too much. "You have no idea what you're talking about," Austin replied.

"Well, it's about damn time." Chris picked up his tools and went back to chipping at pieces of wood from the cabinets still on the walls.

"Is this what I pay you fools for?"

"Why are you always so serious, Boss Man?" Brock clapped him on the shoulder and went on. "Not sure if you realize, but getting laid is supposed to be a good thing."

"Oh, he realizes. There isn't a man alive who doesn't know that."

"I need to get going, but I don't know if I should leave you two alone. I wouldn't want your speculation to get in the way of your work."

"No need to worry. We can handle both," Brock added with a smile.

"Be mindful. Whatever happens, we need to have paint done and be ready for the custom cabinets by Friday. I'd like to see the demo and clean up finished today and if you could get started on patching, that would be good."

"Yep, we're on it," Chris assured. Brock saluted his reply.

Since it was on the way, Austin stopped by a home in a nearby neighborhood where Trevor was working on a wallpaper takedown and paint project. Satisfied with Trevor's work, and not wanting to give the homeowner the impression he lacked confidence in the job, he kept his visit brief, explaining to the homeowner that it was just his way to check in with them when a project was in progress.

He was pushing the mower in the front yard of a house when he noticed a woman on the porch waving her arms in an attempt to get his attention. He released the handle and walked over to where she stood.

"Good morning."

"Good morning. It's Austin, right?"

"Yes, ma'am."

"I'm sorry, I think there has been a mistake, we didn't ask for lawn service."

"No mistake, ma'am. I noticed it was growing up when we were here last week putting in the ramp and meant to get back out before now."

"I appreciate it, but—"

"It's no charge, ma'am. Just hoping to lighten the load a little for your family."

"Bless your heart."

Austin lifted his hand to the brim of his ballcap and nodded slightly. "I won't be long. I'll finish here, hit the back, then be out of your hair. Shouldn't be too much longer now before the weather changes and the grass stops growing for the season."

"Let me get you a glass of cold lemonade. I made it fresh this morning."

"Thanks, but that's unnecessary. I have plenty of water in my truck."

"Well I'll let you get back to your work. Lord knows I appreciate it."

Austin didn't know their story, but he knew there had been an accident that left the man of the house in a wheelchair. He could see the stress and worry on her face. If cutting her lawn took one worry off her plate, he'd be there once a week.

ص

She was five and a half hours into what was supposed to be a four-hour workday. The client had finally accepted their pitch and they hoped to have it all finalized and ready to submit to printers first thing Monday morning.

"That's it. I need food," Lydia said. "I skipped breakfast and since we're obviously not leaving, we need to order in or I have to take a break to go forage for food."

"I could go for a break. I need to cancel some plans," Lora-Beth added.

"I'll order pizza. Don't go far," Mark, their manager, chimed in.

Lora-Beth walked to her office and closed the door. She checked her plant for dryness before dialing Toni.

"Hey, girlfriend. You wanna hang over here for a little girl time after class?"

"That's why I'm calling, actually. I'm not going to make it to class. I'm stuck at work."

"No."

"No?"

"You are not canceling on me. We need to hang out. I need some friend time."

"I can come over to your place after. I'm not happy about missing Pilates either, but we'll still get our girl time in."

"I say yes to that."

"That way I can get my MJ fix. I feel like I haven't seen him in forever."

"Well, that's because you haven't. My baby will be in junior high before you see him messing with you lately."

Lora-Beth laughed. "Why are you this way?"

"He's fully potty trained finally and talking in full sentences."

"I knew both of those things."

"You know them, but have you seen it for yourself? No. You haven't."

"Well I'll change that this evening."

"What did I tell you? I'll tell you what I told you. I said, 'when you get a man, you're going to stop having time for your friends.' Is that not what I told you?"

"I'm hanging up now."

"Mmm hmm. Text me when you know what time you'll be around. I should be home from Pilates by six-thirty."

Lora-Beth sent a text to Austin, mentioning working later than planned, missing Pilates, and spending the evening at Toni's.

A little person crashed into her legs the moment she walked through the door at Toni and Marcus's home. She reached down, picked MJ up, and spun him around, causing him to squeal in delight. She covered his face and neck with kisses, eliciting more giggles. "Titi misses these MJ kisses."

"MJ miss Titi kisses." He returned the favor, planting wet kisses on Lora-Beth's face, exaggerating his *muah* sounds with a long m.

"Hey, Lora-Beth. How's it going?" Marcus greeted when they joined him in the family room.

"Hi, Marcus. I'm making it. How are you? How's work?"

"Um, are you here for the Marcuses or is this girl time?" Toni chimed in.

"Both."

"Well, their time is short. They have agreed to guy time while we have girl time, isn't that right, MJ?"

He raised his little arm in triumph and shouted, "Ninja Turtles!"

"She won't even let me answer you, you can tell she doesn't get much company," Marcus joked.

"Sad, but true," Toni agreed.

"Work is… well, it pays the bills. I got my beautiful wife and my amazing son. What can I say, life is good."

Lora-Beth watched them and smiled. She loved the way he loved her. Her friend was a lucky woman.

"Okay, guys. Scoot. Mommy's about to make some martinis and pry information out of LB on her new boyfriend."

"Titi boyfriend?" MJ's little face scrunched in confusion.

"Who needs a boyfriend when they have this much yumminess right here?" she asked, tickling him.

"Out!"

"We're going. Come on, son, let's get our pizza and make ourselves scarce."

Toni jumped right into conversation as she started putting together the martinis, first catching Lora-Beth up on what she missed at Pilates. After chatting about their favorite shows and talking about their fitness goals for the end of the year, Toni refreshed their martinis and got comfortable on the couch again. "Okay. Enough small talk. Spill."

"I was wondering how long it would take. You lasted longer than I thought. I gave you twenty minutes, it's been more than an hour. Kudos."

"You're stalling."

"Well, like you already know, aside from getting the work done on my house, we're getting to know each other. It's developing into something, slowly, but it's happening."

"What's standing in the way?"

Lora-Beth gave a small smile. "I'll tell you eventually, but not tonight. He's not comfortable talking about it himself and I'm just trying to be there for him. Part of being his friend is earning his trust. For now, I don't think he'd want me to share."

"Secrets aren't good. That's no way to start something."

"It's not a secret, it's just not something we can talk about."

"Is this man married? I mean, how well do you know him?"

Lora-Beth felt a pang. That hit close to home. While he wasn't married, she knew his heart was with someone else. "He's not married."

Toni moved closer to her and threw an arm around Lora-Beth's shoulder. "Oh no! What's that face? Are you going to cry? Don't cry. You know if you cry I'll cry."

She managed to produce a smile. "I'm not going to cry. It's just complicated."

"Damn, you're really feeling him."

"Yeah. He's sweet and kind. A nurturer. He's a good guy who's been dealt a bad hand. He's trying to find normal again."

Toni racked her brain. Hoping to lighten the mood, she asked, "Have I already asked you if he's an ex-con?"

It worked. Lora-Beth smiled. "Yes, you've asked and no, he's not."

"What does it mean; he's trying to find normal? Is he adjusting to his new meds?" Toni was relentless.

"Someone he loves is not doing well. He's trying to figure out how his life makes sense in the face of this change. I don't think he's figured it out quite yet."

"Well, where do you come in? How do you help him get there?"

"I'll let you know when I figure it out."

LB: Hi. Wanted you to know I'm home safe.

Austin: Thank you for letting me know. How was your evening?

Instead of replying, Lora-Beth hit the button and lifted the phone to her ear.

"Hello."

"Hey, you."

CHAPTER ELEVEN

Austin walked in and pressed a kiss to Janet's forehead. "Hey, Janet. Brought you something new this time. I'm told these are called camellias. They're soft, delicate, and pink." Austin busied himself with the task of changing out her flowers. "I'm happy it's warmer in here today. I told them on Wednesday it was too damn cold in this room. You were freezing."

He placed his hand on her face, then her hands. She looked a little swollen to him and he thought she still felt too cold. Austin took in all the tubes and wires and sighed. There always seemed to be something else. Hemofiltration was the latest addition to her plan. The doctors had warned them what to expect as her organs started shutting down, and it wasn't that he was in denial, he wasn't blind. He simply couldn't stop caring for her because things seemed grim.

He'd been cautioned to be careful with his manipulations going further, noting the declining state of her physical body. He took these steps hoping to keep down the myriad of complications known to develop during a coma. Janet had experienced several, including pressure sores from laying in the same position too long, bladder infections, and the most recent, acute kidney failure. Austin decided that today he'd just sit with her and read. He was just about halfway through the book and wanted to see where the story was going. "I can't believe I'm actually enjoying this alternate world stuff, but I'm invested now. I need to see how Sinet's discovery of her powers goes."

Taking the extra blanket from the nearby chair, he tucked it snugly around her legs, making sure her hands were covered. "Okay, here we go."

"Chapter sixteen. Sinet was training with her older cousin Kheive. Six years her senior, Kheive was chosen to aid Sinet in understanding the signs of her powers and how to use them to her advantage. Powers and dreams and interacting with humans from earth in their unconscious state. Where the worlds collided and Djinn and humans existed in the same plane..."

ص

"I thought I'd find you out here." She sat on the chaise lounge on the deck beside him.

"It's a nice night. Figured I'd have a drink out here and wait for the stars."

No sooner than she'd gotten comfortable, the cries of their daughter could be heard from inside. Janet sighed. "Your daughter has mommy radar. She wants me all to herself."

"You relax. I'll get her this time."

Austin turned the corner and stepped into the nursery, but the crib wasn't there. In its place sat his desk and its accompanying shelf. The room was once again his office. He heard the cries again and tried to follow the sound. He left

83

the room and turned to the right, heading for the main bedroom. Finding no one in the room, he panicked. He let out a wail. "Janet! Janet, get in here! Where's the baby?" He rushed through the house, opening every door, turning on every light. "Janet!" He no longer heard the cries of his daughter.

He raced back to the deck in search of Janet and she too was gone.

Austin jerked awake, breathing hard. He focused his eyes and leapt from his seat. He'd fallen asleep. Hovering over Janet's bed, he stared at her and listened to the steady beeping of the machines. He looked her over and his breathing slowed as he watched the illuminated green lines run left to right as spikes and dips ticked by. He needed to get out of there. He kissed her forehead and backed away from the bed, picked up the book, and headed out. It was just a dream.

It didn't mean anything.

It was just a stupid dream.

ص

Raindrops dotted the windshield as he drove down the road going below the speed limit, focusing on the ache in his chest and the hum of his tires on the road. He rolled down the windows, desperate for some fresh air. He didn't register any other cars on the road when he changed lanes and merged off the highway at the next exit. Three turns and several miles later, a familiar house came into view. He parked in the driveway and let himself out before he lost his nerve. He pressed the button on the doorbell he'd installed himself and waited.

"Austin, were we expecting you? Come in, please," Joyce said before calling out, "David, it's Austin."

"Thank you." Austin crossed the threshold and stood in the foyer.

David approached and reached his hand out for a shake. "Austin, how are you?"

"I wanted to speak with you both, if now's a good time."

"Is everything alright, son?"

"Come in, come, have a seat."

The couple spoke at the same time.

"Thank you," Austin said again.

"Can I pour you a drink?" David asked.

"Not tonight. Maybe another time."

"What brings you out this way tonight?" Joyce sat anxiously. She'd been to see Janet yesterday and had a feeling of why Austin had shown up at their door wearing this haunted look tonight. David sat next to his wife and waited for Austin to speak.

Taking a seat opposite them, he looked between them and started. "So, uh, the other day, you asked if I would ever get there." Joyce nodded and he took it as a sign to go on. "I have to level with you and say I don't know that I will ever get there or if I'm even sure what that means." He sighed. "But, I understand where we are. I understand where she is." He paused to find his words.

David was out of his seat and next to Austin suddenly. He placed a hand on his shoulder, a gesture of support. Austin continued, "I, uh, see what's happening, and I know it's exactly what the doctors have told us would happen. And, uh—" He was overcome with tears and didn't finish.

David squeezed Austin's shoulder then. "It's okay, son. It's alright."

"I want to say I appreciate you both considering me in everything and I'll respect your decision. This is probably as close to there as I'm going to get."

Joyce cried silent tears. Tears for Janet. For herself and her husband. For Austin. David went to her and pulled her to him. Austin watched as Joyce found solace in his embrace.

David, a retired Army officer who had come to terms with Janet's fate and was prepared to be strong for his family, added his thoughts. "It's just her body, Austin. A vessel. Our girl is no longer there." Though he tried not to influence his wife's thoughts on the matter, he did not support life-sustaining measures and had since made sure his final wishes were clear. *DNR.* Do Not Resuscitate and no life sustaining measures when his time comes. Should he find himself in the position where his body could not function on its own, he wanted to go be with the Lord and allow his family to grieve and heal. They'd been grieving for Janet, but not healing. Healing couldn't begin when the grief still had a grip on you.

Austin didn't agree with David on everything he'd said over the years since the accident and had often thought it wasn't always good that David spoke so freely about his beliefs. He'd often found it discouraging. Upsetting, even.

Joyce wept silently. She could appreciate it now that she'd needed to know Austin understood and accepted their decision. Even if he didn't agree, he wouldn't harbor any ill feelings when the time came. "We know how much you love her, Austin. She knew. She was so excited about the life you were building. She loved you so much."

He nodded. He knew. He had no doubts of Janet's love for him.

"She wouldn't want to see you this way, so withdrawn. She'd want you to find a way to move on and be happy. We want you to be happy."

Austin knew what Joyce was saying held truth. If the situation were reversed, he would want Janet to be happy in his absence. But while she was still here… well, he would be here with her.

"Never saw her as excited as when she talked about you and the family you were starting. And even though I wasn't a fan of the order in which you were doing things, I couldn't have chosen a better man to love my little girl. Joyce is right, Janet would want you to be happy."

Joyce reached for each man's hand and squeezed. "We are family. You will always be part of this family, Austin."

Austin nodded his understanding. "Thank you. And I apologize, for the other day at the facility. I was caught off guard. I wasn't in the headspace to hear you, but you didn't deserve my anger. I'm sorry."

She waved him off. "Like I said, we're family."

ص

That night, as Austin lay in bed, his mind drifted to the early days of his relationship with Janet. It had been a fast start to their relationship, the on-location nature of his work forced them to make the most of what time they had together, since unlike most new relationships, they had to contend with extended absences. At the time he'd found her, he wasn't looking for anything serious. He'd been happy to keep his career as his top priority, and indulge at his will. It was easier that way, or so he'd tried to convince himself.

Janet's quiet confidence had been especially appealing to him. In just a matter of weeks, he found it was him who was actively pursuing her, taking his one day off to drive from his worksite in Charlotte to Chapel Hill where she was, just to keep more than a week of him not having laid eyes on her in person from passing. His mind called up a particular memory of the first time she'd introduced him to her parents. He hadn't been nervous until they'd pulled up in the driveway and Janet made a joke about her father's shotguns. Yes, with an S. The woman had a wicked sense of humor, that was for sure.

He dozed off with Janet heavy on his mind, and when the ringing phone roused him, it took him a moment to register what was happening. He was surprised to see Lora-Beth's name on the screen. He pressed to answer the call and put her on speaker. "Hello?" he answered with a question in his sleepy voice.

"How are you?" Lora-Beth knew it was his day to visit Janet. And she knew that sometimes, he spent the rest of the evening in low spirits. Not every day was the same, but she tried to put herself in his shoes and knew she'd want someone to check in on her on nights like this.

"I'm okay. Thanks."

"Austin," she coaxed.

He put the phone on his chest and laced his hands behind his head, staring at the ceiling in the darkness. "I don't want to get into it. I need some time to absorb."

"Has there been any change?" she wondered aloud, not meaning to. She wanted to respect his right to keep things to himself, and she did, but she couldn't help wanting to know and understand what he was dealing with.

"There has, but unfortunately, not for the better," he answered quietly.

"I'm sorry, Austin." In the silence, Lora-Beth searched for something to say, some way to move the conversation to a more neutral topic. She'd found that if she could find a rhythm, something she could talk about, he would listen and join in from wherever his mind went when the sadness took him over.

"I appreciate that you called to check on me. It means a lot that you care," he told her honestly.

Lora-Beth accepted his words and moved on, not wanting to dwell or make more of it than he'd intended. "What would you say if I told you—"

"Don't tell me you want to rip out any walls or tear a hole into anything, please."

She laughed. "I hadn't thought of it, but since you mentioned it."

Austin groaned. Lora-Beth chuckled and finished her thought. "Toni wants us to do a half marathon on Christmas Eve."

"It's less than three months from now. Can you be ready?"

She buried her face in her hands. "I have no idea! She's a crazy person. I looked at the race website. I think I'll bargain with her and opt for the 10K."

"That should be doable. How many miles are you running now?"

"Just four, three times a week."

"Is it a women's only thing? It's been a very long time since I entered a race."

"You run? When do you have the time?"

"I get it done first thing in the morning. I've been doing it for many years." He ran five miles most weekdays: five at five. He'd been running in the mornings since his twenties. Starting with a run seemed to clear his mind and set him up for the day and he worked out in his home gym rather than visiting one of the local gyms to hit the weights. It was one of the few things that remained consistent from his previous life.

"Yeah, I have to do it first thing otherwise it won't get done. Running isn't my favorite, if I'm being honest."

"What is your favorite way to exercise?"

"I like to mix it up. Dance, yoga, Pilates, hiking, whatever tickles my fancy. When I can, I like to walk on my lunch break. It gives me a chance to get some steps in and take in some sun."

"Well, you look great, so tickling your fancy is working for you."

Lora-Beth laughed. "It sounds funny when you say it. You don't strike me as a man who'd casually say tickling your fancy."

"It may surprise you to know I have many words in my arsenal," he deadpanned.

"I'm starting to get that. I'm a fan." It was a far cry from when he seemed to speak mostly in grunts and clipped responses.

"You seem to find happiness in many things. What doesn't Lora-Beth like?"

She hummed aloud, as if searching for the answer to his question. "Humidity," she blurted out after a two-second contemplation.

"Humidity?"

"And coconuts. Oh, and fake ice cream. Bleh!"

"What's fake ice cream?"

"You know, those diet ice cream products. The ones that look like ice cream, then you take a bite and realize you've spent four dollars and ninety-nine cents on a pint of disappointment."

He laughed. She was a breath of fresh air. "Fake ice cream. Got it. Anything else?" he asked.

"Seriously, the one thing that irks me is people not doing what they say they're going to do."

"I think I learned that one a little while ago," he admitted, chastened as he remembered the day she'd been miffed at him.

"Oh, yeah." She nearly forgot about that, but try as she might, she couldn't deny she'd been a little upset that he'd flaked and then had shown up the next day out of the blue.

"You're cute when you're irritated," he admitted.

"I wasn't irritated." When Austin didn't argue, she went on, throwing the question back at him. "What about you? What makes you tick?"

He heard the spark of interest in her voice and smiled. She wanted to know more about him. Lora-Beth didn't make that a secret, but she didn't push, and he liked that. He could tell she'd waited for the right moment to ask about him, and if he was being honest, he liked that she was curious. "Ordinarily, I'm pretty laid back. I usually am not particularly bothered by things, but if I had one pet peeve, I'd say it was tardiness. I have little respect for people who waste others' time. I like football and basketball and I love using my hands. I've always liked to build things. My father is a carpenter and brick mason by trade, and when she wasn't teaching, my mother was a seamstress. I think it's in my blood." He paused. "Oh, and if we're exchanging weather gripes, I can do without snow."

"Does your dad still work as a carpenter?"

"Nah. He gave it up about ten years ago. These days he and his wife sell real estate and flip houses as a team."

"No wonder you're so good at identifying what needs to be done over here at Casa Haines. I think that's in your blood too."

"After growing up helping my dad and my uncle who was a contractor on weekends and school breaks, I never thought I'd be making a living doing this." But things change.

Lora-Beth rolled over in bed and stared at the shadows cast from the moonlight shining through the blinds and let the silence linger. How amazingly strong she thought this man was. In the midst of what he was going through, he'd adapted, he hadn't fallen apart. He made changes to be where his heart told him he needed to be. He'd started a business and now employed several people. There were two kinds of people in this world, she thought, those who were faced with adversity and quit and those who found a way to make it work. Austin was the latter. She admired his quiet strength and devotion. "Do you think you'll ever go back to engineering?"

"I try not to think about it. All things considered, my company is doing well. If I start thinking about what might have been, my mind goes places I try to keep it from going."

"To what your life could be," she wondered aloud.

"Something like that."

"Do you ever talk about it? Janet? Your life with her? Is there anyone in your life you talk to about her, I mean?"

"Nah."

"Tell me about her." When Austin didn't immediately reply, Lora-Beth said, "Just one thing. Tell me one thing about Janet that only you know about her."

"She taught herself to speak Mandarin. It's just a thing that she did. She didn't even tell me until she'd learned enough to explain what she was doing in the language. Then she made me promise that one day I'd take her to China so she could put it to use. "

"Did you learn to speak it too?"

"Before, when I was always away working, I never had the time. Then after the accident, I bought the program and would play it for her and repeat the lessons. But eventually, I gave up on it."

"That's a very sweet memory. Thank you for sharing with me."

"She's a terrible singer, but she loved doing it. And even if my voice isn't terrible, I'm no Luther Vandross, so you know, who am I to say, but I can admit, she's basically tone deaf." He told the story with a smile in his voice. It was a fond memory for him.

"You loved it, tone deaf and all."

"I loved how much she got into it. She didn't just sing, she performed. It was terrible and wonderful all at once. You know how on those singing shows, the first few rounds all the terrible people come out and give it their all, it was much like that."

Lora-Beth laughed, happy to hear him talk about good memories. She knew he'd need them. She was filing these in her memory bank. "Sounds like it was."

It was late, but he didn't care. Austin couldn't remember the last time he'd laughed when thinking or talking about Janet. Strange, he thought, that it was Lora-Beth he was sharing the conversation with. There was something about her that set him at ease. She gave him her full attention. Somehow, she managed to be just what he needed when he couldn't admit he'd needed anything at all. "Is this weird?" he asked quietly.

"Not at all. I'm happy you feel comfortable speaking with me about her."

"Yeah?"

"Yes. Your voice changes when you talk about her. It's lighter. More carefree. Less calculated."

"Less calculated? You think my voice is calculated?"

"Yeah, sometimes I can tell you're holding back from being yourself. You think carefully about both your words and actions. Just then, you spoke freely. I could tell you were smiling. I wish I could have seen it."

Austin was quiet for a long moment and Lora-Beth let him have the silence. Words weren't always necessary. Wordlessly, they were communicating just fine.

"Do you believe that dreams are signs?"

"I choose to believe they can be. We're told to dream big. I'm guessing that's a saying for a reason."

"Do you think comatose patients dream?"

She'd not given it any thought before learning of Janet's condition and then a recent movie with a similar subject had come to mind. "I'd like to think they do."

"Would you think I was crazy if I told you I had a conversation with Janet in a dream?"

"No, I wouldn't think you were crazy. Not at all."

His conscious brain told him it hadn't happened and it was the book he'd been reading. His mind swapped some of the details and placed him and Janet in that fictitious world. Maybe his heart wanted so badly to have a conversation with her his brain had made it happen. "I promise I'm not crazy. Just broken."

"Oh Austin, you're not broken."

"I am, but I think you're helping put me back together."

CHAPTER TWELVE

Lora-Beth took a deep breath of brisk air as she took in the bright sunny day. She laced her fingers together and reached them above her head with a groan, stretching the muscles in her chest, upper back, and arms. She reached into the pocket of her workout pants, retrieved the phone vibrating against her thigh, and answered. "Hello."

"Hey, sissy! What's popping?"

"Let me guess, Mama called you and told you to call me," Lora-Beth greeted.

"You know she means well. But can you at least act like you're happy to hear from me?" Latrice joked.

"Of course I'm always happy to hear from you. You and me. Peas and carrots."

"Peanut butter and jelly. Cocaine and waffles." They erupted in giggles.

"You're so silly. So, how much did she tell you?"

"She didn't tell me anything, she just threw it out there that I should give you a call, that you might want to talk. 'Call your sister, she needs an ear' is actually what she said, but listen, if you don't want to talk about whatever it is, you know you don't have to. I know you'll tell me when you're ready. That doesn't mean we can't catch up though, right?"

"I hate that we don't talk more. How's Texas? How are you?"

"Still very hot in October, but good. I'm good. When are you coming back this way?"

"I can't say right now. But let's try to plan something after the first of the year."

"I'm going to hold you to that. Anyway, how's the house? I can't wait to see it in person." At the mention of the house, her mind drifted to Austin and how amazing he had been in helping her pull it together.

"It's really coming along. I love it more and more every day."

"Where are you? What is that I hear in the background?"

"I'm waiting for Toni, we're about to do yoga in the park."

"Sounds like fun."

"When you come out, we'll have to go to a class."

"So, hey, seriously. You know if you want or need to talk, you can talk to me anytime, right? There's nothing you could ever tell me that would make me look at you sideways."

"I know."

"Okay, as long as you know. I will forever be the keeper of your secrets."

"And I am the keeper of yours."

"Well, I'm going to let you go, I'm still at work. Just stepped out to call you on my break. Love you."

"Love you too." They disconnected and Lora-Beth slid the phone back into her pocket.

"Who you lovin' on, girl?" Toni asked, surprising her.

"My sister. She was checking on me."

Toni smiled. "Confession, I did not run this morning. Actually, I haven't run since Wednesday." It was Monday.

"But you're here now. Thanks for not standing me up."

"You mean the way you stood me up for Pilates?"

"That's not fair. It was work. It couldn't be helped."

Toni waved her off. "Yeah, yeah. Excuses, excuses."

Lora-Beth adored their friendship. She really was blessed to have her family and friends.

When class was over Lora-Beth asked, "Are you up for pressed juice or do you need to go get MJ?"

"Juice or a smoothie sounds good. MJ is with Grammy and Papi so he's good."

The two walked the two blocks to Pressed Juicery and, after placing their order, snagged one of two open café tables in front of the windows.

"So, I want to share something with you, but I need you to keep an open mind."

"Well this sounds promising," Toni said, leaning in.

"It's about Austin and what he's going through. I'm not going to go into all the details, but I need to talk to someone about this."

"Let's head to your place. You can tell me there. You never know who owns these ears." She circled her finger in the air, indicating the other patrons. "I want to see the work that's been done in the past couple weeks anyway."

"Yeah, you're right. That's a better idea."

ص

Lora-Beth set her computer on the island and opened it to a Facebook page.

"Who's this?" Toni asked, already scrolling through the dated posts.

"That's what I wanted to tell you. Janet Mitchell is the woman Austin is in love with."

In response to Toni's confused expression, Lora-Beth added, "His girlfriend. She's in a coma. An accident, three years ago."

"Oh." The single word was laced with sympathy. Toni scrolled over the images and pulled up one of Austin and Janet.

"Is this him? They look happy."

Lora-Beth nodded. "Yeah."

"You weren't kidding when you said it was complicated."

Lora-Beth stepped away and placed a bag of frozen shrimp in the sink. She needed sustenance. That juice was not going to cut it. She'd need a meal soon.

Toni was quiet, contemplative as she continued to look over the page. "Wow, LB. I'm sorry. I can't imagine. How is he coping? How are you dealing with it?"

"I'm trying not to think about myself at all for the moment. He really needs to know he has a support system."

"I'm sure he does. And what do you need?" She searched her friend's eyes, hoping to get a read on what she wasn't saying.

"I have what I need. That's what I was thinking about after speaking with my momma and sister. I have a great family, great friends; my life is good."

"What about how you feel about him? How are you managing that with all this?"

"I'd be lying if I said the feelings weren't there. Obviously, they are, but I'm trying to focus on being his friend. No, it's not what I actually want, but I think I would be okay with only being his friend if that's where this ends up. Who knows what this journey will look like for him? What I know is that I'm going to do what I can to make sure he's okay and never feels like he doesn't have someone he can turn to when it all feels like too much."

Toni looked at her and, not for the first time, said, "You really like him."

Lora-Beth didn't respond, just held her gaze. Toni came up beside her and gave her a tight hug. "And when you feel like it's too much, you can lean on me. It's going to be okay."

Lora-Beth released a heavy breath, comforted by the gesture. "Thank you."

"Whatcha making?"

"Shrimp etouffee."

Toni moaned.

"Obviously, you're welcome to have some."

"Obviously. I'm going to walk around and check out the house and check on my guys while I roam."

"Go. Roam."

"Why are there five pink stripes on the wall in this bedroom? Do not tell me you're actually thinking of painting this room pink," she called out moments later.

"I'm seeing which shade feels right. Which one was your favorite?" Lora-Beth yelled back, but Toni rounded the corner just then and propped her hand on her hip.

"A soft pink bedroom? Is there something you want to tell me?"

"No, ma'am. There is no reason other than I like pink and I think it'll be pretty once I get it fixed up the way I see it in my head."

"Umm, okay then. Just checking."

"Toni, cut it out. A second immaculate conception hasn't happened. I have some mockups on my phone. I'll show them to you once I get this sorted."

"Are we done talking about other stuff?"

Lora-Beth wiped her hands on a dishtowel and smiled. "That's all for now."

Chapter Thirteen

Austin arrived at Lucinda's house to assess what she described as a nagging issue she needed him to take a look at to see if it could be an easy fix or if it would be more complicated than she thought. He waited at the door after knocking several times. Her car was in the driveway, so he knew she was here. She opened the door wearing a long, silk robe. She wasn't living in this house yet, so as far as Austin could assume, she had no reason to be in one.

"Austin, please, come inside. Sorry to keep you waiting."

"It's no problem, ma'am."

"Please, call me Cin. I'm nobody's ma'am just yet."

He stepped into the foyer and out of the way enough to allow her to close the door. "Of course." He chose his words wisely. "You said there was an issue," he prompted.

"Right this way, I'll point it out and you can let me know your thoughts."

Austin followed Cin to the kitchen and when she stopped in the middle of the room and stood looking ahead, he stopped several feet behind her. She turned around and revealed her fully nude front, thanks to the now opened sides of her robe. "When I first saw you I wondered what it would be like between us if I managed to get you alone."

Austin turned his back to her. "Lucinda, cover yourself."

She came up behind him and placed her hands on his back. "Don't be shy." He shrugged away from her touch, hating the feel of her hands on him.

He started toward the door. "Don't follow me. I'll see myself out."

"Austin, wait. I apologize for misunderstanding. I thought we were on the same page."

"You did not."

"Wait, please. Let's pretend this didn't happen."

Austin closed the door, walked to his truck and headed out of the subdivision, wondering how the hell this woman could have had even an inkling that they'd been on the same page. Though he endured her flirting, he'd found it harmless, as it was in most cases. Lucinda James wasn't the first client to openly flirt with him. It happened often. He could say, however, she was the first to call him out with seduction in mind. He needed to think about his approach to this project going forward.

For now, he was going to play basketball.

He joined Chris and the guys for a pickup game. How long had it been since he hung out with the guys after work? How long had it been since he did anything after work just for fun? After running two games, he realized that although his legs and lungs were good, his shot was rusty. His team of three had lost the last game and now he sat on the sidelines, waiting to see if he had another in him.

He reached into his bag for his phone and sent a text to Lora-Beth, ribbing himself.

Austin: Guess who's playing basketball.

Speaking with Lora-Beth reminded him of things he'd been keeping himself from for no good reason. The woman was a godsend. His phone buzzed in his hands just as he heard his name being called.

"Austin? Get out, man. It's good to see you, brother." It was Rob, an old friend. The men shook hands and did the one arm embrace shoulder clap.

"Rob, how's it going, man?"

"Good, good. So, how are things? You good?" He was uncomfortable. Nothing untoward had happened between the two men, Austin had simply pulled away from everything and everyone.

"I'm good, man. Let my boy Chris talk me into coming out here tonight. That's all. Been a long time since I've been out here like this."

"Yeah, I don't get out like I used to either. Life is a bit different these days. The wife doesn't let me out much," he joked.

"The wife?"

"Yeah, got married last year, bro."

"That's good, man. That's real good. Congratulations."

"So things are…?" Rob started, unsure how to ask about Janet. They'd been friends for years, and although he hadn't known Janet very well, he certainly knew her and of the accident.

"No change."

"Sorry to hear."

Austin was relieved when the call for the next game came and Rob excused himself, as it was his turn on the court. That was probably the most awkward conversation he'd had in a while.

He looked down and read the message from Lora-Beth. It was two emojis, a smiling face and a thumbs up, and the words,

LB: Score one for me.

Austin: Just ran into an old friend. It was awkward.

LB: I'm sure it wasn't. I bet he was happy to see you. Making shrimp etouffee. If you're hungry when you're done, stop by.

Even if he wasn't before, he was done now. He would come again next Monday, but two games, a win and a loss, an awkward conversation, on top of the fiasco with his customer, was enough excitement for one day. He would take her up on her offer of dinner because he'd be damned if he missed out on homemade shrimp etouffee only to go home and eat a turkey sandwich instead.

He should have gone home and taken a shower. Instead, he was pulling his truck up behind Lora-Beth's car. He'd driven with the windows down, so he was no longer sweating, but still, he was sweaty and smelled like a man who'd worked all day then had gone and run for an hour. He knocked on the door and waited. His mind flashed to when he'd stood at another front door waiting to be let in. How would he have responded had it been Lora-Beth who'd invited him over with seduction in mind? Would he have turned abruptly from the sight of her or would he have stood and drank her in? How would it feel to be seduced by Lora-Beth?

The door opened to a face he didn't recognize. The two looked at each other for a moment. He looked beyond the stranger and saw Lora-Beth in the kitchen.

Toni moved aside and swept her arm open wide. "Come in. LB is in the kitchen. I'm Toni."

He stuck out his hand to shake hers and properly introduce himself. "Austin."

Toni took his hand and shook it firmly. "I usually do hugs, but I think I'll save that for another day. I can't go home to my husband smelling like another man's pheromones." Austin saw immediately why the two women were friends and liked Toni instantly.

"Fair enough," he said with a smirk.

Lora-Beth was approaching and heard Toni being Toni. "Oh my God, Toni. Why are you this way?" She laughed.

Toni held up both hands in surrender. "I was just saying hi to *Austin*."

As Toni walked away, he took in Lora-Beth's appearance in her coral colored yoga gear and appreciated the way it hugged her curves. "Hey."

Lora-Beth came close, leaned on her toes, and gave him a brief hug. "I don't mind your pheromones." His arms wrapped around her automatically and in the brief few seconds of their embrace, he breathed her in and appreciated the feel of her body against his. "Good timing. The rice is done."

"Smells good."

As if it were normal, Lora-Beth took him by the hand and led him to the kitchen. Austin let himself be led, not thinking much of the gesture.

"Let me go wash my hands. I'm starving."

As soon as the door to the bathroom closed, Toni emitted a hushed squeal. "Oh my God! He's fine."

"Shh," Lora-Beth shushed her, fearing they would be overheard.

"LB. I totally get why you're hot for handyman."

"Toni. You've been introduced. You can now call him Austin."

"Maybe to his face, but when it's just you and me…" She shook her head. "Nope. No can do. The nickname has been imprinted in my brain and shall remain there forever."

Lora-Beth busied herself plating three servings of etouffee and white rice and filled a dish with asparagus. "Toni, can you get the pitcher of tea from the fridge and pour us some?"

"Yep."

Austin returned to the kitchen and found them both busy. "What can I do?"

"You can have a seat. Everything is ready."

"The bathroom looks amazing, Austin. Great job in there."

"Thanks but that was all Lora-Beth."

"Ha. Nice try. Lora-Beth has put five shades of pink in that bedroom. I know who's responsible for how the bathroom turned out."

Austin chuckled softly and they both turned to catch a glimpse of it.

Balancing a plate in each hand as she walked over to the table, Lora-Beth added, "I told you both, I'm going somewhere with the pink."

"Yeah, you told me. But I still need to see this vision because I can't picture it. All I see is Barbie nightmare. I'll grab the last one," Toni insisted.

The three sat at the table and Austin picked up his fork, ready to tear into the delicious looking meal. Toni cleared her throat. "So are we heathens now? We don't bless the food around here?"

"Oh my God, Toni!" Lora-Beth and Austin both laughed.

"My apologies. By all means. Let's give thanks for this food," Austin said.

Happy with the giving of thanks for good health, good food, and good company, Toni jumped right back into her conversation. "So Austin, what are your thoughts on the pink walls? And be honest."

Since he'd already shoved a forkful of food into his mouth, it took him a moment to respond. "I believe her when she says she's going somewhere with it. For now, I'm going to trust the vision."

"Um. I get it. You don't want to offend our gracious host and risk missing out on these impromptu dinners. Wise man. This is delicious by the way."

"It is delicious, and I do want to stay on her good side, but I'm confident she'll choose one of the shades of pink, not several. And the good thing about paint is it can always be painted over if your worst fears come true."

"Neither of you are funny. I hope you know this. I have a whole Pinterest board dedicated to the decor for the room. I promise I'm not living out any tween dreams by painting my guest room pink."

Toni placed her empty plate in the sink and slid her purse strap over her shoulder. "Well I better get out of here. I gotta get home to my guys. LB, as always, dinner was wonderful and the company was even better. I'll see myself out and call you later. Austin, it was great to meet you. I'm sure I'll see you again soon."

She leaned in, placed a hand on a still seated Austin's shoulder, then gave Lora-Beth a hug.

"Tell Marcus I said thanks for letting you chill for a bit. Text me when you get home."

Toni whispered, "It's like I can taste the chemistry between you two." Aloud she said, "Will do."

"Be safe," Austin said, now following closely behind the two as they made their way to the door. They stood on the porch and watched as Toni got in her car and slowly pulled down the street.

Austin closed the door and stopped in the foyer. "Toni was right. The food was delicious but the company was better. You're a wonderful cook and host, Lora-Beth."

"I'm glad you liked it. And thank you for having some asparagus."

"They were good too."

"Heading out?"

"Yeah, I better get going. We both need to get out of these sweaty clothes and I really need to wash the day away."

"I'm glad you came. It's good to see you like this."

"Sweaty?"

"Comfortable."

He grabbed her hand and pulled her close. He rested his forehead against hers and confessed, "I'm never not comfortable with you."

Lora-Beth's heart raced at the intimate gesture. "I'm happy about that too."

"Thank you." He wasn't only thanking her for the meal. He was thanking her for being her. For being the kind, patient, caring person she was.

He stepped away, opened the door, tapped twice at the bolt, and closed the door behind him.

Toni had been onto something earlier with the mention of pheromones.

CHAPTER FOURTEEN

She hadn't been planning this. She didn't even know what she was doing, but Lora-Beth found herself outside the hospital annex, preparing to go inside. She couldn't explain it, but she felt compelled to come here, to meet Janet. After finding her social media, then listening to Austin's stories of her, Lora-Beth realized that as time went on, friends and family alike had eventually stopped visiting. She didn't know the details of her condition nor how she felt about whether or not a person in Janet's state could hear what was going on around them. However, she felt incredibly sad when she thought about it. Austin, her parents, she couldn't imagine what it really felt like to be in their position.

"What am I doing?" she asked aloud, talking to no one. She buried her head in her hands and tried to gather her thoughts.

Inside, she approached the nurse's station. "I'm here to visit Janet Mitchell."

Without looking up, the person behind the desk called out, "One twenty-six", and pushed a clipboard toward her. "Sign here."

Lora-Beth signed her name on the sheet, indicating with whom she was visiting and her check-in time.

The lady looked up when she set the clipboard down. "Be sure to sign out before you leave. If you leave and don't sign out, you waste our time having to check for you at the end of the night."

"I will sign out."

"Okay. One twenty-six."

She found the room, knocked twice on the jamb, and took a deep breath before walking through the open door of the room. She stood just inside the doorway, taking in the sight of the woman in the bed, the life-sustaining machines, tubes, and wires, and tried to process it all. She was covered in a comforter adorned with sunflowers, an extra blanket tucked over her feet. Lora-Beth was overwarm in the room and wondered briefly why Janet was so wrapped up.

Nervously, she moved closer and cleared her throat. "Hi, Janet. My name is Lora-Beth. I'm a friend of Austin's. I was hoping it would be okay if I sat with you for a while." She paused, as if waiting for a reply. Lora-Beth took a seat in the chair nearest the bed and tried to think of something to say. "He's doing the best he can, but he misses you terribly." Her face morphed into a sad smile. The steady beeping and whirring of machines seemed to bounce off the walls. "He told me you liked to keep up with celebrity gossip, so I picked up a copy of *US Weekly*. I hope it's okay if I share it with you. Jennifer Lopez is on the cover, looking as amazing as ever. This woman doesn't age. And aren't we lucky, she's going to share her diet and beauty secrets with us. Tori Spelling is getting divorced. There's also a Kardashian story. Is anyone actually surprised by this? I know I'm not. Kevin Hart is in every other comedy movie produced right now.

The latest installment in Keeping Up with Kevin puts him in a serious role about being a single father. I'll have to check that one out."

Joyce listened from outside the door as this woman chatted with Janet as if they were two friends catching up. She stepped away, wanting to compose herself. She knew her daughter would never have moments where she'd hang out with her friends again, being silly and gossiping about the latest celebrity nonsense. She went to the restroom down the hall and sat with her tears for a few minutes before pulling herself together. She splashed water on her face and patted it dry with a paper towel.

When she returned to the room, the woman was still talking, reading from her phone now and interjecting her adlibs at will.

Lora-Beth noticed movement and looked to the door, finding a woman standing there. In the moment, she felt as if she'd been caught doing something she wasn't supposed to be doing. She stood abruptly, apologizing. "I, um. Hi. I'm uh, just—"

Joyce held up a hand to silence her and stepped closer, extending a hand. "I'm Joyce, Janet's mother."

"Lora-Beth. I'm a friend of Austin's. I was just, um, keeping her company. I'll get out of your way."

"No. Stay. Don't run off on my account. Sit, please."

"Um, okay. Sure."

Joyce greeted her daughter by placing a hand over Janet's and leaning down to place a kiss on the top of her head. "Hey, honey."

Lora-Beth noted Joyce's tenderness. She pulled the blanket up over her hands, tucking them in, then sat in the seat next to Lora-Beth. "How is he doing? Really?" Joyce asked.

"I think he's doing the best he can."

"So he's not doing well, then?" Her face wore a sad smile.

"Honestly, he's doing okay. He'd tell you the same."

"He would. But it wouldn't be the truth. He's existing, not living. I know it because I've moved through the past few years the same way. The group I've been going to helps but only so much."

"Everyone has to do things their own way. Sounds like you've found something that works for you. Austin is still figuring out his way. He'll get there."

"He's not himself. Sometimes, I hardly recognize him."

"I see glimpses of him. Mostly when he talks about her."

Joyce smiled at that. "He talks with you about her?"

"Some. He's a man of few words, but he loves your daughter very much," Lora-Beth admitted.

"He hasn't always been that way. I'm hoping one day he'll remember who he was before." She repositioned in the seat, a physical sign of the discomfort she felt at the mention of how things were before the accident. "How did you meet Austin?"

"He started some work on my house a few months ago. He's helped out a great deal, turning the fixer upper I bought into a home I'm proud of."

Joyce nodded. "Thank you for being here, reading with Janet. I'm sure Austin appreciates it."

Lora-Beth looked down at her hands in her lap.

"He doesn't know you're here," Joyce stated and Lora-Beth nodded.

Joyce closed her hand over Lora-Beth's in her lap and held for a moment. "Well then." She patted and drew in a deep breath. "We can keep this between us girls. And you were right, Janet would love that magazine and to know those things you were looking at on your phone. That's just the sort of garbage she kept up on."

"It's kind of nice to know they have regular struggles just like us. Nobody's life is perfect, no matter how good they make it look for the general public."

Janet nodded. "Everyone is dealing with something."

"Well, let me get out of your way."

"You don't have to rush off, Lora. It did my heart good to see you sitting chatting with my daughter."

She didn't know how to respond so she did her best to offer a genuine smile.

"Don't be a stranger."

"Okay."

Lora-Beth left the room in a bit of a daze. She neared the desk and caught the motion of the desk attendant's finger, reminding her to sign out before she left.

ص

"I ran into Rob the other day. Do you remember him? I know it's been a while but you've always been good at remembering names and faces. He asked about you. Well, he told me he'd gotten married over a year ago. Anyway, I know you're curious, but I was playing basketball when I saw him. Yes, you heard that right, I was at the gym, playing basketball.

"It's been too long since I've done anything just for fun. Lora-Beth, the friend I told you about before, she's helping

115

me remember what it's like to enjoy life. I'm trying to show you, to prove to myself that I am okay. That I'm going to be okay, love."

Austin kissed her forehead, then her cheek. "Well, I better get started. I want to finish the book." He sat in the chair and noticed the colorful pages of the magazine tucked into the side. He pulled it free and wondered if Joyce had left it there. It definitely hadn't been here when he'd visited on Sunday. Austin shrugged it off. Probably one of the medical staff taking a break in Janet's room. He made a mental note to speak with someone about that.

He picked up the book and found the earmarked page, Chapter Nineteen.

Sinet sprang from her back, landing steadily on both feet. A figure came charging at her from her left. Kheive was in front of her, on guard, ready for her next wave of attacks. Testing her strength, Sinet leapt in the air, hoping to reach a height above that attacker's head, and landed behind him. She was training to defend herself against the unknown. In the dream realm, there was never a way of predicting what one may find themselves up against...

"Hi. I have a warm blanket here for Janet. Thought I'd beat you to the punch." Her name tag read Tanya and it matched what the board on the wall noted as her CMA for the shift. He hadn't remembered interacting with her in the past, but he must've.

He closed the book and set it on the bedside table. "Thank you."

"I'm Tanya, I'm on duty tonight. If you need anything, let me know." Tanya removed the current blanket from Janet's legs and replaced it with the warm one.

"We appreciate it."

"Good book?"

"Not really my thing, but it's okay. She likes it. I'm reading it for her benefit, not mine."

"You read to her a lot. It's good to see you take time from your busy schedule to spend with her. Too many of the families don't find the time."

"It's no hardship."

"Well, I'll let you get back to it. Like I said, if you need anything."

"Oh, hey, Tanya." He grabbed the magazine and held it up. "I found this here in the chair. Is it yours?"

"No. Janet had a visitor yesterday who brought that in."

"Oh, okay." Austin set the magazine on the table. "Thanks again for the warm blanket."

Austin turned his attention back to Janet. "Looks like we both saw old friends this week." He smiled. The happiness he felt was quickly replaced by the daunting realization that Janet's old friends may have begun to stop by because Joyce had called them, warning them they would soon miss their chance. Soon enough, he wouldn't be coming to visit her here at the annex, but at the cemetery where she'd rest eternally.

He wouldn't think of that now. No. Not tonight. Tonight he had half an hour before visiting hours were over and he was going to read until someone came to round him up.

He wasn't going to make it. His assignment was due in three hours and it was twenty-five percent of his grade. If he was going to stay on the Dean's List and retain his scholarship, he needed to get his ass in gear and pull off a miracle.

The ringing sound woke him and instantly, he panicked. He was slumped over his desk, his assignment unfinished, and he was late for class. The ringing persisted and Austin searched for the source.

Austin grabbed his phone and silenced his alarm. It had only been a dream. He was not in college and there was no report due. He'd simply been dreaming. He was still in Janet's room. Asleep. Well past the end of visiting hours.

CHAPTER FIFTEEN

Austin looked at Janet once the machines had all been turned off and the IVs, tubes, and cords had been removed. His heart pounded too fast, too hard. He stood on one side of the bed while Joyce and David stood on the other. The nurse and doctor who'd just removed all external life sustaining measures stepped away, observing. Waiting.

Holding Janet's hand in his as her mother did the same on the other side, Austin leaned down and kissed her forehead, then placed a gentle kiss on her lips. His tears flowed, unchecked. Her mother stroked her hair and wept.

Seconds, then minutes, ticked by in a haze as he watched her, silently praying Janet would prove to him, to everyone, she was still in there, and that this body wasn't just a shell the doctors believed it to be.

Her body twitched and it looked to Austin as if she was fighting to take a breath. He grasped her hand tightly and met Joyce's eyes before jerking his head in the direction of the doctor and nurse in turn, who each shook their heads slowly, sadly.

The doctor held his hand up, indicating they just needed to wait. "It's a natural reaction," the doctor explained.

In other words, there was nothing they could do for her. Janet wasn't fighting for her life; rather her body was giving in to what was natural now that the machines weren't conducting her bodily functions for her. Their directives were to administer no further measures.

Austin couldn't look away from Janet's face. His tears streamed without sound. There were things he wanted to say to her in her final moments, words he wanted to make sure she heard one last time, but at this moment, he couldn't bring them forth.

He heard Joyce cooing words to her daughter. "It's okay, baby. It's okay to go. We're here. Your father and Austin are here with you and we all love you so much."

Austin brought her hand to his lips and kissed it, finally finding his voice. "I'm sorry I couldn't protect you. I'll love you forever."

Her body relaxed and seemed to expel another breath. It was the second time it had done so and it pained him to know that now, she could be taking her last.

No matter how much time or warning, one could never really be prepared to lose someone they loved. He'd known this moment was coming for months, years if he were able to be honest and admit it to himself. Still, at this moment, after Janet had taken her final labored breath, he felt the overwhelming weight of the loss. Now, he cried for Janet because she didn't get the life she deserved.

Seven minutes. That was how long it took after they removed the equipment before the doctor placed a hand on his shoulder and announced, "She's gone. Time of death ten thirteen a.m." He felt the pat on his back. "I'm sorry."

He nodded his appreciation and the doctor and nurse both left them.

Joyce's wails were excruciating to hear. Austin tuned out everything else happening in the room around him and focused on her face, memorizing it. He'd grown accustomed to seeing her with all the tubes and wires from machines and took comfort in seeing her unobstructed face. She didn't look like she had before the accident, but she was an attractive woman, even now in death.

Joyce and David each embraced him warmly before they left the room. He knew it was time for him to leave as well, but he wanted a moment alone, just to sit with her, one last time.

ص

Lora-Beth stood in the hall fighting back tears. Her heart broke watching his pain. She was here as Austin faced the single-most difficult moment in his life and he needed her to be strong. She was here for him. She didn't know if he'd turn her away or be angry that she'd come at all, but she couldn't *not* be here. From her position in the hall, she could hear their sobs. Janet's room door was closed as the family spent their last minutes with her.

The staff had left the room more than ten minutes ago, but Austin remained inside. She'd wait. She'd wait all day if needed. Whenever he was ready to leave the room, she would be there to help him in whatever way he needed. She felt a hand slip inside hers and saw it was Toni. The two didn't exchange any words. It wasn't necessary. Lora-Beth should have known her best friend would want to be there for her, for Austin.

121

The door opened and Joyce, followed by whom she assumed was Janet's dad, left the room. Joyce caught her eye and Lora-Beth mouthed, "I'm sorry."

The woman nodded in reply, stopped in front of the two of them and took a hand in each of hers. "Thank you for coming," she said. The man pulled his wife to his side and led her down the hall toward the exit, looking as broken as she could imagine two people being.

Austin stopped short and gasped when he saw Lora-Beth and Toni. She moved to him and he opened his arms to receive the hug she'd come to deliver. He clung to her and let out a sound of a wounded animal. She held him for long moments as he buried his head in her neck and together they cried.

If he tried, he couldn't describe how he felt right now in Lora-Beth's arms. Despite his sadness, he was overcome with relief at finding her here, at this moment. He was one ball of emotion and the strength of her hold on him was just what he needed to keep him grounded. Once again his heart beat too hard and too fast. He gave in to his emotions and released the hurt and sadness he'd tried and failed to gain control of before leaving the room.

Lora-Beth whispered reassuring words in his ear as she held him. Cooing, "It's okay", "I'm here for you", "Whatever you need", and "You're going to be okay." Austin nodded and held on a little tighter. He felt the sob leave his throat and gave into his emotions, releasing the hurt and sadness he'd tried so hard to avoid after she asked if he was ready to leave. He was almost ready, but not just yet.

She couldn't say how long they stayed that way, but when Lora-Beth finally looked up, Toni was gone. Lora-Beth took Austin by the hand and asked, "Will you let me get you out of here?" Austin nodded his agreement and allowed himself to be led out of the facility and into her car. The car was silent as they drove. She had a place in mind and hoped Austin would understand her motives.

Forty minutes into the drive, Austin seemed to emerge from his torpor. He looked around as if trying to figure out his surroundings. He fixed his gaze on Lora-Beth in the driver's seat and asked, "Where are we going?"

"We're almost there."

"Where is there?"

"I think you'll recognize it when we get there."

Not five minutes later Lora-Beth pulled into the parking lot and was lucky to find a decent parking spot. "We're here," she announced, unbuckling her seatbelt.

"A shopping center?"

"Yes," she said slowly. "But not just a shopping center. North Hills Shopping Center." When it didn't click, she went on. "The last time you were here it was crowded with people, there was music playing."

"Yes, a music festival."

"A happy day for you two."

Austin stared off into the distance. He and Janet had celebrated the news of finding out their baby was a girl at this outdoor music festival. It was one of his favorite memories they'd made together before the accident. He'd told Lora-Beth about this during one of their conversations when she asked him to tell her about Janet. He said it was one of the happiest days of his life. He thought now of how Janet had sang and danced, brimming over with happiness. He'd loved watching his usually reserved girlfriend so unabashedly open. "I don't know what to say. You didn't have to do this."

Lora-Beth just smiled. "Come on." She popped the trunk and reached in to grab a picnic basket and a folded blanket. "I know it's the middle of the day, and there's no music, but we can still sit out on the green and enjoy the memory you made here. We can spend the afternoon remembering her as she was that day. Remember you as you were that day. I'll even play us some music on my phone if you like," she added.

"You brought food."

She looped her arm through his and crossed the lot. "Yeah. I thought it would be nice to sit out and be by ourselves. I thought you might prefer that to the silence and solitude of your house."

Austin was quiet. In his mind he could hear the beach music playing, he could see the band on the stage, and even feel the steady pulse of the crowd. Lora-Beth set the basket down and spread the blanket out near a tree on one side. She sat and patted the space next to her. Austin joined her, opting to lay flat on his back. Lora-Beth repositioned and lifted his head to rest on her thigh.

When she found a jazz station on her music app and started to play it, Austin spoke up. "Beach music. It was beach music." She changed the music and set her phone on the blanket next to her hips, close to him.

"Knowing it was coming didn't make it easier," he said. Lora-Beth stroked his hair. "I thought it would."

"It was never going to be easy. But you're so strong. You've been through so much, and here you are, still going."

"I don't feel very strong right now."

"Well, for now, you can borrow from my strength."

"I've been borrowing your strength from the moment we met," he admitted.

She didn't see it that way at all. They'd been getting to know each other, and in doing so, she'd found that what he needed more than anything was a friend. Someone he could be himself with. Someone who hadn't known him before, who could accept the man he was now. She was happy to be that person for him. Even if deep down, the last thing she wanted to be was his friend.

The sound of giggles drew their focus and they turned their heads to see a little girl and boy, somewhere between two and four years old, laughing and swatting at bubbles a woman blew in their direction.

"I don't know that there's a better sound than sweet kiddie giggles," Lora-Beth said.

I'd trade it for Janet's off-key singing right now, Austin thought. But he didn't say that. Instead he asked, "What's in the basket?"

"Wraps, pasta salad, chips, cookies, and a thermos of sweet lemon tea. Are you hungry?"

"Not really. I was just curious."

"Let me know when you're ready. For now, I want to tell you a story."

"What kind of story?"

"About the time my sister and I, along with two of our friends, entered a local talent show."

"What was your talent?"

"Think Fly Girls from *In Living Color* meets elementary school performance."

"This should be good." Austin didn't care what she was talking about, as long as she was talking. He was thankful for her thoughtfulness, her kindness. She seemed to always find a way to give him what he needed when he himself didn't have a clue what it was he needed.

"Oh it was something. Though I'm not sure I'd call it good."

Realizing the day and time, Austin tilted his head to look up at her. "Shouldn't you be at work?"

"I'm where I should be." She held his gaze. "Now let me tell my story."

"I'm listening."

It was four twenty-five p.m. and Lora-Beth and her two person team had just arrived back at the office from pitching a presentation to a prospective client. The presentation went well. Despite how well it had gone, the client told them they were meeting with a few other teams and would let them know by the end of the week. She was heading into a meeting with the Senior Vice President of her team, but needed to visit the little ladies room. With three clients left to contact, and an inbox that hadn't been touched since morning, Lora-Beth knew it was going to be one of those days where work didn't leave much time for life.

Lora-Beth tapped on Sam's door and stepped through once he'd waved her in, though he was on a call. She took a seat and waited patiently as he tried to wrap things up.

"Lora-Beth, thanks for your patience. You know how it is. There's always a fire to put out."

She did understand. The steady pulse was one thing she loved about her job. No two days were the same. The clients kept them thinking on their feet. "Yes, I do. But you handle it well."

"I'm just going to cut to the chase. It's looking like there will be a spot opening up soon. I can't give any details, but I'm meeting with you and a couple others to see where your heads are. Nothing is set in stone, so at the moment we're only putting feelers out there."

"What's the hypothetical spot?"

"Senior Brand Manager. It would be a big undertaking, but a great opportunity."

"Thank you for considering me."

"What are you thinking? Level with me. Is that something you think you're ready for?"

She couldn't be totally honest. This was one of those situations where finesse was necessary. Not that she wanted to be dishonest. She needed to figure out, for herself now that it had been brought to her, if she was willing to trade the life she was settling into for a higher spot on the career ladder. "I'd have to give it some thought. I love where I am at the moment, leading the team. I've finally gotten in a groove with this position."

Sam nodded. "I can understand that. You're good at what you do, which is why you're being considered along with others who have more experience under their belts."

"I appreciate that. I do love this job." *This job*, Lora-Beth thought.

"Well, let's keep this between us for now. Like I said, we're just having a conversation. There is no req, because presently, there is no job available."

"Will do."

"That's all I had. Is there anything you wanted to speak with me about? Take advantage while you have me."

"Not at this time. I'll let you know if that changes."

The moment Lora-Beth reached her desk, she reached for her phone, preparing to text Austin and Toni about what had just happened.

LB: Just left a meeting with my SVP. Looks like that job may be opening soon. Details to come. Late day today.

Lora-Beth texted Toni the news about missing yoga in the park and the possible position, then focused on her emails. Maybe she could finish up in enough time to make it to the seven o'clock Pilates class.

Her phone buzzed.

Toni: Where are we on the promotion this week? For or against?

LB: Haven't decided.

Her phone rang, Toni's name showing on the display. Lora-Beth picked up. "Don't be pressured into anything you're not ready for. And that's just good life advice right there, girlfriend. You're welcome."

"I'll take it under advisement."

"Can't stay on long. But I have time, so how's your day? Crazy?"

"Not crazy, just busy. Hate that I'm going to miss yoga, but if I can get out of here, I'm going to try to make it to Pilates at seven."

"Okay. I may skip out on yoga and go get my baby. Ma says he's been fussy today."

"Oh no. Poor thing. I'll call later and check on Titi's baby."

"K, girl. Talk later."

"Later."

Lora-Beth opened a client file, picked up her phone, and dialed the manager of the alt-rock band. He'd left three messages and she needed to know what was so urgent. *This should be good,* she thought.

ص

Lora-Beth set the timer on her heart rate monitor and headed left out of her driveway. It was time to get serious about her training for the 10K. It was only four weeks away and not once since agreeing to enter the race with Toni had she run more than her usual four miles. She needed something to take her mind off Austin anyway, specifically the fact that she hadn't seen or heard from him in four days, since the day of Janet's service.

He'd been so stoic. She respected that he likely needed space, but it didn't stop her worry. She'd feel a lot better if he answered her calls or just responded to one of her messages, letting her know he was okay.

She headed up Radford toward the entrance to the trail, hoping to get lost in the music and focus on nothing but her breathing. There was a nip in the air and Lora-Beth welcomed the feel of it in her lungs. Appreciating the beauty of the rising sun, she steadied her pace, increased the volume in her ears, and logged two and a half miles before turning back in the direction she'd come, making her total for the day five miles.

LB: Hi. Checking on you. Hope you're okay.

Lora-Beth placed her phone on the counter after sending the text to Austin and stepped in the shower, hoping to have a response by the time she returned.

Chapter Seventeen

GRIEVING. Was what he'd been doing. And he needed to do it his way. The problem was, he wasn't sure what his way looked like. He knew he couldn't talk about it. He needed to feel it, live in it for now, and go where it took him. Janet had been buried two days ago and the past few nights he'd drunk himself to sleep. Now he was having the pancake special at The Root Cellar Café. Not because he loved it, but because it had been one of Janet's favorites.

He made some calls and set everything in place before stopping by the jobsite to let Chris know he was taking a few more days and give him the rundown for while was away. Feeling the need to hit the open road, Austin headed home to pack a bag. Lora-Beth had been calling and texting, but as much as he appreciated her cheery disposition, he couldn't handle it right now. Right now he wanted to wallow.

He checked his bathroom once more to make sure he grabbed everything and zipped his bag closed. Then he headed for the car and hit the road. Not thirty miles later, he was pulling up at the rest stop off I-85. His tears had stolen his vision, so for the sake of safety, he pulled into the spot and sat until he regained his composure. He was headed to

Charlotte, straight to that little soul food spot, remembering how much Janet had enjoyed eating there.

Later that night, after checking into a hotel, he found that in his wandering, he ended up at one of the buildings he'd been a part of making happen. Though he hadn't had a large enough role to call it his, he felt a surge of pride looking at the building in all its significance.

SCREAMING. Was what he was doing. Screaming at a building at the top of his lungs in the middle of the night. Austin screamed until his throat was raw, but no tears came. He was at the site he'd been working on when he'd gotten the call notifying him of the accident. He felt nothing for the building. Though he could appreciate its uniqueness, all it was to him was the job he'd been working on when it happened. The project had been in its early stages, so for him, it held no fond memories. He wasn't physically here when the call had come. He was at the condo, asleep. The phone had jarred him from a deep sleep, and before he'd picked it up, he'd known something was wrong. Middle of the night calls were rarely good.

Austin's phone buzzed and he took it from his pocket and hurled it. It collided with the side of the building and shattered. He couldn't listen to one more person calling to offer him their condolences. What the hell was he supposed to do with them? He'd seen enough sad faces and had received enough condolences to last a lifetime. Where had all those friends been for the past couple of years when Janet was still alive? Where was their concern for her, or him, then? He didn't need their pity. The last thing he needed was calls and texts from people who'd all but forgotten about

Janet. They could save their time as far as he was concerned because he was done answering those calls.

DRIVING. Twelve hours after stumbling to the hotel, Austin was five hours into his seven-hour road trip, heading west. He was going home to Nashville to speak with his dad. Last night he thought about how easily his father seemed to get over his mother's death and move on with his life. Faced with losing another significant woman in his life, Austin needed answers. Late-stage liver cancer had claimed his mother's life and within two months of diagnosis, she was gone. *How does a man get over that?*

He hadn't gotten over it. So how had his father been able to do it? The thought made him angry. Or maybe it only seemed like anger at the time. Either way, it was at that moment he realized it was time he had a talk with his father about his mother and how he handled life after her death. He needed to. Because he couldn't reconcile his father's actions with what he was feeling. And the more he thought about it, the angrier he got.

Austin checked his fuel. He was sitting at a quarter tank and had about a hundred and twenty-five miles left on his drive. He changed lanes to take the next exit. He would fill the tank, grab a power bar and a bottle of water in Crossville, TN, and get back on the road.

QUESTIONING. Was what he was about to do. And he wasn't leaving without answers. Austin pulled up at the curb outside his father's house, a different house than the one he grew up in, and shifted the gear into park. He switched the engine off, pulled the keys out, unlatched his seatbelt, and opened the door so swiftly it all seemed like one fluid move.

He waited at the door after pressing the doorbell, shifting his weight from one foot to the other. Anxious. He could hear murmurs growing closer from the other side of the door. He took a deep breath and steeled himself, ready to face whatever was on the other side.

The door opened, revealing a tiny, middle-aged woman, his father's wife. She paused for a brief second but recovered quickly. "Austin, my gosh, what a surprise. Come, come in." She looked happy, albeit surprised, to see him standing at the door. It wasn't that they weren't close, they didn't have much of a relationship at all. Austin didn't step inside, instead he said, "Hi, Susan. Is he around?"

"Not at the moment, but your dad should be home shortly. Was he expecting you? Why don't you come in and wait for him? Please."

"No. He didn't know I was coming. I just got in town."

Susan could tell Austin wasn't interested in her offer to come inside. "Austin, is everything okay?"

"Who is it, Mama?" Austin heard from behind Susan.

She met his eyes when she said, "It's your big brother."

"You're kidding." The girl appeared in the doorway with a disbelieving smile on her face. She stepped around her mom and threw her arms around Austin's middle, hugging him tightly. "Oh my God, I'm so glad you're home!"

Austin froze. He didn't have this kind of warm and fuzzy relationship with them. This was his father's family. When she didn't immediately let go, he melted a little and returned her embrace, meeting Susan's eyes over the girl's head. "I guess I could wait for him inside."

ص

Not long after, Austin sat on the sofa looking at his father, who stood in the doorway looking back at him. He was sitting in the living room with his siblings, Erica and Alex, listening to his sister talk about high school drama club. Apparently, it was a big deal that she held an officer position as a freshman. Alex was not impressed by her role as the club historian.

"There he is. Austin, good to see you." his father said finally.

Austin rose to his feet and started toward his father, extending his hand when he got within a few feet. "Dad."

His father took his hand, gave it a firm shake, and drew his son close. "How are you, son?" he asked as he patted him on the back.

"I've had better days."

Austin's father placed an arm over his shoulder and called to his other children, "We'll be in my study. No interruptions." When he got no response from the teenagers he asked, "Understand?"

"Yes, sir," Erica called.

"Got it," Alex agreed.

Andrew closed the door behind them and Austin took a seat in one of the armchairs. He sat in the other chair. The room smelled like leather and floral wall plug-ins. "Why didn't you call?"

Austin cut a glance his way, offended. "I didn't realize I needed to call ahead before coming to my father's house."

"That's not what I mean. That look on your face, I recognize it. I'm asking why you didn't call. I would have been there."

Austin scoffed. "Why? You didn't even know her."

"No, but I know you and how you felt about her. My presence would have been for you, son." He paused, wondering about the nature of the visit and trying to get a read on his son. "When?" he asked.

"About a week ago."

Andrew shook his head, understanding what his son was going through, having gone through it himself with the loss of Austin's mother all those years ago.

"What's the look that you recognize?"

"The shadows in your eyes. Anger, pain, and disappointment. The mask that's doing a poor job of hiding it."

Austin thought the description was fitting, although he'd have added confusion to the mix. "I'm surprised you know what that looks like."

"And why is that?"

"I never got the impression you felt those things after Mama."

"Then you'd be wrong."

"Guess your mask was better than mine."

"Son, say what's on your mind. You know I'm not one for all this double talk."

"Did you even love her?"

"Austin."

"Did you?"

"Of course I did. I don't know how you could even ask me such a ridiculous question. I loved your mother with everything in me."

"Right. That's why it was so easy for you to move on. Mama was gone one day then you packed her away and got on with your life the next."

"That's just how you're remembering it. The memory is a funny thing. I loved your mother for twenty-two years before I lost her. I had over twenty years of loving that woman while she was here and I grieved her in my own way. But that was nothing for you to see. I still had you to finish raising. I couldn't fall apart because a part of my soul was gone. I had to keep moving. You needed me to keep moving. But oh, I grieved. Trust me, I grieved plenty."

They locked gazes and Austin regarded his father for a long moment, recognizing the sadness in the depth of his eyes. "When did it stop?"

"I'm afraid it never stops, son. The rough edges wear off and you find a way to live with it. It never goes away, but the wounds heal and the scars make it easier to live with the pain of the loss. It never becomes comfortable, but it gets better. One day you'll realize the memories are recalled with fondness and it'll hurt a little less to think of her." He paused before a smile Austin recognized unfurled across his face. Going on, he said, "There are random times I still think of your mother. Things she used to get on me about or things she enjoyed. They're ingrained. I couldn't stop them if I tried, and you know, I don't try. I'm proud to carry her with me."

"And Susan? How were you able to..." He trailed off, grappling with his own guilt for his growing feelings for Lora-Beth. The woman had crawled into his broken heart and started to put it back together from the inside. Part of him soared with the thought, but another, saner, part of him was laced with guilt and conflicted over the fact that she was the only thing that had given him any solace during this impossibly difficult time.

"My love for Susan has nothing to do with my love for your mother, son. I love them separately. What I got from your mother, what I needed at that time in my life, is not the same as what I get from Susan, nor would I ever want it to be. I'm not the same man I was when I belonged to your mama."

"You started over. Got a whole new life."

"No, I went on living. There's a difference. You may not be able to see it now, but one day you will. Nothing you do in the future will change what you had with your Janet. But that doesn't mean you won't go on to have a good life with someone else."

In quiet contemplation Austin let what his father said wash over him. He knew his father was right because he could already feel it and that had been his problem. That *was* his problem. "I was angry," he started. "When I made the decision to come here, I was angry at you, at how you erased her from your life. I was struggling to reconcile my own feelings, and out of nowhere, you popped into my head. And the more I thought about it, the angrier I became. When Mama died, we stopped being a family and became just father and son."

"We've never stopped being a family. You are my family, Austin, and you're a part of this family."

Austin cut another glance his way, then hung his head. "I'm not."

"Well, you're our family, and we're here. You're grown and I don't pressure you, but you've always been welcome. I'm sorry that I've failed to make you feel that way."

He had no response, but searched his father's eyes, looking for the truth in them.

"Stick around for a few days. Spend some time with your brother and sister. They know you, because I talk about you, but let them get to know you *from* you. Seeing them for a few hours every five or six years? You're robbing them of knowing you and they're good kids. You may realize you're not doing yourself any favors either."

"Maybe. I'm going to head out for now. Go bring some fresh flowers to the cemetery."

"Go on, stop by, talk with your mama, but when you're done come back, don't go to a hotel. At least spend one night here, under this roof, with your family."

Austin stopped short when he reached the headstone marking his mother's plot. Rosemary Anne Watts. Loving wife and mother. There was a rosebush that was obviously cared for. The season's final flush of pink blossoms were still on display. Austin set the vibrant bouquet he brought with him down and lowered his face to a rose to get a whiff of its scent. This had to be his father. He planted this rose bush. He tended it. He visited her. Sixteen years he'd been married to another woman and still took the time to do something because he knew she'd loved it. Austin had only visited this cemetery once since he moved away. And his father visited at least semi-regularly. Tears sprang to his eyes.

"Hey, Mama. Your roses are beautiful. Not as nice as when you had them, but the old man does an okay job."

CHAPTER EIGHTEEN

Austin sat with his mother until dusk, then headed back to his father's house to find all eyes on him. Susan greeted him after his father let him in. "Just in time. You haven't eaten, have you? Dinner is just about ready. Maybe three minutes left on this batch of chicken then we can eat."

"Uh, no, I haven't had anything to eat since earlier."

"Well, go wash your hands and join us. Come on you two," she called out to Erica and Alex.

"I'll grab drinks," Alex said.

"I got the table," Erica added.

Fried chicken, mashed potatoes and gravy, green beans, and cornbread, served family-style. Austin's mind went straight to Lora-Beth. His father starting to say grace broke his thoughts thankfully.

"Thank you, Susan, everything looks amazing."

"How long are you in town for?" Alex asked and went on before Austin could respond. "If you're going to be here, I have a game on Thursday."

"What position do you play?"

"Running back, I'm quick too. It's JV. I'm only a sophomore but still, I'm pretty good. Coach says I'm still kinda small, gotta bulk up."

"That explains the two large pieces of chicken on your plate. Gotta add some more of those potatoes too."

"Don't encourage him," Susan joined in, matching Austin's playful tone.

Andrew sat back with a pleased smile on his face, taking in his family.

"Oh gosh, Alex, look at Daddy over there having 'big feelings'." Erica used air quotes to emphasize her point.

Everyone looked Andrew's way and he just smiled. "Okay, that's enough. Eat your food before it gets cold."

"That means he doesn't know what to say but he's happy you're here, Austin. I am too," Erica said.

"Me too," Alex added.

Susan didn't let the moment pass before adding, "We're all happy you're here."

"I do hope you'll be around come Thursday. They're nearing the end of the season and the team is pretty good. You might even run into some old friends. They get great support from the community."

"We'll see. If I'm still in town I will definitely come watch you play." He told Alex.

"Cool."

Austin was exhausted. And hadn't found sleep easily. He was grateful for the blackout curtains in their guest room because they allowed him to sleep until after ten the next morning. He was surprised to find his father sitting in the living room watching TV when he finally left the room.

"Good morning. Coffee is still hot if you're interested."

"Morning. Just gonna grab some water before I head out for a run."

"When you come back from your run, let's go grab some lunch. I want you to ride with me somewhere."

"Aren't you working today?"

"Nah. I'm taking the day off. Wanted to spend some time with you, son, just the two of us."

He met his father's eyes and answered the unasked question he saw in them. "I'm good."

"You're not. But you will be, in time."

"Well, I'm going to head out. Running helps clear my head. I'll be back within the hour. I'll be starving by then so lunch sounds good."

"I'll be right here."

When they turned on Mulberry Street, Austin knew they were headed to the barbershop owned by his Uncle Charles, one of his father's hangout spots. He should have known.

His father cut the engine and said, "Come on, let your uncle get a look at you. I talked to him this morning."

"He will not be cutting my hair," Austin said seriously.

"You can let him tighten you up. Won't hurt nothing."

"No." They shared a laugh at Uncle Charles's expense.

The bell on the door hadn't even fully sounded when he heard his name called. There was no one in his uncle's chair, but another barber, a younger guy, was working on someone.

"Good to see you, my boy!" Charles stood and reached his hand out to Austin who took it, gave it a shake, and pulled him in for a quick hug.

"Uncle Charles. It's good to see you. I see you're still at it."

He waved him off. "I ain't doing much of nothing. I tell you, if I didn't know better I'd think you were Andrew. Man, this boy is still your spitting image."

"Except those eyes. Those are all Rose." Andrew took a seat in his brother's empty chair.

"So, what brings you home? How long ya in town for?"

Austin took a seat across from his uncle. "I'm just in town for a couple days, taking a break. How's business?"

"Doing alright. Andrew tells me you started a business yourself. Guess entrepreneurship in the blood."

Austin took in his father, sitting there looking proud. "I did. It's good. Growing. Always something to do."

"Stay on top of those taxes. Don't let that get behind. And don't give responsibility of your books to a soul. You keep your eye on that yourself."

"Yes, sir."

"My boy has a good head on his shoulders. I'm sure he has it under control, Charles. Don't go lecturing him about his business."

"I ain't lecturing. I'm just telling. Good advice is good advice. Shouldn't matter where it comes from."

Austin spoke up. "That's good advice. I'll be sure to keep it in mind."

An older gentleman entering the shop had Andrew exiting Charles' chair. He shook the man's hand, greeted him by name, and introduced Austin before taking that opportunity to head out.

In the car his father let him know, "One more stop, then I'll turn you loose. But if I don't make sure you stop by Ida's while you're in town, she'll never forgive me."

"That's cool." Aunt Ida was his mother's oldest sister. She lived in his grandmother's house and Austin had lots of fond memories of spending time at that house growing up.

Phaedra, her only daughter, and her two kids still lived there since she needed a little help these days. Quan and Kyle, Aunt Ida's two sons, were in and out, so he didn't remember which of them was living there the last time he'd stopped and checked on her.

"Always a full house."

Aunt Ida was on the porch when they pulled up. She watched warily as they exited the truck and started her way.

"Ida, it's Andrew."

"Who's that you got with you?"

When Austin walked up the porch steps and she could make out who he was, she released a pleased squeal. "Well ain't you a sight for sore eyes. Andrew, don't go springing things on an old woman."

"Aunt Ida! It's so good to see you." He reached down and gave her a hug.

Andrew took a seat in one of the vacant chairs and laughed as Ida held on too long to be considered normal. Austin indulged her, and took a seat next to her, shifting her cane just a bit when she finally released him.

"Look at you. Just as handsome as you wanna be. How's life treating you in North Carolina?"

"I'm grateful for every day. How about you? You doing alright? You look good."

"Good thing I don't look like what I've been through. Some days are harder than others, but every day on this side is a good one."

"I know that's right."

"Y'all had something to eat? I just sent Quan to the store a li'l while ago."

"Yes ma'am, we had something about an hour ago."

"We went and sat down and had chicken fried steak at Arnold's."

"Yeah, they do a good job with that."

Quan pulled up, hopped out of the car, and grabbed three bags from the backseat. "Uncle Andrew, that you?"

"That's me."

"Cuz, man, where you come from? Whassup, man?"

"Ain't nothing, cuz." They dapped and exchanged shoulder bumps.

"Ay, I'm about to let Kyle know you here. What're you up to later? We can throw some stuff on the grill."

"I'll be around. That sounds good."

"Now I see why you're here this time of day. Had me worried something was wrong when I pulled up," he greeted Andrew.

"Nothing's wrong. Just playing hooky while my son is in town."

"Yeah, I know he's in and out so you gotta get it when you can."

Austin and Aunt Ida spoke at the same time.

"Come on now."

"Go put that stuff away before the meat gets warm."

"For real, I'm going to get some stuff together. Swing back by 'round six." Quan said before he stepped inside.

"Sounds good."

"Alright Ida, we'll go ahead and get out of your hair."

"I'll be back later."

"Y'all ain't bothering me none. I'm glad to see you. My sister would be so proud of you," she told Austin.

"Yes she would. I know I am," Andrew added.

Something released in Austin's heart. The frustration, the negative feelings he had bottled up about his father were changing. All these years later, to his father, his mother's family was still his family. He hadn't traded them for a new one. He'd simply added to his family, as he said.

ص

As day two in Nashville drew to a close, Austin realized he was avoiding. Avoiding his life. Avoiding the longing he felt. In doing so, he also realized his father's family *was* his family and they did want him around. And he didn't actually mind being here with them while he avoided everything else. They were a nice distraction. There was a soft knock on the door that broke his thoughts. When he opened it, it was both kids.

"We were thinking you might be in the mood for ice cream. Will you take us to get some? Our treat," Erica offered. How could he say no to that offer when they were both already wearing shoes?

"Ice cream sounds good." He stuck feet in his slides and grabbed his wallet and keys. "Let's go."

"We'll be back. Austin's taking us for ice cream," Alex announced, walking past his parents lounging in the living room.

"Okay," Susan answered as Austin and Andrew locked eyes. Austin nodded.

"Okay, where to?" he asked once they were in his car.

"The Old Fashioned Ice Cream Stand is about ten minutes away. Everything is homemade."

"Left out of the neighborhood, then right at the next stop sign. I'll tell you from there," Alex added from the backseat.

"Who would normally take you on your nighttime ice cream run?'

"That's funny. We would be eating ice cream at that house if you weren't here."

"This is a sibling perk. We're just taking advantage."

"Go through the next two lights. After that you can get over. The stand will be on the left. It's like two more miles.

"Are you always so quiet?" Erica asked.

He thought about it for a moment. "Not always. But I have a lot on my mind."

"Wanna talk about it? I'm a good listener. Ask Alex." She eyed him expectantly.

"She's aight."

"I'll keep that in mind."

"Well, if you don't want to talk to her, you can talk to me. Man to man."

"I appreciate you both."

"Slow down, it's coming up."

When they got out of the car, his sister gave him another big hug. "I'm really sorry, Austin."

Alex clarified, "Daddy told us what happened. I'm sorry too."

"Come here." He grabbed his brother and made it a group hug. Seemed like their dad wasn't the only one in this family with big feelings. "Thank you both."

He was suddenly too warm. His heart pounded. "Let's get that ice cream you promised me. I'm feeling like a double scoop."

ص

On day three he was longing and punishing himself for longing. He enjoyed having the time away with his family, but he was removing the option of seeking solace elsewhere. She'd infiltrated his dream last night, and in it, she'd been sad. It had taken him over an hour to find sleep again. He needed to get a phone. He could only allow himself to be cut off for so long. He had no worries about his business. He knew Chris and the team would handle it. She was the only other thing for him to consider and he'd been avoiding even considering her. He grabbed his keys to head out for a drive. Alex's game was tonight and he'd hit the road first thing in the morning to head back to North Carolina.

"Heading out?" Susan's soft voice coming from the laundry room startled him. He thought he was in the house alone. It was the middle of the day.

"Yeah, going for a drive. Need to clear my head."

She joined him in the hall, wanting to speak with him, but not hold him up. "I'm so glad you're here and getting a chance to spend some time with your brother and sister."

"Me too. Coming was a good decision."

"You know you're always welcome, right? You don't need a reason."

He met her eyes. "I'm starting to realize that."

"You're dealing with a lot. I want to make sure you know that you never have to face anything alone. Everyone here loves you and wants you to be okay."

He swallowed a lump in his throat. "I know."

"He misses you something terrible. He respects that you're grown, and your life is elsewhere, but it did his heart good that you knew you could come home when you needed him."

Austin sat down. "How is he, really?"

"He's good. Healthy. Happy. The kids keep him young." They shared a smile. "How are you, really?"

He gave a deep sigh. "I'm taking it one day at a time."

They heard the garage door go up. Susan patted his hand. "That's about all anyone can hope for."

She walked toward the door as Andrew opened it and greeted him with a quick kiss.

"Let me get back to the laundry."

"Austin, I'm glad you're still here. I want you to ride with me somewhere."

"Perfect, he was just about to head out for a drive." Susan gave Austin a small smile from the door of the laundry room.

In the car Austin asked, "Where to this time?"

"I just want to talk to you, son. Before you get ready to head out."

"We don't need to go for a drive to talk."

"No, we don't need to, but I want to be a little selfish and keep you to myself for a while. Is that okay?"

"Yeah, that's cool."

"Thank you for staying to catch the game tonight. He might not say it, but it means a lot to your brother. He's a lot like you."

"You were right, they're good kids."

"They love you."

Austin didn't respond to that. Instead he asked, "Where are we going?"

"I think you know."

He did know. They were going to visit his mother.

Sitting, talking about their life together, the three of them sharing memories, Andrew hated that Austin now had another loss to grapple with. Another cemetery to visit. He eyed the sky, then looked at his son with glossy eyes. They held gazes for a long moment before Andrew said, "It's hard to believe she's been gone eighteen years."

"Longer than I had her."

"You'll always have her. You'll always have them both. In here." He patted Austin's chest and left his hand there, waiting to feel his son's heartbeat.

"I'm sorry for the distance I put between us."

"I'm sorry for not trying harder."

"She'd be disappointed in us both."

"More me than you." Andrew's smile was sad.

"Yeah, you more than me. I was her sweet boy, it'd definitely be your fault." Austin laughed.

"I know you need to head back, but did you get what you needed?"

Austin sighed. "I don't know."

"What else is on your mind, son?"

"There's someone I've gotten close to. She matters. And I can't reconcile what that means."

"You're allowed to have people that matter to you. Doesn't take anything away from the love you have for Janet."

"My heart knows you're right. But my head's kinda messed up about it."

"Guilt?"

"I guess."

His father listened. And watched. Just sat while he tried to find the words. "Maybe guilt. Yeah."

"Guilt because you think you're doing wrong or guilt because the thought of being happy and she's gone feels wrong?"

"Both in any given moment, honestly. But this friend, she has made the past six months bearable. She's... incredible."

"Does she know what you've been going through? Have you talked to her about it?"

"Yeah, she knows it all."

"Everything?"

"Everything. She's been nothing but supportive."

"And you're in love with her."

Austin nodded his response.

"And you feel like loving her is a betrayal?"

Austin nodded again.

"It's not, son. It's betrayal if it's done as an act of carelessness toward someone. Doesn't sound like that's what happened here."

"No, that's not what's happened at all. Talking to her, being with her, has helped me carry the load. I tried to not cross any lines. I'm not sure if I've succeeded."

"I can tell you this, there is no right answer to the question you aren't asking, but it's not wrong to love someone who shows you they care. I'm happy you have her."

Austin said nothing, so his father continued, "Just take it one day at a time and see how that feels. Don't deprive yourself of joy just because you're grieving. The two can coexist."

"I've seen the truth in that these past few days. I was out of line for coming at you the way I did the other day."

"You were hurting. I knew you didn't mean it."

"I meant it at the time. I was wrong."

"Does that mean we might see more of you?"

"Yeah, I'll do better."

"Then what more can I ask?"

Alex's team pulled off the win, twenty to fourteen. When Austin finally reached the guest room that night, he flopped on the bed, wanting nothing more than to hear her voice as he fell asleep. He really needed to replace his damn phone.

ص

On day four Austin was up and showered before the kids. He wanted to give them a proper goodbye before he hit the road, so he planned to take them to school and grab a fast food breakfast on the way. He stripped the bed and loaded the washer before packing up the remainder of his belongings. There was a soft tap on the door before his sister spoke.

"Leaving already?"

"Yeah, I need to head back. But if it's okay, I want to take you guys to school, we can stop by Chick-Fil-A or something for breakfast on the way."

"Sibling perk?"

"Yeah, sibling perk."

"Okay, let me hurry. Alex! Get up! Austin's taking us to school."

"Keep it down, child," Susan admonished, entering the hall.

"Sorry, Mom."

"Good morning, Austin."

"Morning. Is that okay? Me taking them on my way out?"

"Of course. I know you have to get back to your life, but I've really enjoyed having you here."

"It's been good to be here. Honestly."

"Don't wait too long to come back."

"I won't."

"Your dad's in the shower. He'll be out shortly."

"Okay. I started a load with the sheets."

"Thank you."

Half an hour later they were loaded up and their dad was seeing them off. He pulled Austin in for a hug and held an extra moment. "More big feelings?" Austin teased.

"Don't let your sister rub off on you. Get out of here. Be safe."

"I'll call."

CHAPTER NINETEEN

A WEEK. Seven whole days and not a word from Austin. The leaves were changing and Lora-Beth diverted her increasing anxious energy into work and exercise, but found herself struggling to focus on work at the moment. She'd texted several times. She'd called Austin and left him a voice message last night when she had trouble finding sleep, asking him to call her. Promising she wasn't meaning to be a bother, she reiterated that she just wanted to hear his voice and check on him. Still, he hadn't called. He hadn't texted. She was ready for this evening's yoga class. Maybe finding her chi, and remembering how she spent her days pre-Austin, would help carry her through this radio silence.

They were sitting in the sauna. Having finished yoga, Toni had about half an hour to spare before she needed to pick up her son and they were sweating it out under infrared lights. Both remained quiet for a few moments, before Toni, her head covered with a towel, broke the silence.

"You still haven't heard from him?"

Lora-Beth drew in a breath of hot air and sighed. "Not a word."

"He'll come around. He just needs time."

"That doesn't help."

Ignoring the annoyance in her voice, Toni went on, "I'm sure it doesn't but it's what you have. I know it's hard, but imagine what he must be feeling. Trust me, he'll reach out to you when he can."

"I know you're right, and I'm trying very hard to be patient, but it's difficult because I know he doesn't have very many people he's close to."

"Don't stress. This is temporary. You can't put a timer on it. Try to focus on something else. Find a series on Netflix and fill your evenings binge watching."

"I may have to. But tonight, I'm putting a second coat on the walls. It's coming together."

Toni shook her head. "You are determined to paint this room pink. I can't wait to see how it turns out. You know I'm not going to sugarcoat it, if it's hideous I'm going to tell you."

"It's not."

"Of course you don't think so."

"When the room is ready, I'll invite you over for the big reveal."

Toni laughed. "You've been watching too much HGTV."

Lora-Beth stood and took in her handiwork and decided that tomorrow she would visit her local home décor store and start pulling together the rest of the room. Barely Blush had been the perfect choice. Toni and Austin didn't know what they were talking about. The color was soft and inviting, and truthfully, more neutral than pink in the traditional sense.

She'd done a good job, even if it had taken her three nights to get it done. After taping it off on the first night, she'd called it quits. Luckily, her paint choice had the primer mixed in. Now, the almost white walls were a soft pink that made her happy just standing in the room. *Yes*, she thought, *this had been a good choice.*

Deciding she wouldn't send him another message tonight, Lora-Beth pulled back the covers, climbed in bed, and pulled up her Twitter feed. She needed the distraction.

NINE DAYS. It had been nine days since she'd seen or heard from Austin. She was trying to respect his space, his grieving process, but Lora-Beth was worried sick. She'd texted him at least once each day, just to let him know she was thinking about him. She'd called again, hoping he would pick up and just let her hear his voice. Three days ago, she left a message asking him to reach out and just let her know he'd been receiving her messages. She just needed to know if he was still there. He hadn't responded.

It was Friday evening and she was pulling up at Toni's. Her best friend, recognizing what she was going through, wanted to have a girl's night in, hoping to allow her to take her mind off it, and him, for a while.

Toni opened the door before Lora-Beth had a chance to press the bell. "Hey, girl."

When there were no little arms wrapping around her legs and no screeches of excitement at her arrival, Lora-Beth asked, "Where's MJ?" She'd been looking forward to those sweet baby hugs and kisses.

"Marcus took him to see the new animated movie that came out this week. They should be gone another hour or so."

"Oh."

"I cooked, come on, let's eat."

"I'm not hungry right now. Maybe later."

"A drink then?"

"I'm okay."

Toni didn't like this. She didn't like this at all. Her usually ultra-vibrant friend had not shown up tonight. In her place was a worry-stricken lookalike. She'd witnessed the chemistry between them, but she had no idea how deep their connection had grown. "LB, he'll call when he's ready. You can't worry this much."

Lora-Beth knew that was easier said than done. "My rational brain knows that. But there's a niggling part of me worried that something terrible may have happened."

"Oh God, you don't think he'd hurt himself, do you?"

She thought about it for a moment, trying to sort the anxiety she was feeling at not hearing from Austin. Did she think he'd hurt himself? No. She didn't think so, but if she was willing to be completely honest with herself, she couldn't say for sure what Austin would do. She knew so little about him outside of who he was with her. Could she really say how he would grieve? Can one person ever really say they know what another would do? She didn't know, but he'd been grieving since before she met him and she was sure that wasn't a vibe she'd picked up from Austin. "No. I don't think so." She said finally.

"Then, what?"

"I don't know. I can't explain. It just feels like I need to be with him right now."

Toni was quiet. She held her friend's hand, hoping she would find comfort in her company. She didn't know what Lora-Beth was feeling, but she was clear on the fact that her best friend had deep feelings for Austin, and that, she understood. She tried to imagine if it was Marcus, and he'd closed himself off from everyone in grief, what she would do. She'd be sick with worry. That was what she would do. She would be beside herself. Toni knew that for her best friend, her feelings for this man ran deeper than friendship. This man was special to Lora-Beth and she couldn't bear knowing how worried she was. "I think you should go to him."

"I can't do that. He's never invited me to his home."

"Do you know where he lives?" She nodded and Toni went on. "Lora-Beth, I've listened to you talk about this man for months. I can admit I thought it was odd at first, but you get him. If you can't let this feeling go, then go to him. He may not be able to say the words, or come to you right now, but now is when he needs you most. Don't overthink this anymore."

"What would I even say?"

"It doesn't matter what you say. You may not have to say anything, but if you do, I'm sure you'll think of something."

Lora-Beth keyed his address into her car's navigation system and it told her she'd arrive at her destination in thirty-two minutes. That was thirty minutes ago and she was now parked at the curb in front of his house doubting her rash decision. His truck and car were sitting in the driveway, rather than inside the garage, and she stared at the Honey-Do List logo on the side of the truck. *For all the home projects you never get around to doing* was printed in script below the image of a list. It was a good business idea... and she was stalling.

She picked up the phone and called Toni's number. Before she had a chance to say anything, her best friend started. "Go knock on the door. You can do this. He wants you there. You are not an unwelcome guest."

"Thanks, I needed that."

"I know. Now stop stalling, hang up the phone, and go handle your business. Call me later."

"*Okay.*"

Lora-Beth grabbed her purse and stepped out of the car, moving quickly before she lost her nerve. She rang the doorbell and waited. A minute passed and she pressed the button again, then knocked softly. "Austin, it's Lora-Beth. Austin?"

ص

Austin was prepared to ignore the ringing doorbell until he heard the familiar voice. He sighed, made his way to the door and swung it open, meeting her eyes briefly then turning away and walking back into the house. She let herself in, closed and locked the door behind her, and followed. She hadn't given any thought to what Austin's place would look like, but she was surprised by the clean, modern look of the open floor interior. He flopped down on the sofa, the muted television showing an old Bruce Lee movie. Beer bottles were lined up on the kitchen counter and not much else in plain view. There was no evidence he'd been eating, no dishes in the sink, no takeout containers.

"May I?" She motioned to the couch, asking if it was okay for her to have a seat. He gave a shrug of indifference. Lora-Beth sat on the opposite end of the couch, removed her shoes, and folded her feet under her, facing him.

Without looking at her he questioned, "What are you doing here?"

"Where have you been?" she countered.

"I took some time."

"I was worried about you."

He met her gaze and held it in an obvious challenge. "I'm fine."

"You haven't returned any of my calls or my texts. I wanted to see for myself."

"I had to go out of town."

Lora-Beth looked at him head to toe, reading his body language. It was giving her nothing.

Austin broke the silence. "Now you've seen me. I'm not good company right now. But as you can see, I'm good." Austin slumped down farther on the couch and leaned his head on the back of the sofa, his long legs stretching out in front of him. He folded his hands over his flat stomach.

"Did you lose your phone out of town? Or are they not allowed where you were?"

"Didn't lose it. Launched it into the air. It didn't land well. Wasn't in a hurry to replace it."

Lora-Beth recognized this withdrawn state. It was how he'd been when they met and in the early months to follow, but that had changed and he'd let her in. He hadn't exactly asked her to leave, so she decided not to take offense to his detached demeanor. "Have you eaten?"

"I eat when I'm hungry."

"When was the last time you were hungry?"

"I've been eating. I had something this morning."

"How many of those beers did you have this evening?"

"I'm not drunk if that's what you're getting at."

"I haven't had dinner either. Haven't had much of an appetite the last couple of days. I've been worried about you."

Austin ran a hand over his face and sighed. He hadn't meant to worry her. He just needed to get his head together when he'd gotten back from Nashville this afternoon. The break was nice, but being back in North Carolina was a different story. "I don't have much in there, but you're welcome to whatever you find in the fridge or pantry. Help yourself."

"What would you say if I ordered a pizza?"

"Alfredo's Pizza Village," he answered. "If you like that Chicago deep dish crap, I got no suggestions."

Lora-Beth walked toward the kitchen. She pulled up the number and as she waited for the call to go through, she opened the fridge to see what was inside. Breakfast food, deli meat, condiments, and beer. Okay.

Unable to help himself, he watched her move around his kitchen. He knew she'd be unimpressed by what she found, but it wasn't as if he was expecting company this, or any, evening. He'd barely been home for a couple of hours. He should have been bothered that she invited herself to his home, and was now moving around his space, but he wasn't. Rather, he was curious. She'd never been to his home, he didn't even recall telling her where lived, yet here she was, making herself at home.

He'd never met anyone quite like Lora-Beth. She had reached out to him before they'd ever met and still had a hold of him now. Why else would he have opened the door and allowed her in, when all he wanted to do tonight was be alone in his misery? His legs carried him to the kitchen and he sat on one of the stainless steel barstools at the island. His gaze was fixed on the back of her as she stood, peering into the small pantry. When she turned around, she caught his eyes and smiled.

"Pizza is ordered. I got wings too, but seriously, how do you survive with no food in the house?"

"I eat out."

"Everyday?"

"No. Some days you take pity and feed me."

"Or are you my guinea pig?" Lora-Beth joked as she came and stood next to him.

"Everything you serve is delicious, so it's working out in my favor."

Lora-Beth took his knees in her hands and turned him to face her. She stepped between his legs, wrapped his arms around her middle, and placed hers over his shoulders. "Next time I show up at your door after not seeing or hearing from you for over a week, make sure you greet me properly," she said over his head.

Austin rested his head on the pillows her full breasts created and held tighter and longer than necessary for a greeting. He could feel her heartbeat on his face.

"See, it's not too hard. Act like you like me." She felt, rather than heard, his chuckle.

"You caught me off guard. It won't happen again." He hadn't intended to completely avoid her. He was just taking some time to himself. He'd wanted to go to her on several occasions and the trip had started out as a way to avoid giving into that urge.

"Promise?"

"You have my word. The next time you show up at my door, I'll greet you properly."

"Perfect. See, I don't ask for much," she teased, pulling away.

"You hardly ask for anything," he mused.

"Funny, that's not what you said when I told you I wanted a skylight."

"Still on that, huh?" He was relieved that she let him off the hook and acted as if there was nothing deeper going on. He appreciated it, and her, more than he realized.

"Come on, you know it'll be amazing."

You're amazing, he thought.

Something woke Austin from the light sleep he'd fallen into and his foggy brain tried to register the sound. They hadn't talked about anything heavy. She avoided any questions about how he was feeling and for that, he was grateful. They found their rhythm, talking about everything and nothing, but not mentioning his grief, or her worry, again.

They decided on a Jack Reacher marathon while having their pizza. She'd fallen asleep, pressed to his side midway through the second movie, but he had continued watching. The something that had awakened him, he realized, was Lora-Beth, laughing in her sleep. He couldn't make out any actual words, but it sounded more like she was playing than just laughing. His face settled into a smile and he found it adorable that even in sleep she smiled and laughed.

Austin tried to adjust without jostling her. His couch was fine for sitting, but he was certain now that it wasn't a good spot for co-sleeping. He smoothed her hair, which she kept free, and pressed his lips to her forehead. "Thank you for being patient with me," he whispered and tried to find sleep again.

He needed to wake her. Although it was Saturday, he had to get to work. It had been so long since he'd slept next to someone, he'd forgotten how hard it could be to pull yourself away. He stayed awake way too long thinking about how good it felt just having her there with him. How thankful he was for her presence in his life. He'd hardly gotten any sleep. Lora-Beth was pure sunshine and he felt like a very lucky man to be holding her in his arms as she slept. He almost couldn't believe it was real.

He wondered if there was any way he could extricate himself from her without waking her and knew there wasn't. Somewhere in the early hours, she'd adjusted and was now wrapped around him, her leg thrown over one of his, her arm across his middle, her head on his chest, his vision filled with her hair. She was everywhere. Austin wrapped his arms around her tighter and closed his eyes. Five minutes. He'd give himself five more minutes to enjoy before he woke her. Or maybe he'd be a little late getting to the jobsite this morning. The guys would understand.

Chapter Twenty

It had been several weeks since Janet's passing and Austin was starting to find his new rhythm. The melancholy he felt on Wednesday and Sunday afternoons, time he'd grown used to spending with Janet, had worn on him. So last week, he'd found himself at the gym during that next lonely Wednesday evening. He still brought her fresh flowers every week, only now he took them to her gravesite, visited with her briefly, and then went on a long run or found himself back at the gym. Slowly, he was starting to fill his free time with things he enjoyed doing.

During a conversation where she'd asked him to share a happy memory about Janet, he'd shared a random story and Lora-Beth responded by telling him she could tell how much he loved Janet. It touched him in a way he'd felt as plainly as if she'd reached inside him and massaged his heart. He thanked God for her presence in his life, wondering at times how he would have fared without her in recent months.

She'd become a part of his everyday life. Talking with her via text throughout the day, dinners at her place, or before sleep conversations weren't the exceptions. They had become The Rule. He felt off kilter when he didn't receive a good morning text or random fun facts throughout his day. Things like:

LB: FUN FACT: I'm named after my two grandmothers, Loralei and Bethany.

LB: FUN FACT: I got a broken tooth playing Red Rover. I was six. The tooth was going to fall out anyway.

LB: FUN FACT: Ben & Jerry's chocolate chip cookie dough and Haagen-Dazs peanut butter salted fudge are my two current favorites.

Times where she was too busy to text, he filled the gap and sent her messages, joining her game, adding fun facts about himself or things that interested him that he knew she didn't care about, but was interested in simply because he'd shared.

Just yesterday, he'd texted her:

Austin: The country's oldest African-American architectural firm was located in Nashville.

When she'd gotten back to her phone, she responded:

LB: Maybe we should plan a road trip.

The suggestion brought a smile to his face. Without provocation, she implied the two of them should take a trip together, as if it were a given.

And just a moment ago, he'd sent her a message.

Austin: Sang in the church choir until I was 14. My mother insisted.

She'd quickly come to be his most trusted, most valued confidant. Finding Lora-Beth had been nothing short of a blessing. He hadn't let anyone in in a long time. He wasn't even sure he'd let Lora-Beth in. Strong and tender, she took care of him as if he belonged to her, as if he'd always been hers. From the moment they'd met, he hadn't felt as if they were strangers. The familiarity he witnessed between her and Toni the first night he met her, he felt with Lora-Beth. He was wholly comfortable with her and she seemed to be with him as well.

Austin was okay with Lora-Beth being a fixture in his life.

"Hellooo. Earth to Austin," Chris called out to him.

"What's up?"

"I called you three times. Don't tell me you're so tuned into spackling you didn't hear me."

"I guess so. What do you need?"

Chris leaned against the doorjamb, crossed one foot over the other, and stared at Austin.

"Are you going to stare at the back of my head or tell me what you need?"

"Saturday, after work, a few of us guys are getting together to watch some football and shoot the shit. You in?"

"Sure," Austin answered, without giving it any thought. He continued spackling.

"Sure? As in, you'll come?"

"Yeah. What's the big deal?"

"I guess there isn't one." Chris blinked, surprised by the instant agreement on Austin's part. Usually he'd reply with

I'll think about it or we'll see. First, pickup basketball and now this. Maybe the boss was finally starting to come around.

"Don't you have work you should be doing? Or am I paying you today to watch me work?"

Well, maybe he spoke too soon. "I'm on it, boss." Chris gave a proper salute and disappeared.

Austin felt the laugh spring in his throat and wondered how much of an ass his team thought he was. He'd been surprised to see them all at Janet's service. He was touched by the gesture.

Austin stood in his opened refrigerator door, peering inside, wondering if scrambled eggs would be a suitable dinner. He really needed to visit a grocery store. He tried the pantry in vain. Even if he found something worth consuming, he wouldn't be satisfied. He found his phone where he'd set it on the island and dialed.

"Hey. I have you on speakerphone. Let me know if you can't hear me."

"What are you making for dinner?"

"Who says I'm making dinner?" she teased.

"I can hear it sizzling and it sounds good."

Lora-Beth laughed. "It's just stir fry, but I know it's better than the *nothing* cooking over there. Come on, I'll share."

"You're too good to me."

"Yeah, yeah."

"On my way." Austin grabbed his keys, stuck his feet in his running shoes, and hit the door.

Twenty minutes later he knocked at her door and listened, knowing she'd call out.

"It's open!"

He heard the faint sound, so he let himself in and locked the door behind him. He set the bottle of wine he'd stopped for on the way down, calling out, "Where are you?"

"Here I am," she answered, emerging from the hall.

Austin stepped to her and greeted her with a friendly embrace.

"You're learning," she teased when they pulled away.

"But you're not learning to keep your door locked," he countered.

"Not a fair assessment. I only unlocked it because you were on the way." She walked to the kitchen, ready to plate their dinner.

"I picked up a bottle of wine."

"What's the occasion?"

"No occasion. Thought it might be nice to have a glass with the stir fry. And I wanted to express my gratitude."

"Well, thanks. It's chicken so chardonnay will go great with it. Wanna go wash your hands?"

"Don't have to tell me twice."

Lora-Beth excused herself after dinner and invited him to find something for them to watch. She emerged shortly after barefoot, wearing flannel pajama shorts and a UNC T-shirt. She sat close and pulled her feet under her. "What's it going to be?" she asked, referring to their entertainment for the evening.

"*Ocean's 8* if you're in the mood for it."

"Let's do it."

Austin stretched his legs out and rested his feet on the coffee table. No sooner than he adjusted the pillow under his head, Lora-Beth leaned the other way, lifting her feet to rest on his lap.

He hadn't realized, until he heard her moan, that he was massaging her feet. The sound jarred him and his eyes flitted in her direction. Her head was propped on her hand and her eyes were closed. Absentmindedly, he rubbed each until his hands grew tired and he was sure she'd fallen asleep.

Why was he feeling this way? Could their relationship remain platonic? He was losing the struggle and he was well aware of it.

When the credits rolled, he shut the TV off and extricated himself from beneath her legs, preparing to leave.

"Austin." It was a whisper.

The sound of it had him leaning down to get closer to her face. She was still asleep. He'd only roused her. From his knees, he watched her sleep, finally leaning down to press his lips to her forehead.

Her eyes popped open.

"Austin."

"Lora-Beth."

They spoke at the same time. They were face to face, barely an inch between them. His heart pounded in his chest.

This was it. He was going to kiss her, she knew it. Her heart raced and butterflies started their dance in her belly. The smoldering flame in his eyes encouraged her. Lora-Beth brought a hand to his face and held his gaze, giving him the affirmation he needed.

Austin's eyes lowered from her eyes to her lips and back again before he leaned in and pressed his lips to hers. He enjoyed the feel of her lips against his before tracing her bottom lip with the tip of his tongue, asking for entry. She opened to him, first touching her tongue to his and finally taking him in. He threaded his fingers through her hair to cup the back of her head, holding her to his kiss, stoking the growing fire. Lora-Beth moaned into his mouth and he felt it in his groin. He explored her mouth, thrusting his tongue deep. She rolled her tongue, captured his, and sucked. Suddenly, he pulled away from the kiss and pressed his forehead to hers, breathless.

Lora-Beth thought to ask for more, but found herself speechless, and that didn't happen often. But this was too much for her senses. "Wow," she whispered, struggling to calm her own breathing.

"Yeah."

He pulled away and looked into her eyes, expecting to see confusion, or an admonishment; he saw neither. What he saw in her eyes was validation that the moment had been perfect.

"I better say goodnight." When she nodded her understanding he asked, "Walk me to the door? That way you can lock up behind me." Again, she nodded. He stood to his feet and reached out a hand to help her up.

At the door, he hesitated, searching her face. "I need you to say something. You're giving me a complex. I'm not used to you being so quiet."

Lora-Beth stepped to him and tilted her head to look into his eyes. "Kiss me again."

He pulled her body flush to his, soft curves molding to his firm body, and there in her foyer, he kissed her again. He kissed her for every time he'd thought about kissing her but had held back. He kissed her remembering all the subtle ways she showed him how much she cared.

Lora-Beth went limp in his arms and he held her tighter and kissed her harder. He wasn't just kissing her, he was making love to her mouth. Caressing her tongue and nipping at her lips. Swallowing her moans of pleasure. She was gone.

Lost to the voracious way he kissed her. She couldn't get enough but her lungs were burning, desperate for air. When she pulled away from his lips reluctantly, gasping, he nuzzled her neck and kissed her there, trailing light kisses from there back to her chin.

"My God, Austin." She gripped his T-shirt in both hands at his back. She'd never heard such timidity in her own voice. This was foreign to her; these feelings, this surrender. The prolonged anticipation made this moment that much more intense. Vulnerability was a feeling she loathed and that was the only way she could describe the way she felt right now. Vulnerable.

He was fighting the temptation building inside him. With his hand in her hair, he tilted her head back and kissed the tip of her nose. "I think I better say goodnight for real this time."

When her eyes fluttered closed, he kissed each of them and whispered, "Lock up. Get some rest." But to Lora-Beth's ears it sounded like leaving was the last thing he wanted to do. Unable to find the words, she nodded. When he opened the door to leave, she stepped on the porch behind him, watched him walk to his car and back out of her driveway, wondering how she was supposed to wind down when he'd spent the past five minutes revving her up.

She'd wanted to know what his kisses taste like, how it would feel to have his lips and hands exploring her body, and now she knew. He'd opened Pandora's box and she knew there was no going back.

Blurred lines were all he saw. He sat in his truck at the end of her block kicking himself for giving into temptation. He'd placed the desire he felt for Lora-Beth in a box from the moment their eyes met in her foyer that first day. It had never been just *friendship*. It was lust at first sight and he wasn't a man known to give into lust. But so much more than physical attraction lay between them. She was tender, unselfish, and gave of herself so fully he'd begun to feel as if she gave all she had just to see him smile. Thankfully, he'd regained control of his libido and hadn't embarrassed himself. He'd been without the pleasure of a woman too long and Lora-Beth felt good in his arms, her softness pressing against his firmness, he feared at a single touch she would unman him.

Once he reached his house, he stripped down and stepped into the shower, turned the water on and groaned when the cold water hit his skin. As was the norm for him, this was where he would find release.

Chapter Twenty-One

Lora-Beth felt lighthearted walking onto the floor of her office building at half past eight the next morning wearing her favorite wrap dress, Louboutin slingbacks she'd treated herself to on her birthday this past January, and a smile. Her day was off to a great start. She'd run five miles, had a decent breakfast, and was having the best hair day she'd had in a while. She met nothing but smiling faces on her run this morning, when usually most of the runners on her route seemed not to notice each other at all.

"Good morning. You're looking very chipper this morning, Lora-Beth," Reema, the receptionist on her floor, noted.

"Ah, come on, Reema, don't I look chipper every morning?" she teased.

"You do, but you seem to be glowing today. Whatever it is, get you some more of it."

"I'll take that compliment and go. Have a good one." She stepped away and made a beeline for her office.

She had no idea that last night would be any different from any of the nights before it, but she and Austin had turned a corner and she was feeling very good about it. Now to talk it over with Toni and make sure she wasn't making too much of it. Toni was famous for making mountains out of molehills, but she was Lora-Beth's sounding board. She picked up the phone and typed out a text, then pulled up her work email inbox. She had a meeting at nine, which meant she had less than half an hour to get through the forty-seven new messages staring back at her.

Her phone rang as soon as she'd read the first message. She should have known sending a message that read: He kissed me! would earn her an immediate call.

She picked up the call. "Hello."

"What? Where? How was it?" Toni asked in a dramatic whisper.

"Austin kissed me, on my couch, in my foyer." She dragged out the words, leading her friend to ask more.

"Shut up and tell me everything!"

"I can't do both. Do you want me to shut up or do you want the details?"

"Lora-Beth Haines, do not play this game. I don't have time for it. I just dropped from a work call to hear this story. You better make it worth my while," Toni fake threatened, causing Lora-Beth to burst out in giggles.

"Toni, I literally can't remember any other kiss. I feel like I'd never been kissed before I felt his lips on mine."

"Damn."

"I fell asleep watching a movie, and I woke up and he was there, looking at me with those eyes blazing. I knew it was coming. My brain had time to register it, because it happened in slow motion. When he finally took my lips…" She trailed off. "I can't even explain how this man took control of me."

Toni squealed. "You got it so bad." Lora-Beth could hear the smile in her voice. "Could you imagine waiting all this time, all that build up, and he turned out to be a terrible kisser?"

"No, I can't imagine it."

"Look at you, reminiscing. Come back to the moment and tell me what happened next. He just kissed you and left?"

"After making my knees go weak at the door, yeah, he told me goodnight and left."

"And you let him? Girl!" Toni asked, as if the thought of it were incredulous.

"I may have been a bit dazed."

"Yeah you were!" They shared a laugh. "Okay, now that you've crossed that bridge, don't overthink it. It's good. Let it be good. And don't get weird."

"What do you mean get weird?"

"Just relax and let it happen."

Lora-Beth took a moment to let Toni's words sink in. She'd done a good job of relaxing and going with the flow until now. There was no reason she shouldn't be able to continue doing so.

"When are you seeing him again?" Toni asked.

"You know we don't really make plans, he'll pop over when he pops over."

Toni squealed in excitement. "Maybe it's about time to make some plans."

"I thought you said to not make it weird. Suddenly making plans would be weird."

"No, it would be intentional. You're out of neutral now, but the car ain't gonna drive itself."

"We'll see. I don't want to rush him, with everything. I'm still following his lead for now."

"Fair point. Sorry. I'm getting ahead of myself."

"You're supposed to keep me grounded."

"Nah, not today. Today you get to walk around with your head in the clouds. I'll keep you grounded tomorrow."

ص

Instead of focusing on stripping the hardwood floors he'd been hired to refinish, his mind was on Lora-Beth and the way she'd given in to his kiss in her foyer. Her submission had been complete and his mind raced with thoughts of what it would be like to have her fully. There was one thing he was sure of, he'd taken so much from her, not giving much of himself, and it was time he stopped holding back and let her get to know Austin the man, not just Austin the griever. He'd been finding ways to be in her presence for months and had long since stopped with the pretenses and had embraced their *friendship*. And now, the thought of going two days without seeing her, interacting with her, left him in a foul mood. His guys never let him get away with it either.

Hours later, he was parked in front of her house when she pulled into the driveway after seven that evening. He'd decided to wrap up early, head home, and come to her freshly showered, not still wearing the day. Austin saw the curiosity on her face through the windshield and smiled to himself. He got out of the car and headed to her.

"Hey, you. Don't you look handsome? This is a pleasant surprise."

"I didn't realize you liked surprises. I'll have to keep that in mind." Austin smiled, unable to help himself. She was wearing workout gear and the evidence of the workout she'd had. He took the bag she'd slung over her shoulder. "Good run?"

"Why are you being weird?"

He laughed and Lora-Beth took in the lines around his mouth and his eyes when he did. "I'm not being weird," he started. "But I do want to know if I can take you out. On an actual date."

"Really? What would an actual date with you look like?" she said, teasing.

"Well." He slung an arm over her shoulder and started up the driveway. "It would look like me picking you up, feeding you, and maybe even entertaining you a little."

"How is that different from the other times we've hung out?" she asked after closing the door behind them.

He set her bag down by the door and stepped out of his shoes. "Um, I guess because now we'd call it a date? And because now that I've had a taste of you, you can expect me to kiss you at the end of it." He was rusty, but he still remembered how to flirt.

"So what you're saying is I have to sit through a whole meal before I can get one of your kisses?"

Austin pulled her to him and placed a gentle kiss on her lips. "No. You can have a kiss from me whenever you like." He nuzzled her neck.

Lora-Beth pulled away in horror. "Ew! Don't. I'm all sweaty."

"I don't mind a little sweat."

Lora-Beth blushed. She could get used to flirty, happy Austin. "Are we going on this date tonight? Or did you mean sometime in the near future?"

"Tonight would be good."

"Okay. Make yourself at home. I'm going to shower, then I'm all yours."

Austin watched her walk away, thinking he liked the sound of that. He'd do his best to distract himself from the fact that she was just down the hall in the shower.

Austin stepped out on her deck into the barely lit evening, appreciating the space and taking in the yard. He knew how much Lora-Beth loved the colors of Autumn and though the sun had set, he could still appreciate the view. He decided he'd work on a couple of landscaping ideas and present them to her for adding to her backyard. For all she brought to his world, he'd do his part to color hers beautiful.

Taking her cue from Austin's attire, Lora-Beth dressed in a casual, knee-length nude dress and a pair of colorful pumps, refreshed her hair with a little leave-in conditioner and pinned it to one side. A bright pink lip and large earrings completed her look and she was pleased with it. It gave cute, fun, and sexy without looking like she was trying too hard. *Perfect for a date night*, she thought. She spritzed on Carolina Herrera Good Girl, selected a light jacket to shield her against the night air, and went in search of Austin. She found him standing on the deck, so she placed her jacket on the back of a chair and stepped out to join him.

Austin heard the door open behind him and turned his head in that direction. He took in the sight before him. Lora-Beth was gorgeous and he'd have told her as much if he could have found his voice.

She stood watching him, the look on his face told her he liked what he saw and that was good enough for her. In three steps, he was in front of her, close enough to touch. Close enough to be touched. A moment passed before he reached out, and even when he did, Lora-Beth could sense he was struggling to find what to say.

He ran his bent finger down her cheek, then cupped her face and placed a soft kiss there. "You're beautiful," he whispered into her skin.

Lora-Beth closed her eyes and appreciated the gentle way he touched her.

"Come on." Austin opened the door and ushered her through. "I know this little spot. I think you'll like it."

She'd mentioned to him, in one of their many conversations, that she enjoyed Teppanyaki style food, but didn't eat it as often as she liked. So he checked out a place ahead of time. Tonight wasn't the first time he'd thought of taking Lora-Beth to dinner, but it was the first time he thought of it as a date and had planned ahead to put it in place. He enjoyed spending time with her, but he wanted to make sure she was aware of the difference. Tonight wasn't about just hanging out. Tonight was not two buddies grabbing a bite. Tonight he was a man, asking a woman he was attracted to, to join him for food and conversation. Though he couldn't be certain, he felt confident Lora-Beth knew the difference.

"You're distracting me."

"How am I distracting you? All I'm doing is sitting here."

"You're watching me like you can't figure me out or you can't figure out what's going on. Even when you're not looking right at me, I can see you looking out of the corner of your eye."

"I'm not doing that. I'm just looking around. I can't help it if I'm naturally curious."

"Are you worried I may be kidnapping you?"

She laughed. "Of course not. I'm just... I don't know. I'm something."

He glanced at her before checking his blind spot and changing lanes. "Anxious? Nervous? Unsure?"

"All of those things and none of those things."

"Didn't you just tell me that you liked surprises?"

She thought about what she wanted to say, turning thoughts over in her head before she spoke. "You know how when you were a kid, and it was the night before something big happened, like going to Disney, and you couldn't get to sleep? That's how I feel right now. It's a good feeling."

"So you're excited?"

"If you want to oversimplify it, yes, I'm excited."

"But you have no idea where we're going or what we're about to do."

Lora-Beth looked at him, smiled, and spoke softly. "The what and where are not important. It's the *who* that matters most right now."

Austin reached over, grabbed her hand, and brought it to his lips. He didn't respond. He held her hand in his as they continued their drive.

He pulled into Timberlyne Village and parked in front of Oishii Japanese Restaurant and Sushi Bar.

Lora-Beth appreciated his handsome face and his attentiveness as they shared tonkatsu, bibimbap and orange wasabi salmon family-style. He met and held her eyes as she spoke. The tenderness in his eyes undid her.

When they'd been asked if they wanted a dessert menu, despite being stuffed and having to pack their leftovers to-go, she'd agreed to split a tempura ice cream with Austin. When the waiter showed up with a bouquet of deep pink and white calla lilies along with their dessert, she understood why he'd insisted. She couldn't hide the blush that warmed her face at his thoughtfulness.

"When did you do this?"

Lora-Beth lifted the flowers to her face and brushed the soft petals against her cheek. He loved that huge smile on her face and the gleam in her eye. Lora-Beth's face was so expressive. Her features, striking yet understated, highlighted her natural beauty. Austin appreciated the feeling of instant gratification at seeing her surprise. A couple at a nearby table watched with sweet smiles on their faces at the gesture. He reached over and took her hand. "You like them?"

"They're one of my favorites."

He'd known that. She'd told him in one of her fun facts that calla lilies were her favorite Fall flower. Lisianthus was her number two. Though he'd never heard of the latter, he planned to plant them both in her backyard so she could enjoy them always. He smiled at her. "I know."

Lora-Beth placed her hand on his face and gazed into his eyes. She liked what she saw there. She leaned in and pressed her lips to his in a gentle kiss. "This is so sweet. Thank you."

"You never have to thank me for making you smile."

She loved this man. She couldn't pinpoint when it had happened, but she was sure of what she felt. Austin Watts had captured her heart by simply being his kind, wonderful, wounded self. She brought the flowers to her face again. Not because she needed a reminder of their softness, but because she needed a moment to sort her thoughts. Her throat burned with words she couldn't say.

"How about we give this ice cream a try." Lora-Beth scooped some on the spoon and brought it to his lips in offer. He closed his lips around the spoon and closed his eyes to study the taste. "Well, does it pass the test?"

He took the spoon and returned the favor, offering her a taste of her own. "See for yourself." Lora-Beth locked eyes with him as the spoon grew closer to her lips. His eyes dropped from hers to her mouth and she made a show of sucking the ice cream from the spoon. Lora-Beth moaned, purposely baiting him. Austin wondered if the dessert would taste differently from her lips than it had a second ago.

"It's okay," she said finally.

He laughed. "If that's the reaction okay ice cream gets, then I'll bring Haagen-Dazs next time I see you."

Lora-Beth smiled inwardly as Austin walked her to her door. Before tonight, she wouldn't have given a second thought as to whether or not he was coming inside. It had become the norm for them to "hang out". But now, she wondered if he was walking her to the door to say goodnight or if they were going to fall on the couch and find something to watch on TV. She opened the door without a word, leaving the decision to him. If he didn't want to come in, he'd have to say so.

Austin closed and locked the door behind them and stepped out of his shoes. It wasn't something she required, but he'd gotten in the habit of removing them when he entered her house if he wasn't working. Lora-Beth followed suit and removed her shoes as well, losing three inches off her height, bringing her back to her normal five-seven. She flexed her toes and the bright pink color caught his eyes. She had nice feet.

She took his hand in hers and led him toward the kitchen. "Would you like a nightcap?"

Oh, he wanted to cap off the night alright. "I'll take a beer if you have it."

"Of course." She released his hand and reached into the fridge to grab a beer and the bottle of wine she'd opened the day before.

Austin twisted off the cap and took a long pull from the bottle. Before she could uncork the wine, he was on her. He came up behind her and wrapped his arms around her, burying his face in her neck. "Turn around." She turned, and in the space of a heartbeat, he pressed his lips to hers and slid in his tongue to mate with hers when she opened. He pulled away briefly to check her eyes and was pleased when she pulled his head back to join them again. He lifted her onto the counter and she opened to him, spreading her legs to give him room to fit between.

Lora-Beth was spinning. He'd taken hold of her and she was his to do with as he wished. She smoothed her hand up his back and loved the feel of his muscles beneath her hands. She sucked his tongue and he groaned, pressing the evidence of his arousal into the apex of her thighs. Austin kissed like a man in need.

Wordlessly, she met his eyes and recognized the fire in them. Lora-Beth had seen that look in Austin's eyes before. She touched his lips with the tips of her fingers and he took a fistful of her hair. Holding her gaze, he pulled her head to meet his and took her lips again, as passionately as before.

Austin moved from her lips to her jaw and down her neck. She made the sweetest sounds. He could kiss her for hours. He loved how responsive she was. He wanted to devour her. Austin slid his hand over her breast and held the weight of it in his large palm before circling the nipple with his fingers in the same motion he used with his tongue on her neck. When she moaned and arched into his hand, he felt it in his groin. He pulled away, held her head on both sides, and peered down at her before shaking his head, as if trying to clear his thoughts. He pressed his forehead to hers.

He was communicating to her in all the ways words wouldn't allow. Austin was telling her how much he adored her, how much he wanted her. He was telling her that with her was where he wanted to be. Lora-Beth heard his message loud and clear and answered in kind.

She wrapped her legs around him and held him to her with one hand behind his head, the other around his back. When she felt his hand on her breast again she felt it in her core. He ignited her. She sensed the melee going on inside him. He was holding back and she wasn't sure why. She could see it in his eyes, felt it when they touched. He wanted her as much as she wanted him, but he was exercising restraint.

"I knew it would be like this," he said, almost to himself.

He pressed one more kiss to her lips then lifted her off the counter and set her on her feet. "I think our nightcaps are getting warm."

She needed a moment. The man had stolen her thoughts. And if she had any say in the matter, he'd do it again. She took his hand and led him to the living room. Their kitchen makeout session may have been over, but that didn't mean she was ready to say goodnight.

Chapter Twenty-Two

Lora-Beth walked past Reema's desk the next morning hoping to avoid an exchange like the last one. She liked Reema a lot, but made an effort to keep her private life separate from her professional life. She received a knowing smile and didn't try to hide the one her face insisted on returning.

"Good for you!' Reema cheered as if they'd exchanged words.

Her first meeting of the day had been across town, so she had yet to hit her desk. It was nearing eleven and she had a lunch meeting at twelve-thirty. She lived for these days and was happy she didn't have time to obsess about those damn kisses. She'd have plenty of time for that when she met Toni for their run after work.

Sam poked his head into her office after a rapid string of taps. "How did the meeting go with Sufose? Anything unexpected?"

"Nope, I'll get my notes together and have them ready to share at the afternoon meeting. They have something in the pipeline to try and bounce back from their latest flub and want us to conduct a bit of market research. Pretty basic stuff."

"And the press release for Venusys, how's that coming?"

"Meeting with them at lunch. I should have a draft ready by the end of the week."

Sam nodded. "Sounds good." And then he was gone.

She listened to her voice messages, then scrolled through her emails to respond to anything pressing. Client emails moved to the top of the priority list. Corporate emails came after.

Next, she scanned her usual websites for news that may be interesting for her clients, bookmarked a few articles, and sent two that were relevant to an upcoming campaign they hadn't quite nailed to the team for discussion. The articles may help them find a new angle.

She put the final touches on a press release. Pleased with it, Lora-Beth sent it out to the appropriate contacts.

Hours later, they both were struggling for breath when Toni's watch finally beeped and she exclaimed that they had reached their target. Lora-Beth leaned over, placing one hand on a tree, trying to steady her breathing. Running with Toni always pushed her to pick up her pace.

Toni came up beside her and started stretching. "Good run, LB!"

"Girl, I struggled for it today," Lora-Beth said, still panting, but now balancing on one leg as she held her other foot to her butt, stretching the leg. She switched feet to stretch the other.

"Yeah, well, that was actually six and a half miles. So, like I said, good run."

Sitting on her butt and folding her body over one extended leg, she groaned, "I hate you."

"You love me," Toni said from her position already on the grass. "Hey, at least now you know you're ready for the race."

"I have plenty of time to be ready for the race."

"I know. Which is why I don't know why I let you talk me into the 10K."

"Next time, we'll do the half."

Toni laughed. "Sure, LB. Anything you say."

"I'll even book the race."

"So, your man candy has you in neutral."

She looked at her friend and rolled her eyes. "I thought you said you would call him Austin?"

"Did I say that? That doesn't sound like me. When did I say that?"

"Austin…" Lora-Beth enunciated, "…doesn't have me in neutral. We're taking things slow."

"Slow? Girl, you've known this man for how long? Seven, eight months?"

"Come on. That's not fair. You know it wasn't like that."

"Yeah. You're right." Toni gave a small smile. "How's he doing with everything?"

"I think he's handling it well. He hasn't seemed too sad or down, at least not when we're together. He's been doing some of the things he used to do before. He seems good."

"And you're…"

"It's good to see him this way. He's a joy to be around."

"I admit, in the beginning, when you told me what was going on, I thought you were crazy for getting involved with someone who wasn't emotionally available, but once I saw you two together, I got it."

"What did you get?"

"I've only seen you together a couple of times, but you're comfortable. You feed off each other like you've known each other forever."

"I don't know if I've felt this connection before," Lora-Beth admitted.

"Not even with Brian?"

Her eyebrows drew together. "Where did that come from?"

"So no?"

"I hadn't thought about it, or him, at all for that matter. Where is this coming from?"

"Yesterday, he stopped by. He asked about you."

Lora-Beth paused to take that in. Brian was back. Now, when she'd finally found someone she was interested in, he was back. Lora-Beth couldn't believe it. "He stopped by? What do you mean he stopped by?"

"LB, he's back. He and Marcus have been hanging out."

"How long has he been back?"

"Coupla weeks."

"And this is the first I'm hearing it?" She gave her a dramatic side eye. "Well, what did you tell him?"

"I can't speak for Marcus, but I didn't tell him anything. I let him know that your number hasn't changed and if he wanted to know how you were, he should call and ask you himself."

"He's back, as in local? Permanently?"

Toni searched her face before replying. "Would it matter?"

Lora-Beth thought about Toni's question. Would it matter that the man she thought she would marry was back in town? Of course it would. But how? "I don't know."

"I didn't want to tell you, but that wouldn't be right of me to keep it from you. Lora-Beth, I know you thought your happily ever after would be with him, we all did, but hon, he made his choice and it wasn't you."

She shut her eyes tightly and held her closed fists to them. "Yeah." Brian had always been motivated, determined, and charming. But it was his drive that had drawn her to him. In her heart of hearts, she'd known it was that he was afraid to fail, afraid to be like his father. For the three years they'd been together, he'd been the one person she'd given her whole self to. He was the man who'd held her heart. It was with him she learned how she loved. But then, her love hadn't been enough.

"Ready to get out of here? I need to get home to my guys."

She didn't know how long her friend had been trying to get her attention. She'd zoned out, lost in her thoughts. "Yeah," she agreed. "Let's get out of here." Brian being back changed nothing. Not for her anyway.

In her car, Lora-Beth let down the windows, despite the crisp November air, and drove in the opposite direction of her house. She was going to Fresh Market for a Bistro Power Plate.

Brian. She scoffed. Two years and a half years she'd spent alone, getting over him, building a new dream. He *would* show up now and pick up with their mutual friends as if he hadn't walked away from their lives. Of course he would.

ص

One project had turned into three and it seemed as though his company had gained another regular, faithful client. The only problem was that the client was Lucinda. Even though she'd been relatively tame since their incident, Austin wouldn't list her among his favorite clients. They'd still not moved into the house, and he had yet to make the acquaintance of Mr. McCarthy, but she told him she was traveling back and forth. Her husband was still up north, but would be retiring soon. It was her hope that she'd have the place ready, just as she wanted it. The open architecture, lakefront home had been built in 1993, but renovated just eight years ago. It was beautiful in his opinion, but he understood everyone had their preferences. Today, he and Brock were changing out lighting fixtures in the entire house and installing several fandeliers. He'd learned to avoid being alone with Lucinda when possible. He was sure she'd received the message, but saw no sense in risking it. The last thing his company needed was for him to be accused of something improper with a customer when business was really starting to soar.

Austin grabbed his ringing phone. This was the fourth call he'd received within the hour. He'd made appointments this morning for Trevor and Chris for the afternoon and several appointments for Saturday. Not that he was complaining, but he wouldn't get any real work done at this rate. Maybe he should think about hiring an answering service, or an appointment setter.

After hanging up, but before resuming his task, he sent a message to Lora-Beth mentioning his recent increase in business and his pleasure in it. He didn't receive an immediate reply, so he went about his task, assembling the second chandelier for Lucinda's dining room. The things had at least three hundred crystals each. And while he understood why they weren't shipped assembled, that didn't mean he liked putting them in place. *At least they were on strands*, he thought. Sitting on the floor trying to get it fully assembled was a better option than what he'd attempted with the first. Standing on the ladder and attaching all those pieces? Yeah, that had been a bad idea.

"Aren't they lovely?" Lucinda asked, breaking his thoughts.

He looked up to meet her gaze briefly. She was dressed appropriately and he thought she wore the dress well. If he had to guess, he'd say she didn't look a day over forty, but he knew she was in her fifties. "Yes, they're nice. I didn't realize you'd come back. How was your lunch, Lucinda?"

"Austin, please, how many times do I have to tell you? It's Cin. Nobody calls me Lucinda, my mother didn't even call me that for heaven's sake." She waved a hand. "The name is so stodgy and I am neither dull nor uninspired."

He wouldn't argue with her about that. He could think of a few adjectives to describe her and dull or uninspired wouldn't make the top one hundred. He nodded by way of reply.

Satisfied, *Cin* went on. "Lunch was lunch. Nothing to write home about. I remember the days when food had flavor. Everything didn't need to be covered in a sauce or drenched in butter or oil to taste like something. Nowadays, everything in a bowl of steamed vegetables tastes the same. If I couldn't see it, I wouldn't know if I was eating a zucchini or eggplant. I swear the flavor has been sucked right out of everything."

Austin's mind flashed to Lora-Beth's amazing meals. He didn't know whether what the woman was saying was true or not. But for his part, he was eating well these days and he was grateful. His phone started ringing again and he lifted it and looked at the screen. "Excuse me. Duty calls."

"Sure, sure. Don't let me keep you from your work."

She stepped away, but didn't go far. He could see her shadow so he knew she was just in the other room. This caller wanted to know if they worked on HVAC units. Sadly, he had to tell them no, but referred the caller to a company he trusted. When he ended the call, he noticed the reply from Lora-Beth. It was just a thumbs up emoji. He smiled, knowing that meant she was having a busy day, and though she didn't have a lot of time to text, she wanted him to know she received his message and thought the news he shared was good. He hadn't seen her yesterday and had plans to play basketball tonight.

Tomorrow. He would make it a point to see her tomorrow.

"That company you referred that caller to, are they friends of yours?"

"No, but I've never had a problem with their service. Do you have a need for an HVAC guy?"

She smiled sheepishly, almost embarrassed she'd admitted to eavesdropping on his call; almost, but not quite. "I'm moving into a house, I need an *everything* guy. Since I have you for most things, I figured it wouldn't hurt to have an HVAC guy in my list of contacts. I can admit my husband isn't very handy. It's just not something he's ever bothered with really. Mainly, he's left running the house to me."

Austin nodded his understanding. "I see," he said, but he didn't see. He didn't understand why what she was saying was relevant to him. That was someone else's business. "I'll be sure to give you their contact information."

"The message, was it from someone special?"

Austin quirked an eyebrow.

"I don't mean to pry. I just noticed your smile when you read it. You are a very handsome man, Austin. You should smile more."

"Lucinda."

"Cin," she corrected.

"Mrs. McCarthy," he challenged.

Lucinda held up her hands in protest. "It was an observation. A compliment. Not a come-on. Lighten up, Austin. You're far too serious. If you're not careful, you'll turn into a grumpy old man."

"Better safe than sorry. I'm not a fan of crossing boundaries. I make an effort to keep my professional life and personal life separate." It wasn't a total lie. In fact, it had been true until he'd met Lora-Beth. And he was entitled to one pass, wasn't he?

"I told you, it won't happen again. It won't. I'm a woman with a healthy sex drive, whose husband is not only six hundred miles away, but also past his prime. I made a pass at you. You turned me down. Don't hold it against me. I'm not holding it against you."

Brock cleared his throat. "Excuse me, ma'am. I have two broken units here; these will need to be returned."

"Are you kidding me? Did we order extras?"

"Not that I'm aware of, ma'am," Brock answered.

Austin wondered who made up the "we" she referenced. She'd ordered the fixtures and called to schedule their installation last week.

"Thank you. I'll call them now and see how quickly they can get replacements sent out."

"I went ahead and opened the remaining packages after I found the first one. These are the only two that are broken, but we won't really know until we've had a chance to turn the power back on and test everything. Maybe you oughta wait until then."

"I'll call now, and if I need to, I'll call again later." She excused herself.

"Hey man, what time do you think we can break for lunch? I'm starving."

Austin checked his watch. It was after one and he'd hardly noticed. "Give me fifteen minutes to finish with these crystals, then we can go."

"Here, let me help you, man."

ص

The gym was crowded and he'd already run three four-on-four games before his team lost. He was hoping to get in one more good run before he called it a night. It was nearly eight-thirty and the gym would be closing at ten, but he wouldn't stick around that long.

Chris took a seat beside him on the sideline and started talking. "So, you're not going to take her up on her offer?"

"Who?"

"Cin, man. How many offers did you get today?"

"Brock doesn't know what he's talking about."

"You could do worse."

"I'm good."

"Austin, hey man." Rob came up on his left and reached his hand out for a fist bump.

"What's good, bro?"

"Well, we're having a few friends over this weekend. Think you can make it? I want you to meet my wife."

"I can probably swing by in the evening. I work on Saturday, but should be finished by seven."

"Bet. Is your number the same? I'll text you the address."

"Yep. Same number."

"We're up," Chris called. "You running or are you done?"

"I'm running one more before I roll. Rob, man, send that text. It'll be good to get caught up."

"Count on it."

Austin was wiped and ravenous. He knew he shouldn't be there when he pulled up at the drive through window and asked for the bacon double cheeseburger with fries and sweet tea. The sad part was he doubted the meal would fill him. He wondered what deliciousness Lora-Beth had cooked up tonight and felt a pang of sadness that he was missing out on whatever it was and that he hadn't had much time to even speak with her today.

He picked up his phone and dialed her number. Lora-Beth answered on the second ring.

"Hello. How was basketball?"

"Good. Ran into Rob again. He invited me over on the weekend. But I called to say guess where I am."

"Uh, let's see. You're at a bar."

"Good guess, but no. I'm in the drive-thru line waiting for my bacon double cheeseburger." He laughed a guilty laugh.

"Hmm. I made gumbo tonight so I don't know who's winning this one."

"Definitely you." Austin handed his card to the cashier at the window and she handed him his drink.

"I made enough for you. You should have called before going with the fast food option."

He accepted his card and the bag and declined her offer of ketchup before asking Lora-Beth, "Leftovers?"

She laughed. "Yes, I have leftovers and you're welcome to them."

"Tempting. So tempting, but I'm sweaty, and probably smelly."

"You can take it to-go this time."

"I'll be there in fifteen."

"I'll be waiting."

CHAPTER TWENTY-THREE

Lora-Beth shut down her laptop and went to the kitchen to pull the bowl of gumbo out of the fridge. She'd been watching TV and doom scrolling at the same time, so basically, she was doing a whole bunch of nothing. It gave her joy knowing Austin enjoyed her food enough that he never minded coming out of his way to have a taste. It was a source of pride for her, and she knew her grandmother would be proud.

When she heard the knock, she picked up the bowl, brought it with her to the door, and opened it with a flourish. "Special delivery!"

"You're too good to me." He stepped inside and closed the door behind him. Austin gave her an appraising look and found her adorably comfortable in her natural element. He needed to find a way to show her just how much he appreciated her. She truly was good to, and for, him.

Lora-Beth's heart swelled with tenderness. He really had no idea how easy it was to be good to him. "I think we make a decent team. We both have our talents. You're good with your tools and I'm good with mine." Holding the container in both hands, she offered it to him.

He thought it was sweet she thought of them as a team. She really was special and he was thankful that even in the midst of everything he'd been dealing with since before they'd met, he'd been able to recognize it. He hadn't been in a good place then, and now, at this moment, he wasn't at his best, but he was healing, getting there, and she was helping him along the way.

He was exhausted from a long day and sweaty from the gym, but he didn't want to take the dish and leave. He wanted to come in, sit a while, have her talk to him while he enjoyed the dinner she cooked and had so graciously offered. He reached for it and grasped her hands along with it. "Is it okay if I eat it here? Will my sweatiness offend you?"

He stared at her so intently she knew he was reading her. He wasn't just waiting for her words. She softened, as if she weren't already open to this man. The realization that he wanted to be in her presence, even when he was visibly tired, pulled her even closer. He was handsome, captivating. She loved that despite his well-constructed walls, he'd let her in, when he'd kept others at arm's length. "I'll deal. Come on, I'll heat it up for you while you go wash your hands."

He headed down the hall without a word. Austin noted the opened door of the guest room and when he finished washing his hands and splashing water on his face, he stepped in, flipped on the light switch, and was pleased at what he saw. The room had turned out well. The soft pink and gold accents were beautiful. It didn't look like a little girl's room as he'd imagined it would. The gold bedding on the poster bed looked regal. He ran his fingertips over the fabric and closed his eyes at its softness. He stepped closer to an antique-looking dresser and examined the items she'd placed there. A jewelry box, a ballerina music box, two gold framed photos—one of an older black lady, the other an older white lady—and several old perfume bottles sitting on a round mirror.

Lora-Beth found him in the guest bedroom. She stood silently, watching him peruse the space. "My grandmothers, Bethany and Lorelai."

He didn't flinch at the sound of her voice. He'd known she was there. He realized he could feel her eyes on him. She came up beside him, pressed herself to his side, and placed her hand on his back. She pointed to the frame on the left. "This is the woman largely responsible for my cooking abilities, but any baking you can credit this one for."

He looked at her through the mirror, liking the feel of her softness against him, liking her scent filling his nostrils. "I can see both of them in you."

"I like to think they both left me with a little something and I don't just mean physically. They were so different, but they loved me so much, in their own ways."

He turned to face her then, took her hand in his and started out of the room. "So, even after your dad left, your grandmother was in your life?"

Lora-Beth liked the way her hand felt in his, and Jesus, Toni had been right about those pheromones. Her body hummed whenever she got within a couple feet of him tonight. "Yeah. She lived in a small town in Kentucky, but I saw her several times a year and spent two weeks with her in the summers until I was old enough to have a job."

Austin sat at the table where she'd served the gumbo and a glass of sweet tea. She sat in the seat to his left. "Are you in contact with your dad at all?" he asked before taking his first bite. He moaned at the flavor.

"I know how to get a hold of him if I need to, but I don't see the need. He decided he didn't want to be my dad, so I don't try to force him. I haven't seen him since my grandmother's funeral seven years ago. Before then I had only seen him twice since he left us."

He didn't understand how any man could leave his child, but to leave Lora-Beth? What kind of fool was he? "I'm sorry."

She waved him off. "I do believe I've managed to deal with those feelings. My actual dad, my stepfather, is amazing and he and my mother made sure I never felt like I didn't have a dad and he gave me my sister. And I feel safe enough to admit to you that I've had my share of counseling because they wanted to be sure I didn't have any deeper issues about being abandoned. I don't."

He set the spoon down and placed his hand on top of hers on the table. "You'll always be safe to be yourself with me."

She held his eyes, "What about you? Have you had any sort of grief counseling?"

"No."

"You know it's okay if you ever need to talk to someone right? You're also safe to be yourself with me, but if it ever gets to be too much, there's no shame in talking to someone."

He took his hand in hers and closed his eyes before responding. "I'm so lucky to have you. I appreciate it. All of it."

"I know you do." She decided to cut him some slack and back away from the heavy stuff and gestured to the food. "How is it?"

"Delicious, as always." He fought the urge to take her in his arms, cradle her close. He didn't want her to worry. And she may have come to terms with it, but she couldn't hide the hurt in her eyes when she talked about her father's absence from her life.

Austin was nearly done with his gumbo when Lora-Beth spoke again. "What are you doing for Thanksgiving?"

He looked at her for a moment before responding. There was a gleam in her eye. His voice was laced with teasing when he said, "Why do I have a feeling you're about to tell me?"

"Because you know me so well." She was happy he had a lighthearted response and gave one in return. When he smiled, she went on. "If you don't have any plans, I'd like to invite you to my family's Thanksgiving dinner." Wordlessly, he met her gaze, checking it to see if he could decipher the meaning behind her offer. "We keep it low key these days. Just the immediate family. My sister is flying in from Texas on Wednesday."

Austin took his time before responding. "And you want me to come? Have Thanksgiving dinner... with your family?"

"I want you to come have Thanksgiving dinner with my family," she confirmed.

An easy smile spread across his face. "Okay," he agreed easily. "Do you make anything special?"

"I'm usually on pie duty. Apple and sweet potato, but we do most of the cooking together. Though Mama usually does most of the prep work for the meal."

Lora-Beth smiled. She wasn't sure where that had come from. Thanksgiving was just over a week away and sure, she'd thought about how he would be spending the holiday, but she hadn't planned to ask him to come with her to Asheville. At least, she hadn't planned to ask him tonight. "So be prepared for a long day. Although we'll have dinner with my parents in Asheville, we have to be back that night. Toni and her husband host a game night for the adults over at their place and I can't miss it."

"Game night? As in watching football games or playing board games?"

"Playing games, although not necessarily of the board variety. It'll be fun. Trust me."

"What have I gotten myself into?"

"Get ready for holidays Lora-Beth style."

He'd take just about anything Lora-Beth style. He placed his hand over hers on the table. "I'm looking forward to it."

Lora-Beth thought about the changes she'd witnessed happening with him and exhaled. He smiled regularly now. Engaged in small talk and not so small talk alike, and without having discussed it, they'd fallen into a certain level of comfort that negated pretense. He didn't need a reason to reach out to her and she didn't either. They just did. Communicating with each other had become a part of their day. It was rare that two days passed without them laying eyes on each other. They'd shared heated kisses, but so far, it hadn't progressed beyond that.

"How's the race training going?" Austin asked, breaking into her thoughts.

"Honestly, better than I thought. Toni tricked me into a six and a half mile run recently."

"Wishing you hadn't backed out on the half, aren't you?"

She thought about it. "Maybe a little, but I promised her we'd do one."

He nodded.

They spent an hour talking about their respective fitness routines, favorite holiday meals, and the busy past couple of days. He lingered as long as he could without being obvious.

At the door, Austin drew her close to his chest, and without preamble, lowered his head and took her lips in a soft, lingering kiss. He pulled away and stared down into her heated face. He read the lustful look in her eyes.

Lora-Beth wrapped her hand around the back of his head and pulled his lips back to hers. She bit his bottom lip then soothed the spot with her tongue. Then she felt her back against the wall and Austin devouring her mouth. He pressed his body into hers. Her breath quickened and she moaned at the feel of his erection on her stomach. With one hand in her hair, his other slid down and found her breast. He palmed it, teasing the nipple with fast flicks of his thumb.

Austin's lips left hers and grazed her neck. "I love the way you respond to me," he whispered huskily in her ear then bit the spot just below it as she felt the pressure from him pinching her nipple.

"Austin," she gasped and leaned her head to the side, giving him more access. He ran his tongue where he could feel her pulse before he kissed her lips again. He hiked up her dress and closed his lips around her bare nipple, licking and sucking, as he rolled the other between his thumb and forefinger. His kisses were slow and gentle. He was exploring, enjoying the feel of her, the taste of her.

Lora-Beth was afraid that if he didn't stop what he was doing, she would come soon. She tried to call out to him, to give him that warning, but the words came out differently. When she opened her mouth, "Austin, yes, yes," was what came rasping out.

He'd thought about little else since he walked in the door and realized she wasn't wearing a bra beneath her T-shirt dress. He wanted to kiss her the moment she opened the door to him. He'd been a good boy until now, but Austin decided he wouldn't leave without showing her just what he'd been feeling. He wanted her. He wanted her to know he wanted her.

Austin slid down her body and knelt at her feet. He kissed down to her belly button, placing open mouthed kisses on her not-so flat stomach before hooking his thumbs into the waistband of her panties. He looked up at her with lustful eyes, asking for permission. She met his eyes and in them, he saw what he needed to see. He slid her panties down and when she lifted a leg for him to remove them, he turned his head and kissed one thick thigh, then the other, before he completely divested her of the garment. And then his mouth was on her. There were no timid kisses. There was no uncertainty. He got down to business. He lifted one leg over his shoulder and buried his face between them, greeting her with hungry lips and a probing, greedy tongue.

She felt her knees weaken. It was already too much. Lora-Beth ground her hips in small circles, gripped his shoulder, and dug her foot into his back, pulling him closer. At her urging, he closed his lips around her clit and suckled. Lora-Beth was overwhelmed, she was spiraling and damn it to hell she was already coming. She cried out unintelligible words as her orgasm claimed her. Her legs shook and she felt his hand press flat to her chest, holding her in place with one and holding her open with the other as he continued to lick and suck through her climax. Then came tender kisses on her thighs and belly as she came down.

If he could get her there that fast with his mouth, what it would be like when he finally got her in a bed, she wondered.

Satisfied for the moment, he rose to his full height, wrapped his arm around her waist, and snatched her against him, moving her against his swollen length, letting her feel how affected he was. He smoothed her hair from her face and peered down into her eyes. "Next time you come for me, I want to see your face."

She shuddered, an aftershock sending a curve to her spine. "Austin." It was a whisper. Where had all her words gone? She was always talking. Austin had given her an orgasm and stolen her words in the process. She held him to her tightly, her hands fisting his shirt at his back.

He trailed gentle kisses on her jaw and down her neck. His breath was hot on her skin. Austin pulled her earlobe between his teeth then soothed it with gentle licks. "Kiss me and tell me goodnight. We both need to get some rest."

She shook her head against his broad chest. She didn't want to say goodnight because she didn't want him to leave. Not after he'd just given her the first orgasm that wasn't self-induced in more than two and a half years. She wanted him to take her to her bedroom, or the couch, or right here on the floor of her foyer and finish what he'd started. "Not yet. Don't let go just yet."

He held on, letting her take what she needed from his embrace. He ran his hand up and down her back and placed a kiss on top of her head. "You okay?"

She tilted her still flushed face for his kiss and he obliged, lingering but not moving to heat things up again. "I'm better than okay. I just can't find the words. You've poleaxed me."

"It's about time we start to get on equal ground. I've been under your spell from the first phone call," he admitted quietly. Then, wanting to change the subject after his admission, he fell to his haunches, retrieved her panties, helped her back into them, and pulled her to the door. "You're good on so many levels, Lora-Beth. You've been patient with me and often what I needed even when I didn't know what that was."

When she moved to speak, he placed a finger at her lips to silence her. "If only I could figure out how to be as good to you as you are to me." He shook his head. "I would like nothing more than to take you to your bed and keep you there for days, but not tonight. I didn't come by to seduce you. I just wanted to see your face. When I take you, and it will happen soon Lora-Beth, it will be intentional, and it won't be because I lost control in your entryway and had to get my mouth on you before I went crazy."

Lora-Beth kissed him. She was so turned on by his words, his promise of what was to come, that she had to have her lips on him. "You are good to me. I get that it doesn't seem like it to you, but your presence in my life has been as good for me, as mine has been for you. I'm with you, honey, right there with you, and I'm not going anywhere."

He pulled her close, and again, she felt his hardness. He held her eyes. "Goodnight, Lora-Beth."

"Goodnight, Austin."

He released her, opened the door, and tapped the jamb twice as he walked through.

"Be safe getting home," she called after him.

"Always."

He pictured her perfect lips wrapped around him and his fingers laced through her hair as he fed her his length. Water pelted his skin and he could hear his own sounds of pleasure bouncing off the walls of the shower as he found his release as soon as he made it home.

When Lora-Beth stepped out of her front door the next morning for her run, she found Austin in her driveway, stretching. "Good morning."

"Hope its okay that I'm here. I thought we could run together this morning," he said by way of greeting. She walked up to him and lifted her lips for a kiss. Surprised by the gesture, he placed a chaste kiss on her lips. "Good morning," he said.

Her eyes danced. "That's better. And of course I don't mind, but go easy on me."

"We'll take this at your pace."

"Let's do it." She took off, heading left out of her driveway, and he gave chase.

CHAPTER TWENTY-FOUR

It was the day before Thanksgiving and she and Austin were hanging out at his place. He'd phoned her this afternoon, invited her to dinner, and told her to pack a bag and plan to sleep over. They were heading to her parents' house in the morning.

She was sure this was it. Tonight would be the night. She'd hardly been able to focus the remainder of the day. She'd been a bundle of nerves, too anxious to focus in her yoga class. She was ready to get home, get showered and ready for their evening. She drove to his place and was surprised to find dinner. He'd picked up an Italian meal from one of his favorites. They enjoyed the quiet, candlelit dinner and easy conversation.

Now she sat on his couch, watching him walk in her direction. He'd topped off her glass of wine and grabbed himself another beer. He was comfortable in shorts and a tank. Lora-Beth wanted to run her hand down his sleek abs. She was still wearing the jeans and fitted teal sweater she'd chosen for the evening.

"I think I'm going to put on my loungewear, get comfortable, if that's okay?" she said.

"Of course."

Lora-Beth stood to leave the room, but Austin caught her, pulled her flush against his chest, and kissed her. "This color looks really good on you."

"You've seen me in this color before."

"And I always think you look amazing in it."

"Thank you."

He let her go and watched as she walked out of the room, thinking maybe he should join her and save her the trouble of getting into anything else.

In his bedroom, she went to the bag she'd packed and pulled out the pink, silk chemise. It wasn't exactly lingerie, but it wasn't the leggings and tank top or oversized T-shirt dress she usually lounged in either. She toyed with the idea of packing something totally risqué, but landed on this happy medium. She wanted to be clear, but a little subtlety went a long way, or so she'd heard. She stepped into the bathroom and changed out of her outfit, donning the dress and matching thong underwear, washed her face, rinsed her mouth, applied a fresh coat of gloss, and fussed with her hair. Satisfied with the whole package, she set her bag aside and went to join Austin.

When she turned the corner into the living room Austin's eyes turned to hers and she saw his nose flare at the sight of her. Inwardly, she smiled. He was pleased with what he saw. He set his beer on the table and reached a hand toward her. Her stomach fluttered and her nipples hardened a little more with each step. She wanted him and if he didn't make the move tonight— Her thought was cut off when he stood abruptly and closed the remaining distance between them in three long, quick strides.

Austin reached her, threaded his fingers in her hair, and tilted her head for his kiss. His kiss was hurried, frantic even. He slid his hand down the soft material, gripped the globe of her ass, and groaned. He stiffened against her. Her long legs, confident smile, sweet kisses, those hard nipples pressed against his chest… it all drove him wild. He wanted her, and unlike the other days, his body was refusing to listen to his head. He lifted her from her feet and instinctively, she wrapped her legs around him. She yelped in surprise before he fused his lips with hers. He walked her back to where she'd just come from. He lowered her to the bed and gazed down at her.

Lora-Beth looked up at him and desire simmered in the depths of her eyes. She was wet. Her skin flushed. She was charged with anticipation. He lifted his shirt over his head and gave her his lips again. She placed both hands on his back and loved the feel of his smooth skin against her palms. And then his mouth was gone, he lifted from her, and removed her panties, then the dress, and she was naked before him. He ate her up with his gaze and she watched as his eyes roamed her body. He touched her softly, letting his hands feel skin that was new to him.

He removed his shorts and Lora-Beth stared at his nudity. This man was beautiful. His body was six feet, one inch of lean, muscled perfection. Unable to help herself, she reached out and took him in her hands. She stroked his thickness and he groaned. Gently, he removed her hands and brought them to his lips. "I've thought about nothing else for days, I don't want it to be over before it begins. I need to be inside you."

Her eyes clamped shut at his words. Her body hummed with excitement to feel him inside her. She heard the drawer open and the package rip. She opened her eyes and watched as he rolled the condom on. Then he was back in bed with her, his mouth on hers, and without preamble, he hitched her leg and joined them. Her mouth gaped and her breath hitched as he filled her. He stilled, buried to the hilt, and pressed her forehead to hers.

"Jesus, Lora-Beth." He moved slowly, taking his time. He'd gone without being inside a woman and if he didn't pace himself he feared he'd embarrass them both.

She wanted him to go faster, or slow down so she could savor the moment, she wasn't sure. She touched him everywhere her hands could reach. They were all hands, mouths, and moans. "I'm close, please, Austin," she practically begged.

She grew slicker around him. His thrusts became harder, deeper, and faster than Lora-Beth expected. Her breasts danced in all directions as he drove into her. Her orgasm came and she yelped. With no control, her body vibrated with his thrusts and the sweetness of her orgasm. He watched her go over the edge, noticed the way she closed her eyes tightly and arched her back when it grabbed her. He buried his face in her neck and groaned as he came inside her, repeating her name and random expletives. He gave her his weight and she wrapped him in all four limbs, holding tightly as they caught their breaths.

"So, you like my nightie?" She felt his chuckle.

He rested on his elbows and brushed her hair from her face. "Yeah, I liked your nightie."

The room was dark, the moonlight from the tiny holes in the blinds was all that allowed him to see a glimpse of her face. Her low moans had roused him from his sleep. Austin curled his arm around her and held her there. There was no place he'd rather be and no one he'd rather be with than Lora-Beth. She was draped on his chest, skin to skin. He'd been at her half the night it seemed, and still, he wanted her again. He shifted, rolled her onto her back, and slid down to rest between her thighs. He loved her legs. Loved having them wrapped around him.

Lora-Beth felt his kisses and knew this wasn't a dream. Unabashedly, she spread her legs to allow better access. "I love your mouth on me." At her words, he moaned his acknowledgment, the sound sending vibrations through her clit. She reached for his hand, and when he laced his fingers with hers, she pulled at them. "But not as much as I love you inside me." She handed him a condom she'd grabbed from the nightstand.

Austin rolled the condom on and pushed inside again.

Hours later he slipped out of bed and got started on breakfast, the one meal he was decent at cooking. They'd be hitting the road to her parents' house soon. Then, after a three-hour drive, he'd meet her parents. The thought reminded him that he should reach out to Joyce and David to make sure they weren't expecting him. He'd enjoyed the holiday with them the past couple of years. Realizing that six sixteen a.m. was likely too early to phone them, he made a mental note to call them before they got on the road.

While bacon cooked in the oven he whisked the eggs in a bowl and set it aside, going to flip the pancakes. Though always from an instant mix, he made good pancakes. He hoped Lora-Beth agreed.

There had been a moment, just a moment, last night when he'd hesitated. His brain was so conditioned to his loyalty to Janet, he had to remind himself he wasn't doing anything wrong and was free to have feelings for Lora-Beth. In his heart, he knew he'd always love Janet. But, as his father had said, there was room for Lora-Beth. Even before he realized there was, she'd found a way in. She befriended him, regarded Janet as precious to him, and had given him the opportunity to talk about her and his life with her. Not once had he sensed any ill feelings. She'd taken her time to sit with Janet and read to her because she heard the pain in his voice when he'd spoken about the fact that their friends had stopped coming long ago. He never thought he'd love another woman. Janet had been his love and one was all he'd wanted. So after the accident, when he was hopeful she'd come back to him, he'd loved her even harder.

Now, as much as he was sure he'd always love Janet, he felt himself struggling to imagine his life without Lora-Beth. Could a man be so lucky as to have two great loves of his life? Austin wouldn't speak for other men, but for his part, he was almost certain it was possible. It definitely seemed to be true for his dad.

Austin reached into the oven to grab the pan with the bacon in it and when he turned again, Lora-Beth was sitting at the bar. "Smells good." She was wearing shorts and a tank top. For a moment, he was disappointed she wasn't wearing the pjs she'd worn the night before.

He set the pan on the counter, removed his mitt, went to her, and kissed her lips softly. "Good morning."

Lora-Beth wrapped a hand at the back of his neck and moaned her good morning into his lips.

"How'd you sleep?" he asked after pulling away and getting back to his task. The pancakes were ready to be removed and he needed to get the bacon onto the paper towels to drain.

"Best three hours of sleep I can remember having," she admitted. When he brought his eyes to hers and smiled, she asked, "Is there anything I can help with?"

"Nope. I need to show you I'm at least a little domesticated, lest you think you will always have to do the cooking."

"You know I don't mind cooking, but I can appreciate you feeding me."

"Luckily, I can feed you, and still not cook, because this is pretty much as good as it gets." He gestured to his spread.

Lora-Beth observed him moving about his kitchen. He was happy and she liked that she was there to witness it. "Well, it looks and smells delicious."

"You want coffee? Tea? Juice?" he asked.

She hopped off her stool, went to the fridge, and removed the carton of orange juice. "Juice is good." She grabbed two glasses as he removed the pancakes and plated their food.

Casually, she asked, "What were you thinking about earlier?" He turned to face her in confusion. "When I came in you were wearing a look. You didn't notice me standing there."

Austin wouldn't lie to her. He hadn't before and he wouldn't start now. "It occurred to me that I should reach out to Joyce and David so they aren't expecting me for dinner."

Understanding, she regarded him, checking his face for any sign of change. "How are you feeling about everything?"

He placed the two plates on the bar and grabbed the syrup. "I'm feeling a few things this morning. I'm not sure how to categorize them, but I can try."

"I'd like that." She took a bite of one of the strips of bacon he placed on her plate.

"I'm feeling happy to be here, like this, with you. I've thought about it many times and I'm a bit relieved we're on this side of it." Lora-Beth blushed. She agreed. "I feel a twinge of anxiety about meeting your parents. And I feel a little sad." When she opened her mouth to speak, he rushed on. "I hope that doesn't come across more harshly than I meant. Spending the last few holidays with her parents has been more somber than happy."

"It's okay to miss her today or any day. She was a large part of your life for a long time. Though I've never experienced it, I'm not so sensitive that I can't understand what you're going through."

He didn't want to start the day this way. He'd woken up with her wrapped around him, and here she was in his kitchen, enjoying breakfast. This was not a sad moment. He leaned over and took her mouth in a quick, passionate kiss, meant to let her know that beyond these words what he was feeling was unchanged and he wasn't having second thoughts about what they shared. He explored her mouth with his tongue, enjoying the sweetness of the pancakes mixed with the sweetness of Lora-Beth more than he'd enjoyed them from his own fork. He broke their kiss and whispered softly above her ear. "I can't explain how much it means to have you here. To have you in my life. I hope one day I will be able to make you understand how much you mean to me." He kissed below her ear. "Last night was amazing. You are amazing."

Lora-Beth left her stool to get closer to his touch. She stepped between his thighs and they wrapped each other in a tight embrace, much like they'd done when she'd shown up at his home the first time. "If you never said the words, I would know how much I mean to you."

Chapter Twenty-Five

"Are you still nervous?" Lora-Beth looked over at him from the passenger seat amused.

"Um, did I say I was nervous? Should I be nervous?"

"No, my parents are easygoing, but meeting the parents is usually a little nerve-racking. I'd be a little nervous if I was meeting your parents. And we're barely official. I don't want to run you off."

Austin took her hand and laced their fingers. "I can't imagine anything running me off."

"Good."

"Barely official?"

"You know what I mean!" She tried to wave him off.

He didn't let her. This felt significant. "Let's say I don't. Talk me through it."

"I just mean it's early. Being an 'us' is new."

"Did you just casually claim me?" He couldn't hold back his smile.

"Did you think you were going to do the things you did to me last night, and this morning, and not be claimed?"

He tilted his head back and laughed from deep in his belly. He met her eyes briefly to see her blushing. "I'm up for meeting the parents responsible for making you, you."

Her phone rang then, breaking the moment. It was her sister.

"Helloooo! We're twenty-five minutes out."

"Good. I can't wait to see you and meet this man."

She hit the speakerphone button. "Say hi to Austin."

"Hey, Austin."

"Good morning, Tricey."

"Where's your other half?" Lora-Beth asked.

"Outside with Daddy."

"Where are you?"

"I'm in the kitchen, chopping veggies for dressing and on my second cup of coffee. Hurry up. I'm bored."

"Bored? Where's Mama?"

"Um… I think she went to take something to someone or pick something up from someone. I don't know, girl. All I know is she's gone and I'm here slaving away in the kitchen."

"Is the turkey in the oven?"

"Nope. That's what Daddy and Damon are doing outside, getting the fryer set up."

Austin groaned and Lora-Beth chuckled. "Right," Tricey said.

"We'll be there soon."

"Hurry."

"Hurrying," Austin answered as Lora-Beth ended the call.

"This should be interesting."

"It'll be fine, he's done this before. Although, usually there's a backup turkey, so there's less pressure."

Tricey pulled the door open before they reached it and squealed, "Sissy!"

"Sissy!" Lora-Beth returned and wrapped her sister in a bouncing hug, unable to contain their excitement.

"You didn't say he was this fine," Tricey stage-whispered.

"Nice to meet you, Tricey."

She gave him a quick embrace as well. "Same."

Just then her mother's car turned into the driveway. "Perfect timing. Is that Aunt Mary?" Lora-Beth asked, cupping her hands over her eyes to shield them from the glare of the windshield.

They worried for nothing. The fried turkey turned out great. Once her uncle Stan showed up to supervise, it all went off without a hitch. By the time it was done, the ham, dressing, greens, mac 'n cheese, and all the other fixings were ready to go, and the pies were cooling on racks. Cousins Chantal, Jared, and Edwin rounded out their Thanksgiving dinner count. Austin had fared well, fitting right in with the family.

The cousins agreed to give Aunt Mary a ride home and Uncle Stan "had another stop to make". The remaining men—Austin, Damon, Tricey's longtime boyfriend, and Art, their dad—were watching the Cowboys and Commanders battle it out. Arthur had championed the Washington team long before the Carolinas had a team to call their own, and every year, he looked forward to the Turkey Day showdown. With Tricey living in Texas, things had been kicked up a notch two years ago when Damon, a Texas boy and Cowboys fan through and through, had come around.

"So you went out and found Lance Gross's brother to bring to Thanksgiving dinner?" Chantal asked.

"He is fine," Tricey added.

"He is a good looking young man," Cora, their mother, chimed in.

"Not you too?"

"And such a sweetheart. That one is a keeper," Cora added.

Lora-Beth smiled her agreement and had every intention of keeping him. "I happen to agree with you, Mama."

"Wait. Is Damon a keeper? I don't know that I've ever heard you use those words about him," Tricey asked jokingly, but not. She wanted to know.

"I wasn't so sure at first. A little rough around the edges, but he's grown on me and I'd have to be blind to not see he makes you happy. Yes, that young man of yours is also a keeper."

Tricey went and gave her a hug. "Thanks, Mom. That means a lot."

Lora-Beth threw the dish towel over her shoulder and eyed her sister. "Is there something you want to tell us?"

"Something like what?"

"Like why Momma gets a hug for telling you something you already knew."

"Oh shush." She waved her off. "Dry those dishes before she gets you."

Cora squeezed them both. "It's so good to have you two home. And you too, Chantal. Get over here."

"And we're happy to be here," Lora-Beth answered for them all.

"Mmm hmm. Is that why you're only here for the day?" her mother asked pointedly. "And you have no excuse. You still live in town." Chantal did not escape her aunt's chiding.

"I know, I need to do better."

"Come on, Momma! Don't give me a hard time about that. You know Toni has her Thanksgiving night thing. It's the only time I get to see some of my friends."

"Also, about that…" Tricey piped in, hesitating before she went on. "We're actually going to head back with them tonight as well and see you all tomorrow evening, or Saturday morning."

"This, on the heels of telling me how happy you are to be here," Cora teased lightly.

"I live too far away. LB, and especially Cuz, have no reason not to visit more often."

"Wow, Tricey," Chantal said.

Lora-Beth looked at her with a hand to her hip, a gravy boat in the other hand. "Seriously, sissy? Throwing me under the bus and asking to come with me?"

Cora threw her hands up. "It's like you're teenagers all over again." She walked out of the kitchen, a fit of giggles ringing in her ears.

"I'm going to head out. I'll call you about coming out your way soon to check out the house," Chantal said.

"Anytime. Just let me know."

"I'll see you when I get back, we don't fly out until Monday," Tricey added.

Austin was happy to find he wasn't the only other guy besides family in attendance. Damon's presence helped him feel less like an intruder on their family time. He'd been pleased to find that Cora shared Lora-Beth's sense of humor and open, chatty nature, and that Art, her husband, lit up in the presence of his wife and daughters. He could certainly relate to that feeling. Dinner had been delicious and now, as they watched the football game, he found he didn't feel out of place at all.

It was the third quarter and the Cowboys were up seventeen to six. The former 'Skins had yet to gain control of the game. "You fellas want another beer? These boys ain't talking 'bout nothing right now."

"I'll take one more," Austin said.

"Got you." Damon excused himself, leaving Austin and Art in the den.

Art cleared his throat. "My wife told me about you and everything you've been going through," he started. The statement surprised Austin, but he nodded, not sure what else to do. Art went on. "Don't know if Lora-Beth shared, but I lost my first wife, Tricey's mother, to cancer."

"I had no idea. I'm sorry."

"Long battle. It was hell, and for a long time, I was in a bad place. Nowhere to bring someone new if you follow me."

The man met Austin's eyes and held. "I follow."

"She may not be my blood, but I love that girl as if she was, and as her father, I gotta ask if you're ready to love her or if she's your way out of your grief?"

"Although it wasn't my intent, I believe both of those things are true. She's helped me more than I can explain, but what I feel for your daughter is far beyond that. I don't have to tell you how great she is. She's captivating. And even when I was in the thick of it, in my darkest days, she shined her light on me and I wanted to find ways to make her smile. That's my goal every day. Make her smile."

Art regarded him as he spoke, and though the younger man seemed to have slipped into a trance, a genuine smile spread across his face as he considered the right words to say to convey his thoughts. The boy was in love. Plain and simple. A whimpered sound captured their attention and Austin turned his head in the direction from which the sound had come and found Cora standing in the doorway to the room, a hand placed to her chest. "How sweet."

"Woman, why are you intruding on our football game?" Art asked playfully.

"Is that how the menfolk watch football now? Mute the television and engage in sensitive talk?" she teased, sliding onto the seat beside him.

Art put his arm around her and she leaned into him. "Let's pretend you didn't hear that."

"Hear what?" She looked at Austin and winked.

Austin smiled. He'd watched this family all day and understood the vibe Lora-Beth had created in her home and within herself. She'd grown up in a home full of love and affection, shared and expressed openly and often.

"Are you hiding from Daddy?"

"What? No. Just grabbing a couple beers for me and Austin." Damon came up behind Tricey and kissed her cheek. Unsatisfied, Tricey turned and kissed him fully.

"What time are we heading out?"

"That's a question for LB." They both looked at her.

"Oh, I didn't realize you guys knew I was still in the room." They all laughed. "Let me go see if Austin needs rescuing and see what time he wants to get on the road. I'm a passenger princess this weekend."

"Me too!"

"When are you not?" Damon asked with a laugh.

"Huh? I drive myself all the time."

"When was the last time we went somewhere together and you got behind the wheel?"

She waved him off, "Oh, if you're in the car, the wheel ain't none of my business." Lora-Beth joined in on her laughter.

"Right."

"So, yeah, somebody better get in there. Austin is alone with Momma and Daddy." Tricey pointed out.

"Your folks are harmless."

"Is that how you felt your first time meeting them?"

"Good point. Let me go take him this beer." Damon offered.

Lora-Beth reached for it. The bantering was fun to watch. "Here, I'll take it. It'll have to be the last one or I might be forced to drive after all."

CHAPTER TWENTY-SIX

"Come in, come in! Take off your coats, make yourself at home." Toni ushered them in and closed the door against the cold. She greeted each guest with a hug, starting with Lora-Beth and Austin, greeting him with a "Good to see you, Austin", making a show of using his name and not referring to him as hottie handyman or any of her other monikers for him.

"It's good to be seen. Thanks for having me."

When she embraced Tricey, she pulled back to look at her. "When are you moving back this way? Don't tell me you're letting this one keep you in Texas forever."

"Toni, this is Damon, my boyfriend."

"Yeah, I got that. Your sister briefed me from the car. It's nice to meet you," she said to Damon, greeting him with a brief embrace as well. "Welcome. Everyone is at home here, so yeah, let's have some fun."

"What have we missed?" Lora-Beth asked.

"Welcome shots. But don't worry, you're not too late if anyone wants one," Toni said.

Marcus, coming up beside them, interjected, "A few rounds of Taboo and Charades. A couple of guys have a game of dominoes going."

"Marcus, I'd like you to meet Austin and Damon. You know my sister." Marcus shook the men's hands in turn and greetings were exchanged.

"Why am I an afterthought though?" Tricey joked. "Hey, Marcus."

He brought her to him in a one-handed hug, as he'd done Lora-Beth. "What's good, fam?"

Instinctively, Austin's hand found the small of Lora-Beth's back as they walked through the space, checking out the madness around them. Toni and Marcus had a full house. Lora-Beth recognized most of the people there: Toni's younger sister Michelle and husband Brad, her older sister Vonda and husband Eric, Marcus's brother Michael and his girlfriend Keisha, as well as their baby sister Missy. Several of their mutual friends were also milling about.

"Drinks are in the kitchen, but if you want beer, there's a cooler on the back porch. Toni made her punch if you're up for it. It's fruity, but don't be fooled."

"Babe, are you up for it?" Damon asked, knowing Tricey liked fruity beverages.

"I think I am."

Austin threw his arm over Lora-Beth's shoulder and whispered, "I'm not sure about drinking a punch that comes with that kind of warning."

"Good call. Stay away from that stuff. But I'm sure we can find something to sip on. Their bar is usually well stocked."

"How about I go grab a beer while you figure out what you're going to drink. I think I want to see what that dominoes game is looking like."

"Okay, but don't think you're getting out of playing any other games. I want to see what you're made of."

"You know what I'm made of."

She blushed. "Fair enough. Still, you're my partner, unless Toni pulls some men versus women stunt, then we're sworn adversaries."

Her eyes danced and he loved the way they looked. He kissed the tip of her nose. "You have a deal. We're partners, unless the woman of the house says otherwise."

Austin walked in the direction of the back door and Lora-Beth turned to go the other way and met the gazes of Tricey, Toni, and Marcus. "What?"

Marcus exchanged a look with his wife before excusing himself. "What?" Lora-Beth repeated.

Her sister raised an eyebrow and Toni looped her arm through Lora-Beth's. "Spill."

"Toni, girl, stop it. There's nothing to spill."

"Is that what we're doing now? We're lying?" Tricey asked as she served herself a cup of Toni's special brew.

"When?" Toni asked. "I don't need to know the details, but there's been a change. It doesn't take a genius to figure out what that change is. Also, I am gonna need all those details."

"Well, I can't speak to any changes, but I know when my sister is getting some and well, sissy, it's about damn time."

"Latrice. Filter," Lora-Beth said sternly, causing the other two women to erupt in laughter.

"What are we laughing at?" Missy asked, entering the kitchen with an empty cup in hand.

"My sister's particular brand of crass. I swear I don't know where she gets it."

"Ladies, hurry up with those drinks." Toni raised her voice over the steady hum of the crowd. "It's time for some fun, Minute to Win It style. I hope you're all ready to play. Where is my husband? Has anyone seen my husband? Tall, brown, handsome? Anybody?" she called dramatically.

In true Toni fashion, they were pitted men against women for Minute to Win It. Going head to head against Austin, Lora-Beth lost twice. Once during the game aptly titled The Nutstacker, where they were charged with stacking nuts using a single chopstick. He'd stacked his eight bolts in thirty seconds, and her stack, despite only reaching five high, had fallen twice during that time. And now, when they battled moving M&Ms from one plate to a plate on another table using a straw. In the one-minute period, Austin had moved nine pieces. She'd only moved eight, having dropped one along the way.

"Your legs are longer, of course you can get across the room faster than I can."

"Last time it was my hands were steadier so obviously I would win, this time it's my legs. If I didn't know better, I'd say these were excuses," he teased.

"Men are up nine games to five. So it's not just you, Lora-Beth. You women might want to regroup," Mike joked.

"Let's see if you guys are still saying that when we pull out Taboo again," Michelle piped up.

Missy stretched her hands out and popped her knuckles. "Okay, what's next? Since these guys think it's going down like that, I'm ready to show them a li'l something."

"How much of that punch have you had?" Toni asked.

Missy held up her thumb and forefinger, centimeters apart. "Just a little."

"Right," Marcus agreed with a laugh. "Justin, you're up. Go easy on her, she's drunk."

Lora-Beth started toward the kitchen, looking to refill her martini and heard the doorbell chime. "I got it!" she called behind her.

Austin stepped closer to Toni and touched his hand to her elbow. "I never got a chance to thank you for being there."

Toni waved him off. "No thanks necessary. We support each other. That's what friends are for."

Austin smiled and Toni went on. "Didn't you know that when you take a Lora-Beth you get a Toni for free? As long as you have her, you're stuck with me."

"I'd say that's quite a deal."

"Also, it comes with a side of Marcuses."

Austin laughed. "Keeps getting better."

Toni touched his arm. "You both look happy. So I should be thanking you. Have another beer. Let me see who was at the door."

Lora-Beth opened the door and came face to face with Brian.

The two stood looking at each other for a moment. Brian broke the awkwardness by saying, "Fancy seeing you here. You look amazing."

"Brian. I heard you were back."

"You heard right. I'm back."

"Who is it?" she heard Toni call out, coming up behind her. "Oh damn. I didn't know he was coming, LB, swear."

"I hope my presence isn't a problem." Brian directed his comment to Lora-Beth who shrugged. He looked at Toni and continued, "I told Marcus I might swing by."

When Lora-Beth walked away, Toni gave him a half hug and turned on her heel. "Well, everybody's welcome, so come on in. You know where the drinks are."

He caught her arm. "Hey. I thought maybe she'd be a little happy to see me."

Toni tilted her head to the side to examine him. "No you didn't," she said.

"I did nothing wrong, Toni."

She got close and spoke quietly, but forcefully, "She's seeing someone. It's new but it's good. She's happy. Whatever you were thinking would happen now that you're back, won't. It's too late. You missed your chance. Deal with it. Don't screw with her head. She doesn't deserve it."

"I've never—" he started but Toni held up a hand to silence him.

"Tonight is about playing games and having fun. You get that? This is not the time or place for you to try to win her back. Do that on your own time."

He sighed in defeat. Already, the night wasn't shaping up the way he'd hoped. "Got it."

Lora-Beth plopped onto the seat next to Austin and leaned heavily into his side. He brought an arm around her shoulder and kissed her hair. "Tired?"

"Walk out on the porch with me for a moment?" she asked and stood. He followed her out of the room. Outside he drew her to him, sensing the sudden tenseness in her shoulders.

"What's up?"

She pulled away to look up at him. "The guy I just let in the door is my ex."

"Okay?"

"And uh, well, I haven't seen him for a long time. Things ended badly between us." When his hand stiffened on her arm, she went on. "Well, not so badly, but suddenly."

"Yeah. And?"

"And I only just learned he was back in town. It caught me off guard to see him standing there."

"So, now what? You're uncomfortable? You want to leave?"

"No. I just… I didn't want you to be in the same room not knowing our history."

"I still don't know your history, and unless it has some bearing on what we're building, I don't know that I need to know much of it." When she didn't respond, he lifted her chin to see her eyes. "I'm going to ask you a few questions. Answer with the first word that pops into your mind. Can you do that?" She nodded. "What do you feel when you look at me?" She smiled. "You're supposed to give me a word."

"Flutters."

"Did you feel those flutters when you saw him standing at the door?"

"No."

"You were all friends, so these are his friends too, are they not?"

"Yes."

"Do I come across as a man who cares about the man you used to date?"

"No."

"Did he leave you?"

"Yes."

"Did he hurt you?"

"Yes."

"Are you going to let a man with such poor judgment ruin your night?"

She smiled again and pressed herself to his chest.

"Words," he reminded.

"No."

"Good." He held her to him tightly for a moment and let her breathe him in. As he often did, he threaded his fingers in her hair and cupped the back of her head, lowering his lips to hers in a slow, soft kiss. He held her to him with an arm wrapped tightly across her lower back. Austin pulled her tongue into his mouth and let it dance with his. Kissing from the corner of her mouth to her ear he asked, "Did you get what you needed?"

"Yeah, I think I did."

"Then how about we get back inside to this butt whipping in progress? Your stalling tactics are worse than your excuses," he teased.

"I agree with Michelle. Let's see how well you fellas do when we play an intellectual game."

"Challenge accepted."

A couple of hours later Brian caught up with Lora-Beth in the kitchen. "Can we talk for a minute?"

She'd just reached into the fridge and produced one of MJ's mini bottles of water. "What's there to talk about?"

"Can we get together and have a conversation, maybe this weekend or next week? There are some things I want to say to you."

She rested her hip on the counter and faced him. "You can say them now. Go ahead, I'm listening." She opened the bottle and took a sip.

"Not here. This is neither the time nor the place. I've been forewarned."

"I'm seeing someone."

He almost snarled. "I noticed."

She released a deep sigh. "So having that knowledge might alter what you want to say to me."

"It doesn't. At all." He shot her a look with raised eyebrows, challenging.

"Sorry, Brian. I don't think it's a good idea. But welcome back."

Brian watched her walk away, thinking the night was going terribly. Marcus had failed to mention she was seeing someone. He would have liked to have been prepared. Though he questioned if there was anything that could have prepared him for what he felt when he'd seen her on the porch in another man's clenches.

It was after three o'clock in the morning by the time they left Toni and Marcus' place. Damon suggested a late night snack.

The four of them were at Lora-Beth's, digging into leftovers from Cora's Thanksgiving meal. His deep rumble of laughter broke the silence. "Are you okay, LB? It doesn't look like you're going to make it until the microwave stops."

"Long day and I didn't get much sleep last night."

"Mmm hmm. I just bet you didn't," Tricey chimed in.

"Hush, you."

"Weird," Austin teased. "I felt very refreshed this morning. Maybe I need to get you to bed."

"Ooh, I like him!"

"Don't encourage her," she warned Austin.

"What? I'm just doing my part to take care of you."

"See, this. This is what you needed all along. Not that uptight fool who showed up out of nowhere earlier looking like someone dropped his candy in the sand."

"Babe," Damon said.

She waved him off. "Let's not act like we're not going to talk about it. Besides, Austin's not worried about that lame."

"I'm not."

"See. It's nothing. So there's no reason we can't talk about it. I never liked Brian. Sure, he's fine, but too cocky for his own good. Best thing he ever did for you was to leave."

"What am I going to do with that mouth of yours?" Damon asked.

"I think you'll just have to live with it, brother. It would seem as if that mouth runs in the family," Austin piped up.

"You love it," Lora-Beth teased.

Austin chuckled and met her eyes across the island. "Yeah."

Lora-Beth froze. Did he just kind of say he loved her? She searched his eyes. Even if she never heard him say the words, she knew how he felt about her, just as she was sure he knew how she felt.

Tricey gasped. Reaching for her man she said, "Oh my God. Babe, did we just witness a moment? I think we did."

"Babe, eat, please," Damon pleaded.

Austin dropped his gaze and placed a forkful of turkey, dressing, and cranberry sauce into his mouth. He hadn't said he loved her, had he? No, he said he loved her mouth. When he gave her those words, it would be intentional. He wouldn't slip them in casually. No, there was nothing casual about telling a woman you loved her.

Later, when they crawled into bed, Lora-Beth snuggled close. She burrowed into his side and rested her face on her chest. Austin drew lazy circles on her back.

"Thank you, for today." Lora-Beth said.

"I should be thanking you. I don't know that I've ever had such a fun Thanksgiving. I like that you feel good bringing me into the fold."

"Into the fold?" she questioned.

"Your family, your friends. You showed no hesitation inviting me into both worlds. Because you did it with grace, I didn't have to feel a certain way about it. Your family seemed happy I was there. Not like they were tolerating me because I was tagging along."

"They were happy to have you."

"Even though your dad hit me with the 'what are your intentions with my daughter?' talk."

"He didn't?" She gasped in shock.

"Oh, he did. Don't worry, I think I passed the first round of his tests."

"First round?"

"I'm thinking there will be more next time we visit. They want to see more of you."

"He told you that?"

"He didn't have to."

"So Christmas in Asheville then? We can stay a few days if you can swing it. Check out the Biltmore."

"I've never been."

"It's stunning. Particularly at Christmastime."

Austin stifled a yawn. "We can leave after the run."

"Oh. I almost forgot about the run."

"Can't forget about the run."

After a moment of quiet she said, "Hey."

"Yeah?"

"I'm happy you're here."

He kissed the top of her head. "Me too. Now sleep."

ص

They were making breakfast, this time as a team in her kitchen. She was actually letting Austin help her. This was huge for her. She had made the homemade biscuits, and they were baking, and now she was working on the grits and sausage. She delegated bacon and eggs to Austin. He laid bacon on a pan as she grated cheese for the grits when Damon joined them and took a seat on a barstool.

"Morning."

"Morning," Austin returned.

"Good morning. How'd you sleep?"

"Great. Except your sister snores when she is drunk. Can I help with anything?"

"Yes, you can keep us company. You're a guest."

"Ouch. I thought I was family."

Horrified, Lora-Beth corrected herself. "You are, I meant, you're a guest in my home and this is your first time here. I won't have you helping in the kitchen."

"I think he's messing with you."

She looked to Damon, who wore a smirk, for confirmation, then waved him off. "Help yourself to coffee. That I don't mind."

"Thanks. I think I'll take a cup to your sister if you're okay with her having it in the bedroom."

"That's fine."

When he left the room, Austin spoke. "Nice to know I've been moved up from guest status."

"You haven't been a guest in that sense in a long time."

Austin continued to crack eggs into a bowl. "But now that I'm in your kitchen, helping, I think that makes it official, wouldn't you say?"

"I will concede that point," Lora-Beth agreed, then went on, "Do you have any jobs today?"

"Yes, but the guys are on them. I don't have to be at any of the sites until later, around noon. Business has picked up. It's looking like I am going to have to hire someone else. I thought I would be able to get through the winter without doing so, but I need another body. I'm thinking either an HVAC technician, electrical guy, or another general contractor, so I can free up some of my time to focus more on the business end of things."

"About that..." she started as she stirred the shredded cheese into the pot of grits. "I may have had something to do with the increase in your calls lately."

"How so?"

"Well, I wanted to do something nice for you and I couldn't think of what. The idea came to me while I was working on a project at work and I figured it wouldn't hurt."

"Still haven't said what you did to make my phone start ringing more," he pointed out.

Lora-Beth peeked at her biscuits and decided they were brown enough. She donned an oven mitt and removed them from the oven. As nonchalantly as she could, she said, "I may have created and socialized a media kit for your business and sent it to a few contacts." He raised his eyebrows. "It didn't cost me anything other than a little time.

I called in a favor. I'll show it to you. I should have gotten your permission before making a move like this on behalf of your business but I know how much you love what you do and just want to see you succeed and be happy. And I know your work makes you happy." She was working herself up.

This woman truly was taking care of him. She was invested in his success and without provocation, had done something to help him. She was in the position to do so, so she made a move because she knew he loved his business.

"Are you mad?"

He went to her, drew her into his arms, and peppered her face with kisses. He backed her into the oven and took her lips full on, darting his tongue into her mouth. He had to be inside her somehow and this would have to do. "Man, I love you," he groaned when he pulled away. To his delight, she responded with a heated look and he didn't need the words. He knew.

She felt the tears sting her eyes and smiled up at him. Her heart danced and her stomach fluttered. He loved her. "I love you, Austin." She kissed him this time and got lost in the feel of being kissed by the man you loved knowing he loved you back. Moments later, they heard someone clear their throat.

"Umm. The bacon. I would get it, but you're kinda blocking the ovens," Tricey said.

Austin released Lora-Beth and opened the oven to check on his bacon.

Tricey moved to give her sister a hug. "What I just witnessed was beautiful. As if I'd missed it yesterday, even hung over from mystery punch, I can see what's between you two. I'm happy for you, sissy. Love looks good on you."

"Thanks."

"After breakfast, can I get the grand tour, full description, walkthrough of the house?"

"Of course. Though it's not a finished product, I'm proud of the job we've done." She looked to Austin. "He has a really good eye. But I won't let him take any credit for the guest room. He doubted my vision for that one big time."

"I'm glad you didn't listen to him on that. It's lovely."

"I agree. The room turned out nicely. The entire house is. I think it suits her personality." Austin joined the conversation as he finished removing strips of bacon and placed them on the layers of paper towel sitting on the rack he'd laid out for that purpose, then whisked the eggs once more before pouring them into the hot skillet.

Lora-Beth stirred the grits. "Where's your man?"

"He hopped in the shower."

"Well, as soon as he's done, we can eat."

CHAPTER TWENTY-SEVEN

It'd been a week since Thanksgiving and a new routine had formed. Some nights they spent at her place, others they stayed at his. They hadn't gone more than a night without ending the day together. Their lives had become intertwined and it felt good. Unorthodox, sure, but it had been a natural progression, them getting to know each other, falling in love.

Today was Friday and Lora-Beth sat at her desk, fresh out of a status meeting and feeling mentally drained when the intercom on her office phone buzzed and Reema's voice came through.

"Lora-Beth, you have a delivery that requires your signature."

"Okay, I'll be right up. Thanks, Reema." A delivery? What kind of delivery required her signature? Lora-Beth wondered as she smoothed her skirt and blouse into place before walking toward the reception area.

She reached the desk and looked at Reema in question. She gestured with her eyes toward the man standing a few feet away with his back turned. The two women continued their non-verbal exchange, before finally, Lora-Beth sighed in resignation.

Taking a few steps to where he stood, Lora-Beth stopped a few feet away. "Brian."

He turned and presented the bouquet of flowers he held in his hands. "Special delivery."

She took them. "Thank you."

"Can we step into your office and talk? Or maybe I can steal you away for lunch?" he asked.

"Come on. We can talk in my office." She turned and headed back in the direction she'd come.

Brian followed, happy to at least be welcomed to have a conversation. It really was all he wanted, to talk to her. He'd called her twice, but the calls had gone unanswered and unreturned.

When he stepped into her office, she closed the door behind him and gestured for him to take a seat in one of her two guest chairs. She rounded her desk and sat behind it, intentionally putting it between them.

"The flowers are nice. Thank you, but you shouldn't have."

"I'm just going to cut to the chase. I want back in your life. I want to know what it's going to take to make that happen."

A year ago hearing those words from Brian might have made her dance. In the early months after their breakup, she'd prayed he would find his way back to her, and even if she hadn't been willing to admit it, she'd waited for it. Waited for him to come to his senses and come for her. But not anymore. That time had passed. She'd done the work to heal and realized that the dream she had for their future was gone. "I'm flattered. And I'm with someone."

"And from what I understand it's new. Something new can't compete with what we shared. We had years of loving each other, which has to count for something."

"What did it count for when you left? You chose your career over us. You decided what was most important to you and it wasn't us." She leaned back in her chair, challenging him to disagree with what she said.

"That's not at all how that happened. I asked you to come with me."

"What you were really asking me was to choose your career over mine."

"Is that how you saw it?"

"That's how it was. We were doing fine, Brian, but that wasn't good enough for you. Our life wasn't the life you wanted."

Brian leaned forward, put off by her version of what ended them. "That's not true."

"There I was, thinking you were ready to propose when what you were really doing was planning your escape."

He flinched. "Lora-Beth, come on, that's not fair and you know it."

"Isn't it? How about this? You tell me how you see it."

Brian sighed, rose to his feet and began to pace. "I wanted to focus on my career, that much is true, but I wanted you with me. I didn't think of it like I was asking you to choose my career over yours. I didn't think it mattered to you as much." Lora-Beth didn't reply, so he went on. "I wanted you to understand that I needed to focus on that aspect of my life first. But that didn't mean I didn't want you or us. It was you who made me choose one or the other. That was never what I wanted."

Lora-Beth leaned back in her chair, watching him. "I didn't make you do anything, Brian. I let you. And I know you don't want to hear this, but it was the right decision."

He stood in front of the window, folded his hands in front of his face, and exhaled an exaggerated breath wondering when had she turned so cold? "Can we just take a moment, Love, please?"

She winced. "Don't call me that."

"Habit. Sorry."

"Brian, why are you here now?"

"I'm here for you. I'm back for you."

She sighed. "What's the truth? Why are you really back?"

He approached the desk and reached a hand out to her. She didn't take it. He didn't pull it back. "Because even after all this time, it's still you I want. Please, have lunch with me. It's lunch, Lora-Beth. I'm not trying to seduce you, I'm just trying to feed you."

"Fine. I have half an hour before I need to head out. You can buy me a sandwich in the café on the first floor," Lora-Beth relented. Even as she said the words, she wasn't sure why she had. She didn't want to go to lunch with Brian. Though she held no ill will, she wasn't looking to be chummy with him. Not now. She was good.

Still, he brought his hands together in a prayer motion and said, "Thank you."

CHAPTER TWENTY-EIGHT

Austin picked up his phone to send Lora-Beth a message.

Austin: FUN FACT: Going through resumes trying to determine who's worth an interview isn't my idea of a good time. Also, good morning.

It was barely seven o'clock and he'd already run five miles, showered, had breakfast, and looked at enough resumes to be bored. He opened the app on his phone he'd been using to draft the remodel of Lora-Beth's kitchen. He'd drafted the plans for two large skylights with the addition of a larger, two-level island and he was working on a 3D design to get her approval. His phone rang with a call from her and swiped right to answer the call immediately.

"Hello."

"Good morning, hard worker."

"Good morning, Sunshine."

"Now, tell me, what *is* your idea of a good time?"

"These days, anything involving you."

"Good answer."

"I do what I can."

"So, do you want some help weeding out the applicants?"

"It's sweet of you to offer, but I can handle it. Trying to find the right guy, the right fit for the team, isn't as easy as seeing their qualifications on paper."

"I get it, but if you change your mind, the offer stands."

"Thanks. It means a lot that you're willing to help. How was morning yoga?"

"Just what I needed. How was your run?"

"Five easy miles. Although, the sidewalk was a little icy this morning."

"Be extra careful, Honey. Maybe now is the time to use the treadmill."

He smiled at the endearment and wondered if she even realized she'd said it. "It wasn't too bad. I was able to navigate the patches, but you may be right. I don't want to risk getting injured."

"No, we definitely don't want that."

"Shouldn't you be getting showered and ready for work?"

"Yes, but right now, I'm lying here on the floor, talking to you. I have plenty of time."

"I have two guys from the stack I'm going to call today, and Trevor knows a guy, so I'm going to talk with him too. Whoever I go with, I'll likely bring him on the first of the year."

"See, you had it under control all along."

"Are you still laying down?" he asked at the sound of her sleepy voice.

"Yes."

"Are you going to fall asleep?"

"No, but I have you on speaker with my eyes closed, listening to the sound of your voice fill the room."

"Just like I was there."

"Nothing like if you were here," she insisted.

"I'll be there tonight."

"Yes. Tonight. And what about tomorrow? Remind me what we're doing…"

"Nice try."

"Give me a clue."

"I gave you a clue."

"Honey, 'wear comfortable shoes' is hardly a clue."

"Isn't it? It tells you I'm not taking you somewhere we'll be sitting the whole night. That in itself allows you to eliminate certain things. Like, the movies. I'm not taking you to see a movie."

"Are we going bowling?"

"I already gave you your clue, now you're asking for another? This from a woman who loves surprises."

"I do love surprises," she agreed with a laugh. "Okay, fine. No more clues. But if I embarrass you with my attire, you'll have yourself to blame."

"You could be wearing a potato sack and paper bags on your feet and I'd still be proud as fuck to be seen with you."

"Austin, that's the sweetest thing you've ever said to me."

He wasn't trying to be sweet. He meant every word. While she looked great in everything she wore, and even better when she wore nothing, there was so much beauty in who she was, what showed on the outside could never be anything other than beautiful. "So tonight then. I'll pick you up at six-thirty."

"I'll be ready. Goodbye, Austin."

"Later."

Austin refocused his attention on his skylight project when they disconnected the call. He still had half an hour before he needed to leave to make it to his first job of the morning.

While Chris and Brock installed laminate floors, Austin and Trevor were on day three of laying a limestone patio and installing a stone fire pit on the other side of town. It had taken them weeks to decide, but finally the homeowners picked out the stones and called him when they'd been delivered last week. The area had been measured, laid out, and dug with a rented Bobcat skid steer, courtesy of Home Depot. The patio stones were laid and set to dry overnight before they left the site that day. Today, they were working on erecting the fire pit. The circular fire pit was to be two and a half feet tall with a five foot total diameter.

He and Trevor were working together, laying out the heavy stones to determine what pieces worked best where, mixing the sizes and colors of the stones, and selecting stone faces that were attractive and best matched the curve of their outline, hoping to need as little hammering to chip at the stones as possible.

Austin was thankful Chris had agreed to field incoming calls today, so he wouldn't need to contend with them as it was necessary for him and Trev to work together. Still, he responded when he received random text messages from Lora-Beth, but only when his hands weren't full. He never kept Trev waiting on him to proceed.

Just a moment ago, he'd responded: Apple , to her texted question: What's your all-time favorite pie flavor?

And twenty minutes before that she'd asked:
LB: How do you feel about roller coasters?

And when he'd told her:
Austin: It's been a while, but I'm a fan.

She'd made him blush when she'd texted:

LB: Well, you know that feeling you get when you're on the way up the incline and the car pauses before the drop? That's how I feel when you say things like you said this morning.

"I'm feeling like some barbecue," Trevor said as they walked to the truck.

It was lunchtime and Austin could admit to being more than a little hungry. "Pulled pork barbecue or ribs barbecue?" he asked, thinking of their options on this side of town.

"Pulled pork. Two or three sandwiches. Extra slaw. Hushpuppies, fries, and all the sweet tea I can drink." Trevor called off his order as if Austin had asked "what will you have?"

"I guess that means you have a place in mind." Austin started the truck and pulled out of the driveway.

"Cross Ties."

"Alright, I'm following your directions because I have no idea where that is."

"Bet."

Sitting at the table a short while later waiting on their order Trevor said, "Your girl makes better sweet tea."

Austin looked up from his phone at Trevor's words. He was back on the app, fiddling with Lora-Beth's kitchen design, changing the cabinet colors from soft cream to bright white and the island countertop to a butcher-block top to see what it looked like. "What?"

Trevor lifted his cup. "This sweet tea. It's good, but your girl makes it better. It's that lemon she adds that doesn't kill the sweetness or the flavor of the tea. Good stuff."

"Right," Austin agreed skeptically, wondering when his crew had started referring to Lora-Beth as his girl.

"Don't you agree?"

"Yeah, she makes good sweet tea. She's a great cook."

"Lucky. When I had a girl, she didn't cook and I could barely manage a package of noodles. Why do you think I know where all the good food is served across the Triangle?"

Austin grunted his reply and went back to his phone.

"What are you working on?"

"Minor reno for her kitchen. She wants a skylight. Here, take a look." He placed his phone on the table so Trevor could see. "I have two versions and I'm working on a third. I want to have options when I come to her with it."

"Damn man, that's pretty cool. How do you know how to do all this stuff?"

"I guess you could say some of it's in my blood. My dad is pretty good with his hands and taught me a lot of what we do now, but I'm an engineer and got my general contractor's license shortly after starting this business. I worked with architects and designers so I picked up a few things along the way, I guess."

"Man, that's cool. Is this a project we'll work on?"

"Not the skylight, I'll hire that out, but the rest of it, yeah. I have to get her approval first though."

"She doesn't know you're doing this?"

"No. She mentioned putting a skylight in her kitchen next year when her budget allows but I'm hoping she'll accept it as a Christmas gift from me."

"I want to see this last one when you're done. What is that, white oak? That really changes the look. I think that may be the one. Nice bright white countertops. Yeah, that'll be nice."

Austin decided to send her a text before digging into his pulled pork platter with smoked Gouda mac and cheese and roasted Brussels sprouts.

Austin: Guess who's having Brussels sprouts with lunch.

Her reply was swift.

LB: Eating your veggies when no one is watching? I'm such a good influence on you.

Austin: More than you know.

He replied before lifting his fork and taking his first bite. Trevor was halfway through his first sandwich.

"Good, right?"

"Yeah, that's good, man."

"Mmm hmm. I told you. I know good food."

Back on the jobsite, they were nearly done, only two more levels and the top pieces, then they could line the interior with high heat furnace cement and barring clean up time, this project would be a wrap. "What's on for tomorrow?" Trevor asked as he mixed another batch of mortar and Austin chipped away at stones.

"There were three jobs as of this morning, but now, I'm not sure. I'll have to talk to Chris to see what he's put on the schedule today. Do you need some time?"

"A friend has tickets to the Duke game that starts at five-fifteen, just trying to see if we'll be done for the day in time for me to make it."

"Go. Watch. We'll manage. Even though I'm not a Duke fan."

"Not this again."

Austin said nothing. Trevor continued anyway. "What? Are you really about to talk trash about Duke coming off a thirty-two and seven, championship winning season?"

Austin lifted his hands in surrender. "I'm not saying anything. Hey, I used to go to Duke games, too. Still not a Duke fan though."

"Don't be a hater all our life. It's okay to come on over to the Blue side."

"I wouldn't hold my breath if I were you."

"I can see if my buddy has another ticket if you want to join."

"Maybe the next one. I'm meeting up with some old friends tomorrow evening."

"I'll see if I can snag us some tickets when Carolina and Duke face off, that's always fun."

"You do know Lora-Beth is a Tarheel, don't you?"

Trevor shook his head. "Well, nobody's perfect."

CHAPTER TWENTY-NINE

Austin grabbed the bags, determined to make only one trip. He closed the door with his back and moved to the front door, tapping lightly with his foot.

"Hey, what's all this?"

"I made a grocery run," he said as she ushered him in.

"You did? For me?"

"Yep. I figured as often as you feed me, I should probably pitch in on your grocery bill. And since I was certain you would say no to that, I picked up a few things I know you keep on hand." He set the bags down on the counter.

Austin rifled through the bags and produced a pint of ice cream in each hand, her favorites. "Got the good stuff too."

"Come here and kiss me." She pulled his face down to hers and gently kissed his lips. "This is incredibly sweet. Thank you."

"You're welcome."

"Let's put this away so I can check your shopping skills."

"I know I did well because I checked the fridge and pantry last night after you fell asleep and made myself a list."

He couldn't be real. Lora-Beth was sure now. This man was not real. "Have I told you how amazing I think you are?"

He stopped his movements, as if considering her words. "I don't know that you have."

"Well, you are. You're so good to me." She touched his face, loving the feel of his low beard on her palm. "Is there something else? Is there a shoe that will be dropping?"

Austin sat on a stool and let her stand between his legs. "This is me. What you see is what you get. You met me when I was in the shadows. You held my hand and walked with me, shined your light on me, and now, we're together in the sunshine. You can relax and enjoy this. I'm able to give to you as you give to me. I may never be able to pay you back, but if it's okay with you, I want to spend my days trying. Can I do that?"

She nodded. "Yeah. But one random question I've been thinking about: Are you going to want to go back to your engineering job and travel?"

He paused to consider her question. "I actually hadn't given it much thought. Building my business is going well. If the urge strikes, I can always look into consulting. For now, I'm happy where I am. Where is this coming from?"

She sighed. "I had lunch with Brian today. He stopped by my office and I agreed to go with him. I figured it was better than trying to hash it out in my office."

"Let me guess, he wants you back," Austin said dryly.

"Pretty much. He's back in town. He wants to see if we can make things work again, etcetera. Of course, I told him, no, I was with you."

"Would it be a yes if I wasn't in the picture?"

She sighed. "Honestly, I don't know if I can answer that. For a long time, I wanted him to come back. I was sure he and I would get back together and make it work."

"Lora-Beth, level with me. I can't handle another heartbreak right now, so if you're unsure, I need you to tell me now. If you need time to sort out your feelings, I can give you time. Lord knows you've been patient enough with me for me to give that to you."

She caressed the sides of his face. "No. Definitely not. I am so sure about us that you asking the question doesn't bother me. I get how you could have heard it that way, but let me clarify. I want you, us. I love you and I don't even want to think about moving forward without you. It was complicated, and may have only become official recently, but you've had me for months. Even when you weren't mine to have, you had me. I knew I was yours the moment you opened up to me about Janet and poured your heart out. I love the way you loved her."

"You love me because of my love for her?"

"That's a part of it, yes, but I love you for the man that you are. The kind of man that would change his whole life to be near the woman he loves. The kind of man who put her first for no other reason than because you loved her that much."

"So he didn't put you first?"

"Austin, that wasn't about him. My feelings for you have nothing to do with him. Nothing at all."

He hoped that was true. He recognized the look on Brian's face as he watched the two of them interact. The man was not simply going to accept that she had moved on.

ص

256

Lora-Beth finally decided on an outfit to wear. It was Saturday evening and Austin was taking her on a mystery date. He'd told her to wear comfortable shoes because they would likely do a bit of walking or standing. He was being aloof, and she liked it, even if she wished he'd been more specific. That would have spared her the last forty-five minutes deciding what to wear after she decided the ankle boots she'd picked up at Nordstrom Rack when she and Tricey hit up their Black Friday shopping were the shoes for the night. Now that she'd gotten dressed, she applied her makeup, light and understated as always, then pinned the right side of her hair back, leaving the rest of the five-day-old wash and go to do as it pleased, and slid the large hoops in her ears. She was brushing on mascara when she heard his truck pull up in the driveway. After a final check of her lipgloss, hair, and overall look, she left the bathroom, picked up her jacket and purse from the bed, and went toward the front door where Austin waited. She smiled at the flutters in her stomach as she entered the foyer, visions of a special moment they'd shared there still fresh in her mind.

"Hey, you," she greeted with a broad smile when she opened the door for him.

Austin thought she looked amazing in her fitted black sweater, faded jeans, and sexy smile. He stepped inside and pulled her to him to take her mouth as he closed the door behind him with his foot. He backed her into the wall and slid his hand around her waist, holding her to him. He stroked across her tongue with his, giving a moan of his own in response to her whimpers. She was his and he loved the way she gave herself to him anytime his primal instincts got the better of him. Her body responding to his touch, his kiss, added fuel to an already raging fire. He loved capturing her this way, sucking up some of her goodness just for himself.

Lora-Beth's mind was full of fog when his hand found her nipple and pinched. She stopped kissing him long enough to whisper his name. It was a plea. A plea for what she wasn't sure, but she never seemed to be able to manage coherent thoughts when he touched her this way with greedy hands and mouth.

"I just needed to get my mouth on you," Austin breathed into her neck. "But we have somewhere to be. Stop distracting me."

"What? Now?" she whined.

"Yes, now, let's go. You're going to make us late." He took her by the hand and before leading her to the door asked, "Do you have everything you need?"

"I'm not sure. Tell me again where we're going?" she tried.

"Out."

"Out? Just out?" At his nodded reply she sighed, noting he was similarly dressed in jeans and a hunter green button down and said, "Then yes, I think I have everything I need."

He reached for her keys, led her through the door, switching off the interior light and on the exterior light, and locked up behind them. He opened the passenger door of his car and got her situated, reaching across to secure her seatbelt before crossing in front to let himself in. A car slowed in front of the house before he reached the driver's door, and he glanced that way, noting the luxury sedan before folding himself inside.

Lora-Beth recognized the place immediately when they pulled into the shopping center. Southern Season, also known as Chapel Hill's culinary Mecca, had been on the list of things she wanted to try but never actually got around to. From what she'd heard, visiting the Mecca one could expect samples from featured vendors, handcrafted coffees from the full service coffee & tea bar, an ice cream cone from the old-fashioned soda fountain, a glass of wine from the full service wine & beer tasting bar, or a cooking class taught by a celebrity chef.

Austin watched her eyes widen with realization and wondered if she had any idea just how captivating she was. The joy that emanated from her warmed him to his core. She really was easy to please. She'd mentioned to him in one of their many "fun fact" exchanges that she'd always wanted to try this place and he thought learning to cook a Spanish dish would be fun. She was such an amazing cook and truly enjoyed it. "Taste of Spain is our class for tonight."

"We're taking a cooking class?" Lora-Beth practically screeched.

"We are, but we'll be able to browse and take a tour before the class starts."

She stared into his eyes for a moment, appreciation glowing in hers. Lora-Beth released her seatbelt and leaned over to place a gentle kiss on his lips. "You remembered."

Austin kissed the tip of her nose. "I remember everything you tell me."

"Thank you."

"Don't thank me yet, let's get inside and see this place for ourselves."

"Yes! Let's do it!" She was out of the car before the sound of his laughter could fill the space.

Austin watched as Lora-Beth listened intently as the chef instructor went over the class menu in its entirety: white gazpacho with almonds and grapes, mussels and chorizo paella, roasted pork tenderloin with romesco sauce, gambas al ajillo, and Catalan tomato-garlic toast. For dessert, there would be Spanish almond cake and of course, wine pairings throughout the meal. To him, it sounded like a lot for a two and a half hour class, but what did he know? It would likely take him two and a half days to pull this together if he was trying to do it on his own.

Lora-Beth broke into his thoughts. "I'm so excited. Aren't you excited? Everything sounds so good. I hope they give us recipe cards so I can make what we like at home."

He wasn't excited, but he was happy as hell to see her so excited. He kissed her cheek. "You're blushing."

"I can't help it, my emotions come out of my face with reckless abandon."

"I know. I love it, particularly when you've lost your words and I only need to look at your face, into your eyes, to know exactly what you're feeling."

"So, is everybody ready for a taste of Spain?" the instructor called out from less than five feet away.

Austin grinned. "Saved by the chef."

"And now we make roast pork tenderloin with romesco. Made with red peppers, tomatoes, and nuts, romesco is to Spain what pesto is to Italy," the instructor said. "And when we finish, this pork will be tender, it will melt in your mouth." This was their final dish of the evening and Austin could admit to having enjoyed working with Lora-Beth at the chef's instruction. Lora-Beth had a way of purposefully tasting the food she tried, seeming to identify ingredients individually, able to tell what they needed more of or what she'd use less of when she made the dish later.

"I know you're excited for this. You love pork chops," she said to him.

"I love your pork chops. But this is pork tenderloin, not chops," he pointed out.

"Do you know the difference?"

"Ask me again when class is over."

"So. What did you think?" Austin asked as they walked to the car, carrying bags of goodies Lora-Beth had to have. Most of the necessary ingredients to recreate the dishes they made tonight, several bottles of wine, a few small kitchen gadgets, one for her and one for Toni, and two flavors of ice cream among them. There were a few items she'd wanted to get for his house as well, but he asked her plainly what she thought he would do with an olive pitter or a vegetable spiralizer.

"Are you kidding? Look at me. Do you even have to ask?"

"So what you're saying is I did good?"

"You did better than good."

Austin opened the trunk and loaded their bags before ushering Lora-Beth to the passenger side and securing her in the seatbelt.

"Why do you always do that?" she asked once he'd climbed in and fastened his own seatbelt. "Not that I'm complaining."

"Why do I do what?"

"Fasten my seatbelt for me."

He looked at her and shrugged. "I like to know you're safe, I guess."

"Well, I like it."

"I don't even realize I'm doing it."

"I like that even better, it's instinctual for you to take steps for my safety." He seemed to do things that pleased her without even trying. It was endearing the way, seemingly from the start, he'd found ways to make her life easier. It felt natural. Easy. Good.

Austin gazed at her. Giddy. That was how he'd describe her mood tonight. He doubted she'd be more excited to be at Disneyland than she was to be at Southern Season. She was as adorable as she was sexy and if he wasn't driving, he would kiss her sweet lips. The woman had no idea the depth of his feelings for her, but he planned to show her. She was an open book who wore her heart on her face. He'd never experienced a woman as content and grateful as Lora-Beth. He was convinced that if he lived a thousand lifetimes he'd never be able to give as much as he took from her. Plain and simple, this woman lit his once dark world and he was eternally grateful she'd chosen to shine her light on him.

ص

"Lora-Beth," Austin groaned. The words sounded as if he were in pain the way he'd barely managed to croak them out. Everything inside him tightened and his body grew still as she took him deep in her mouth. His erection grew harder still as he met the back of her throat and felt it close around his girth. "Fuck. Baby, please." She'd been teasing him for what felt like hours. He was dying for release and damnit, he wasn't too proud to beg.

She drew back, gliding a firm tongue along the base of his shaft as he left her warmth. And when she flicked her tongue over the tip of his engorged, hypersensitive head and dove deep again, he reversed their positions, settling her beneath him on the bed. "That's it."

Lora-Beth yelped in delight. She'd been waiting for that. The moment she knew was coming when he had all he could stand and took charge.

Austin grabbed the condom he'd placed on the nightstand, sheathed himself, found her entrance, and joined them.

"Finally," she moaned.

The soft kisses to her face and neck were incongruous with the savage way he was taking her. He moved fast and deep, holding her in place with his hands under and around her shoulders as he drove into her, barely maintaining his control.

"Open your eyes. I wanna see them."

Lora-Beth gave him his desire and opened her eyes to meet his. He stared into her eyes, evaluating what he saw there. His movements slowed to an excruciating pace. Slow and deep. "You're beautiful. Inside and out, Lora-Beth."

"Austin." Her eyes closed on their own.

He kissed her chin, each of her cheeks, her nose, and forehead. "Look at me." When she gave him her eyes he said, "I love you." And then he took her mouth, increased the pace of his strokes, and rode her the way she loved. Without holding back.

Her orgasm came too fast. She wasn't ready. She wanted to enjoy the feeling of him moving inside her, their bodies connected, for the rest of the night. She wrapped her legs around him.

"I feel that. You're close. Come for me. Let me watch you enjoy the pleasure I give you." Austin released her hands and pulled one taut nipple between his fingers and Lora-Beth cried out from the extra stimulation. Her body jolted and she exploded around him, calling out his name repeatedly. Austin followed soon after, losing it the moment her face contorted with pleasure and his name left her lips. He buried his face in her neck and growled his release freely, not holding back the intensity he felt. Even to his own ears the sounds he made were feral.

She pulled him fully onto her with the strength of all of her limbs. He gave her his weight and rested there, cocooned in Lora-Beth. She was around him in every way and he was inside her. The thing was, she was just as deep inside him, had been long before he'd ever felt what it was like to make love to her.

Austin rested his weight on his elbows and stared down at her sated face.

"I love you, too," she said with closed eyes.

"I know you do."

They were lying in bed, eating ice cream from the carton. Austin had gotten up, saying he needed water, and returned with one of the pints they'd bought earlier but had been too stuffed to eat. Now they'd worked up an appetite.

"How'd you get this scar?" Lora-Beth asked, tracing the faint line with the tip of her finger.

"You've kissed me there a dozen times. I was beginning to wonder if you'd ever ask." Austin fed her a spoonful of the ice cream and answered. "Bar fight. I was in a bad place for a while shortly after the accident. Drinking too much, feeling sorry for myself. Looking for trouble because I needed to do something with the anger. And one night, I ran into someone who wasn't dealing with my shit. He hit me over the head with a beer bottle. Seven stitches."

She kissed it then. Still not being able to imagine the hurt and pain he lived with. She knew it was something he'd never really get over. "And what about the nose? Looks like it may have been broken."

"It was. But not from a bar fight. High school basketball. I caught a flailing elbow. It may surprise you to learn just how much a nose can bleed. Hurt like hell, too."

She imagined what it would feel like to have someone's elbow make contact with her nose and the thought of it made her cringe a little. She kissed the bridge of his nose, then took the spoon from his hand and served him some ice cream.

"Are you going to kiss all my old boo-boos?" he teased.

"Yes. The new ones too." She leaned down and kissed his chest, right about where she thought his heart would be.

Ice cream set aside, he brought her to him and held her to his chest. Warmth radiated from the very spot she'd kissed and formed into a ball of heat that reached his belly. Her words had the ability to reach the very soul of him. Would he ever get over the surprise and delight at how sweet she was? Austin didn't know what he'd done to deserve her love, but he was sure he would do everything in his power to make sure he never lost it.

Austin rolled her to her back and slid down her body. He parted her thighs and she let them fall open. He kissed each before he licked his way to her clit. He alternated between slow, soft licks, fast flicks, and deep sucks. Lora-Beth gripped the sheets at her sides and moved her hips to her own rhythm. When he gave her two fingers, she whimpered. Austin licked her clit and she rode his pumping fingers. Her moans were music to his ears.

Lora-Beth felt her temperature rise and knew she was close. When she worked her hips to help him go deeper, he responded by giving her a third finger and sucking her clit into his mouth. She came with clunky, jerky motions. Austin stroked her through it and brought her back down with tender licks to her hypersensitive clit.

When she was done, he pulled her into his arms, placed her head back on his chest, and held her.

CHAPTER THIRTY

"It's my sister's thirty-fifth birthday and we're going out; just us girls. Tell that man he needs to learn to share," Toni rambled when Lora-Beth picked up the incoming call.

"Why are you telling me something I already know?"

"I'm just making sure plans haven't changed. Mr. Fix It has been taking all your time lately."

Lora-Beth laughed at the new moniker. "Mr. Fix It? What happened to Honey for Hire? And anyway, no he hasn't. Time spent with Austin hasn't stopped any girlfriend time. I see you just as often."

"Then why haven't I seen you since Thanksgiving?"

"Toni, that was like a week ago, and you'll see me this evening."

"Has it only been a week? Well, it seems longer. I miss you!"

"It wasn't me who bailed on yoga on Wednesday."

"The Marcuses are to blame for that one. Hubby had to work late, so I had to pick up MJ. That one was out of my control."

"Not blaming. I'm only reminding you of why it feels like it's been a month since we've spent any girl time."

"So, is there anything you want to tell me?"

Lora-Beth searched her short-term memory for something chat worthy. Not coming up with anything, she said, "Not that I can think of?"

"So does that mean you haven't heard from Brian? I had a feeling he would reach out to you."

"I actually have. He showed up at the office wanting to take me to lunch the other day. " She said dismissively.

"What? Why am I just hearing about this?"

"Nothing to tell really. He showed up and invited me to lunch. I had half an hour so we grabbed a sandwich downstairs. Nothing noteworthy."

"Um, well, then this may not matter." Toni hesitated, unsure if the conversation was warranted.

"What may not matter?"

"Ok. Well, you know it's hard to rely on anything relayed through a man, so take this with a grain of salt, but according to Marcus, Brian still has it bad for you."

"Yeah, he mentioned it."

"Well, he told Marcus, and Marcus told me, that rekindling your relationship is *the* reason he moved back to the area."

Lora-Beth sat on her sofa, having just brushed on a second coat of OPI's We the Female nail polish. She blew on them gently. "Well, that's too bad. His revelations are too late."

Toni huffed. "A day late and a dollar short."

"Too bad he didn't think to, I don't know, reach out to me when he realized he'd made a mistake two years ago, or even a year ago when I still might've been open to the idea of taking him back."

"Too bad he didn't think, period. Good looking arrogant fool."

Lora-Beth laughed at her best friend. The woman had her back. "A fool doesn't know he's a fool."

"Hmph. As long as the rest of us know."

"Where are you?"

"Southpoint. I'm supposed to be trying to get some shopping done for my baby. Christmas will be here before you know it and I can't be bothered with that last minute mess."

"Where is MJ?"

"Marcus took him to the barbershop. Since MJ has lost his spot, where's the top guy in your life today?"

"MJ will never lose his spot and Austin works on Saturdays."

"Making a mental note of that so I can be sure to schedule some of your time for Saturdays now." Then out of nowhere, Toni started singing her version of Chanté Moore's song in perfect pitch. "LB's got a man at home."

"And he's so good to me!" Lora-Beth finished the line.

"Ay! That was on time," Toni cheered.

"Why are you this way?"

"Hey, I'd rather be savage than average. Besides, you love me."

"I must."

Toni changed topics. "What are you wearing tonight?"

"Little black sweater dress, thigh high boots."

"Maybe I should be shopping for myself. You know I don't get out much. I need my fly to match your fly."

"I'm sure you have plenty of options in your closet."

"How about we pretend I don't and you support my mission to buy a new dress?"

"Too bad you didn't call me and let me know you were heading into Durham. I would have gone with you. And this from a woman who just got done complaining about missing girl time."

"How was I supposed to know you'd be willing to tear yourself away from Mr. Fix It to hang out with me this afternoon and tonight?"

"He's working!"

"Ain't no love like new love. I may give you a hard time, but I'm not actually trying to get in the way of that."

"You never do. Even though you gave Brian a hard time, you never tried to get between us."

"I like Brian, but he's always been too full of himself for his own good. He's cool but he thought he was too good for you. I did my part to make sure he knew he wasn't. And now… Well, let's just say there's a part of me that will enjoy seeing him pine after you."

"Toni!"

"A small part, but still, it's there. He screwed up walking away from you. And he has some nerve showing up out of the blue talking about he 'wants you back'. The hell you say? I'll tell you what I say. I say no, sir. Not today. Not tomorrow either. Too little too late. That train has left the station."

"Feel better now that you've gotten that out?"

Toni blew out a breath. "Whew! I actually do."

"Good. I'm starving, so I'm going to put together a quick lunch. Oh! I have something for you by the way. Austin took me for a cooking class at Southern Season last night and I picked up a couple things for us both."

"Remember when I asked you earlier if you had anything you wanted to tell me?"

"Yes."

"For future reference, cooking class date nights qualify as something to tell me."

"Bye, Toni."

"Just saying."

"See you tonight."

"Bye."

It was said that wine brought out the best in cheese and chocolate. Well, apparently, it also brought the inner artist out of Lora-Beth, or so she thought.

"Well ladies, I walked in here a regular nine-to-fiver, but I may be walking out an artist. Feel free to call me LB Van Gogh."

Toni looked over at her canvas and raised an eyebrow, "Um, more like LB Van No."

"Come on, have you ever seen such a magnificence?"

"Yes, I can see three other magnificences from this seat," Toni deadpanned.

"If you want to see a masterpiece, wait until I finish over here," Vonda, the birthday girl, proclaimed from the other side of the row of easels, paintbrush in one hand, wine glass in the other.

Toni's eyes met mine. "Too much sauce," she mused and the group erupted in a fit of giggles.

There were nine ladies helping Vonda celebrate her special night and putting their artistic skills to the test at the local Wine & Design. Tonight's painting was of branches of a pine tree with pine cones covered in snow against a turquoise background. Difficulty scale was somewhere near a three out of ten and Toni doubted either of the two ladies who'd claimed it would end up with masterpieces. If history was an indicator, Vonda was putting her personal spin on what they were instructed to do.

"Those branches need more needles and why don't your pine cones have any scales?" Tamara, one of the ladies in their party, offered Vonda advice she didn't want.

"Eyes on your own canvas. It's my birthday, so however I paint it, it's the right way."

"You tell her, V," and "Someone get that woman a refill," were called out by two of the women at the same time.

"Who was that? Devin? If she's counting needles and checking for scales, she definitely hasn't had enough wine," Lora-Beth agreed. She took out her phone to snap a few pics and noticed the message from Austin, who was hanging out with some old friends.

Austin: Have fun tonight. No drinking and driving. If you need a ride, call me and I'm there.

She typed a quick reply before resuming her picture taking.

LB: Carpooled with Toni and Michelle. Restaurant is a three-minute walk away. Will err on the side of caution and call if it's questionable when we're done.

Thai Palace was a brief walk away, even in her stiletto boots. She was confident she could make it there and back with no issues. She snapped several pictures of the group and got back to her own canvas before his reply came through.

Austin: Call anyway. I want to fall asleep with you tonight.

She turned her back to her canvas and snapped a pic to send to him.

LB: Will definitely call. Artist @ work. Cheese!

Austin: Gorgeous

They all posed with their artwork when the painting portion of the night was over, and as expected, Vonda had veered a bit off track and done her own thing. And if she had to judge the pieces, Lora-Beth would say it was clear the five bottles of wine they'd brought with them had all been served.

"So, is thirty-five the age where I stop thinking of a girl's night out as a night of dancing and debauchery? Or is that just my sister?" Michelle, Toni and Vonda's younger sister, asked the crowd once they'd all placed their dinner order selections. Several of the ladies had bowed out of dinner and six attendees—Vonda, Michelle, Toni, Lora-Beth, Devin, and Tamara—remained.

"And just what sort of debauchery are you used to?" Vonda asked.

"Yes, do tell," Lora-Beth added.

"This should be good," Toni chimed in.

Michelle started on her explanation and Lora-Beth mused that at twenty-seven she likely still had quite a bit of debauchery left in her system. Dinner passed in a blur, partly due to the fact that Austin had top billing in her mind since his earlier proclamation of his desire to end his night with her. It was always surprising how often her thoughts drifted to Austin. More than once Toni had chastised her for being on her phone instead of being in the moment. They were settling their tabs and, at his request, she'd told Austin where they were. He agreed to end his night with the guys and come to pick her up rather than leaving Toni with the charge of getting her home safely.

"Excuse me. I need to visit the ladies room. If our server comes while I'm away, this is all set." She gestured to her check presenter.

"I'll come with."

"So, is he coming over tonight?" Toni asked no sooner than they'd stepped away from the table.

"Actually, he's coming to pick me up. He should be outside by the time we're done."

"Really?"

"Yes. He was out with his friends, reconnecting, and wanted to end our night together."

"Aww, that's so sweet."

Austin's handsome face appeared in Lora-Beth's mind and she smiled at the image of his smiling face. He was always attractive, but was simply beautiful when he smiled. "Yeah, it is. He is."

Lora-Beth blushed.

"Oh my god, you've got it bad. But that's okay because he clearly has it just as bad."

Lora-Beth was usually much better at compartmentalizing her thoughts, but lately, it'd been all Austin, all the time. She knew it was good that they spent time with friends separately, and even liked that he was reconnecting with his friends, but that didn't mean she didn't think about what the two of them might be doing had they not been out doing their own thing. And it was then she realized, as usual, Toni had been right. Apparently, now that she had a man....

She was so lost in her musings after she'd done her business and stood at the sink applying a fresh coat of lipstick, she hadn't realized Toni had joined her, washed her hands, and was now waiting for her to be done with her primping.

When Lora-Beth faced her, in her amusement Toni asked, "You done? Sure you don't want to check your hair? I think maybe there's a curl out of place."

Lora-Beth winked at her. "He likes my curls out of place."

"I bet he does." Toni laughed, shaking her head. "Let's get out of here so we can get you to this man. I think he has his work cut out for him tonight."

She winked and added, "I'm sure he's up for it."

CHAPTER THIRTY-ONE

"I'm out, guys. It's time for me to call it a night," he said to his friends, Rob and Brick, as he made his way to the door. He and Brick had been friends for years, and when he'd started back at the gym for pick-up games, they'd had a chance to reconnect. He was glad he let Chris talk him into joining him. It was now part of his routine twice a week.

"Don't forget what I said," Rob said, clapping him on the back. "We'd love to have you. Bring your lady, I'm sure my wife would love to get to know her."

He hadn't mentioned anything to his friend about having someone new in his life, yet somehow, he'd known.

"I'm going to be there," Brick added. His real name was Patrick but he'd been given the nickname thanks to his lacking on the basketball court.

Rob and his wife were hosting a New Years' Eve party and he extended the invitation to Austin. He'd run it by Lora-Beth to see if she was interested.

"Thanks."

"It's good to see you looking like your old self again, man," Brick called out to his back as he left the room. Austin silently agreed. He felt like himself again.

They were at Tobacco Road Sports Café watching the Tarheel game. It just so happened, he was less than ten minutes away from where Lora-Beth was out celebrating with her friends, which was why he told her he would pick her up and drive her home. No other reason. It wasn't because he hadn't seen her since early that morning and was already missing her company. No, that wasn't it at all.

Smiling to himself, he walked to his car and climbed in, then sent a reply to let her know he would be outside when she was done.

Austin pulled into the first spot he saw when he spotted the restaurant. He got out, slid his jacket on, and walked toward the building. He stood out front, stepping out of the way of the smoke coming from the couple nearby, and waited.

The door opened and three women walked out before her face appeared. She was in the middle of a conversation, talking animatedly, as was her way. Though her boots were over her knee, he could still see the smooth skin of her thighs before the dress's hemline stopped his search. Then Lora-Beth looked at him and stopped mid-sentence when their eyes met. His breath caught in his lungs at the sight of the smile on her face.

He started in her direction before he realized he was moving. Lora-Beth walked straight into his chest. He wrapped his arms around her, lowered his mouth to her ear, and kissed her there before saying, "You look absolutely amazing." He heard her quiet "thank you", as he buried his face in her neck and inhaled. She smelled amazing as well. The black dress fit her curves like a glove. He was thankful for the short jacket she'd worn. It did nothing to mask her amazing figure. Not that he hadn't already known how amazing her figure was, but he'd never seen her dressed this way, for a night out like this. The ultra-sexy boots were doing things to him. At five foot seven, Lora-Beth was tall, but with those boots, those legs that he loved seemed to go on forever. He'd have her keep them on when he finally got her home.

Toni cleared her throat. "Can the rest of us say hello? Sheesh. Hello, Austin. And how are you tonight?"

Austin felt Lora-Beth's laugh against him. "Hi, Toni. I'm good. I hope you are."

Lora-Beth turned in his arms and faced her friend.

"Why are we formal all of a sudden?" She stepped closer and gave him a half hug. "I guess that'll do since this one is all over you."

Lora-Beth spoke up then, introducing Austin to the rest of the group. "Austin, you've met Vonda, the birthday girl and Michelle. And this is Tamara and Devin." She pointed to each of the latter two in turn. Hellos and nice to meet yous were called before everyone dispersed in the direction of their respective vehicles.

Austin opened the door and let her in, then reached across to fasten her in. She lifted her hand to his face and brought his mouth to touch hers. "Thank you." She loved that he did that.

"For?"

"I don't know, I just feel grateful."

He knew the feeling. "Well then, you're welcome."

"How'd it go with the guys?" she asked as he pulled out of the parking lot.

"It was good. I'm glad I went." He thought about it for a moment before continuing. "It was like no time had passed. The guys were as they'd always been. And at some point, I realized it hadn't been them who had changed at all. It was me. I'd pulled away, isolated myself, I guess."

"Why did you?"

"I think it was guilt. I felt guilty about living my life as usual while hers was on hold. Since I felt as if I was alone, it became easier to be alone than to force myself to carry on as if everything was okay."

"Must've been difficult feeling that way."

He shrugged. "I dealt with it."

"And now?"

Austin looked over at her in the shadows of the streetlights. "Now, the only *alone* I think about is being alone with you."

She smiled and rested her hand on top of his on the gear shift. "Have you always been so charming?"

"I don't think so." He brought their joined hands to his lips and kissed hers. "We're going to my place. I hope that's okay." He changed the subject.

"That's fine."

An hour later Austin was finding his pleasure watching Lora-Beth move above him. He'd gotten her home and had taken her over the back of the couch, boots on, fully dressed, taking only a moment to expose the necessary parts to allow him entry. She had been as into it as he was and made no objection to the frenzied way he'd taken her. Now they were in his bed and it was the Lora-Beth show.

Her hips rolled in painstakingly slow rhythm. She twisted her hips on an upstroke and called out his name. She was torturing him. Austin lifted his hand from her hips and pulled her down to his mouth and grinded his hips into hers, setting a faster pace. She moaned deep in her throat and he felt her grow slicker around him. She loved to tease him until he couldn't take it anymore and took over.

Now she complied, pulling away from his hold and sitting up on him again, riding in earnest. He drew one of her nipples into his mouth, sucking gently before nipping it with his teeth at the same time he grabbed two handfuls of her luscious cheeks. She shuddered at the feel of it, the multiple stimulations causing her breath to hitch. She moaned his name, begging him not to stop. Austin switched breasts and paid this one the same attention he'd given the first. Lora-Beth lifted her hand to his head when he closed his lips around the sensitive peak, holding him there. Still, they moved together, sweat slicked bodies sliding against each other.

She knew what he was doing. He was making her ask for it, teasing her as she'd done to him. He knew what she wanted, knew what she needed. She pressed a little harder on his head and commanded, "Bite it."

"What was that?" He flicked it with his tongue.

"Austin, please. Please."

"Please what?"

"Bite it."

He closed his teeth and at the same time pressed his thumb to the sensitive spot between her legs and rubbed. He was rewarded with a string of yeses and calls to Jesus' father and Lora-Beth coming apart. Austin chased his own release, holding her tightly to his chest as he took what he needed from her body.

Lora-Beth felt his limbs go loose and released a contented sigh. She tried to roll off but he tightened his hold and kissed her hair.

"Sleep now."

"I can't sleep on top of you, you won't be able to breathe."

"I'll risk it. Now sleep, sweetie. I'm drained."

Lora-Beth smiled into his chest and nuzzled. She loved when he called her sweetie. Loved when he was spent from the love they made. And loved how easy it was for him to fall asleep in her arms. She'd get cleaned up in a moment, For now, she would enjoy the afterglow.

ص

Austin stared at the ceiling. He'd been awake awhile, just watching the room grow brighter with the morning sun and listening to her breathing. At some point during the night, their positions had switched and he was no longer inside her, but they were wrapped in each other still. She was sprawled over him and one of his legs was between hers. Her head rested on his chest and his hands rested over her shoulder and on her thigh. One of the things Austin loved most about Lora-Beth was that she was bold and proud to be who she was. She was happy with herself and gave without reservation to those around her. He'd known how she felt long before she ever said the words, maybe even before she did. From the start she'd made him feel like her house was a place he was welcome, a place he belonged.

She noticed something inside was broken, and without asking what it was, she accepted him. What little he gave to her, she'd taken it and made it good. She brightened even his darkest days, had seen the pain on his face, heard his story, and still, she'd been there, giving him what he needed and asking for very little in return.

Austin closed his eyes and focused on her breathing, feeling the rise and fall of her chest against his side and matched his breath to hers. He envisioned his heart beat synching with hers. He could feel his heart beat getting stronger. He laced their fingers and kissed her hair. "Thank you for loving me, Lora-Beth Haines."

Lora-Beth smelled food. She rolled onto her back and stretched her sore muscles. Austin had given her a workout last night. She groaned as she felt her stretch from her toes to her fingertips.

"Good morning. I hope you're hungry." She turned her face toward the sound of his voice and found Austin standing in the doorway shirtless, a tray of food in his hands.

Yummy, she thought. And the food looked good too. "Breakfast in bed? What did I do to deserve the royal treatment this morning?"

Austin placed the tray on the nightstand and leaned over to give her a brief kiss. "You loved me." Lora-Beth sat up and he placed a pillow at her back, between her and the headboard. He sat on the edge of the bed next to her.

"Loved?"

"Yep. Hungry? We have cheese eggs, turkey bacon, fruit, and croissants. Though I must confess the croissants are store bought. I didn't whip up a batch of dough while you were sleeping. I did, however, pick them up at the bakery yesterday and heated them just a few minutes ago."

"I also buy my croissants from the bakery, so I'd say you did great. Let me have a bite of those eggs."

"Made with cheddar-Monterey Jack cheese blend and scrambled soft, just the way you like. Taste for yourself." He forked some eggs and raised them to her mouth.

Lora-Beth savored the first bite Austin offered her and moaned. "You nailed it. You're so good to me." She patted the bed beside her. "Climb in, let's eat."

He'd driven her home at noon, getting her settled inside before he'd taken off to handle something. The *something* he needed to handle was his weekly trip to the cemetery. It was forty minutes away in Siler City where Janet's family was from. He was now at Fresh Market because he'd long ago learned he liked the selection of fresh flowers they offered. He picked up a bouquet of winter jasmine for Janet, remembering it was a scent she'd sometimes worn.

Austin nearly leapt with joy as his eyes landed on the purple tipped white flowers. Though he was sure, he checked the card and laughed when it confirmed these were, in fact, lisianthus. He picked up three bouquets, went to the clerk working the floral department desk and asked, "Do you have a vase big enough to make this one arrangement?"

The clerk—a young lady likely in her early twenties, with long straight black hair and gray eyes—looked at him and smiled. "Sure. I have two orders to put together before yours, but I can have it done in about forty minutes. If you'd like, you can do your shopping and it'll be ready by the time you're done."

"How about if I pick it up in about an hour and a half?"

"That's no problem, sir. Is this for a special occasion? Would you like to select the vase and ribbon or do you want to leave it up to me? I do a real good job. I've been doing this for five years. You can see here, behind me…" She gestured toward the two arrangements. "This is my work."

"They look great. No special occasion, she just loves these flowers. So I'll leave it in your capable hands."

"You won't be disappointed."

Lora-Beth was making a grocery list. She was preparing to cook a traditional Southern-style Sunday dinner and didn't have all the ingredients she needed to make it happen. She pulled her cell from her pocket and dialed Toni's number. Her friend answered on the second ring.

"Hello."

Forgoing pleasantry or greeting Lora-Beth asked, "Sunday dinner at my place? Dinner served at four-*ish*?"

"Oh thank God! Baby! LB is making Sunday dinner!" her friend yelled.

"Did you really just scream that in my ear?" she asked when she heard Toni speaking with MJ.

"LB, my baby wants mac 'n cheese. Is that on the menu?"

"For MJ? Of course it is. And I'm sure he'll share with the rest of you."

"She said yes, there will be mac 'n cheese," Toni told her son, who then squealed his excitement. "Girl, you must have read my mind. I did not feel like cooking today. What should I bring?"

"You don't need to bring anything."

"Except my container for leftovers you mean, right?"

Lora-Beth laughed. "If there are leftovers, you may have to battle Austin for them."

"See, I didn't agree to that. I don't remember anything about agreeing to your man taking priority on leftovers. What about me?" Toni and her dramatics.

"Don't you think it's time you learned how to share?"

"I agreed to share my best friend, now I have to share my leftovers too? Where does it end?"

"You don't even know what's on the menu, how do you know you'll want leftovers? I could be cooking up chicken feet and succotash."

"Well, I know you, so I know better, but if you're serving it with cornbread I would find a way to make it work." They shared a laugh.

"I'm getting my list together. Where does MJ stand on chicken these days?"

"Girl, I doubt he'll eat anything other than the mac 'n cheese you promised him."

"Alright, well, my list is complete and now I'm going to run to the store and get what I need. See you by four."

"That's it? Just dinner plans? No convo about last night?"

"Last night was nice. Vonda enjoyed her night out. It was so sweet of her hubby to let her have the night with her friends while he stayed home with the kids."

"Yeah, but that's not what I'm talking about and you know it."

"Oh?"

"Your man showed up, looking all manner of handsome, and you couldn't even finish your sentence. Mr. Tall, Dark, and Handsome stole your entire train of thought."

"Oh, yeah. That."

Toni could hear the smile in her voice. She laughed. "Wow. You're terrible. Is he there?

"Sunday afternoon," she said simply.

"Ah. Forgot. But he'll be there for dinner though?"

"Yep. He'll be here."

"Does he talk about it? Or does he avoid the subject altogether?"

"He mentions her or references his life before occasionally."

"Does it bother you?"

"Not at all. I hope I will always be able to say that. What happened changed his life. I want him to feel comfortable talking to me about everything, and she's no exception."

"Damn, you really love him, huh?"

"Yes, I do."

Just then, Toni yelled out again, "Say what, Baby?"

Lora-Beth could hear muffled sounds in the background before Toni spoke to her again.

"Marcus wants to know if you're making something sweet and if your man will be watching the game."

"There will be something sweet and if I had to wager a guess, I'd say yes, he will be watching football."

"You see how it is? Good company and good food isn't enough for these men. They have to have those things *and* football on the TV. Why do we bother?"

"Because we love them. And they're handy to keep around," Lora-Beth joked.

"Yeah, there's that."

"Okay, let me go. I'll see you soon."

"Later."

Three hours later she opened the door for Austin and gasped at the large bouquet of flowers he extended. Her eyes grew large and she exclaimed. "Oh my God, Austin, they're beautiful? Gimme, gimme."

"I may have been just as excited when I saw them." He laughed.

"I've never seen a bouquet this big. It's so beautiful." She set the vase down to thank him properly.

"You're welcome. Smells good in here."

She led the way and he followed closely behind. She set the bouquet on the kitchen table. "We're having guests. Toni and her guys are joining us for dinner."

"Okay. What are we having?"

"Fried chicken, mashed potatoes and gravy, fresh green beans, and cornbread. Oh and mac 'n cheese for MJ." When Austin raised an eyebrow in question, she assuaged his curiosity by saying, "Don't look so worried, I'm sure he'll share."

"You're kidding, right?"

"Did I mention I'm making you a peach cobbler?"

"No you hadn't, but my mouth is watering just hearing those words. Come here and kiss me." He lifted her to the counter, stepped between her legs, and kissed her long and hard. He pressed the palm of her hand to his heart and held it there, then did the same with his on her chest. He looked into her eyes just as he'd done hours earlier, matched his breath to hers, and envisioned their heartbeats synching.

"I can't think when you look at me like that."

"You don't need to think. Just feel. Let me feel you."

Chapter Thirty-Two

"Brian?"

Brian zoned out while he sat in the sandwich shop staring out of the window, lost in his thoughts. Honestly, for a moment there, at the sound of her voice, he thought he'd been daydreaming. But when he looked up and saw her face, his transformed into an easy smile. Surely it wasn't a coincidence they'd ended up in the same sandwich shop. It had been two weeks since he had seen Lora-Beth and he'd been a good boy and resisted contacting her. Now, running into her at a random sandwich shop, Brian thought the universe was trying to tell him something. And who was he to ignore signs from the universe?

"Lora-Beth?" He stood to give her a brief embrace and hoped she didn't avoid the contact. He loved looking at her. Her warm brown eyes danced in the sunlight, and from them he got that she may have been happy to see him. At the very least, she wasn't unhappy. The dress she wore showed off a healthy body he used to love having pressed against him.

She allowed the greeting, briefly remembering the way it felt to be in his arms. "Would you mind if I join you for a minute? I got mine to go. I don't have long, but…" She paused. "I think it's good that we ran into each other."

"Sure, of course." He cleared his throat and gestured for her to take the seat across from him. Was it possible that he wasn't the only one listening to the universe's signs today? God, he sounded pitiful. The truth was that he wasn't prepared for this. Sure, he had every intention of winning back her heart. It had been all he could think about the last year he'd spent in Washington, which was why he'd taken a lateral move to get back to the East Coast, back to her. And it was a good call. She still brought butterflies to his stomach and that made him feel like a teenager with a crush.

He watched as Lora-Beth seemed to get her words together in her head. She'd never been short on words and he steeled himself for what might pop out of her mouth. He remembered when they'd met in grad school. He had been different back then. More confident. Sure he was a catch, and any woman who'd garnered his attention could count themselves lucky, but his very first words to her had been, "Man, you are beautiful." Lora-Beth had blushed, but recovered enough to respond, "You're not so bad yourself."

Every day following that first meeting, he reached out to her in some way. After a month of build-up, Lora-Beth agreed to a date. Their first date went like many first dates, nothing out of the ordinary. Dinner, then a movie and a walk around the promenade where an ice cream shop was still open for the express purpose of capturing business from late movies. He found out then just how easy it was to be around her and he wanted more of her time.

"That's a pensive look. Is everything okay?" Lora-Beth asked.

"Yes, everything is cool. Just thinking about old times, I guess, and what happened to get us to where we are now." The last time they had lunch they'd spent the time actually getting caught up, asking about each other's families, talking about his life in Washington, her career moves here, the house, keeping things light. Even then, he made his intention clear. He wanted another chance with her.

Lora-Beth sat back in the chair and sighed. "We didn't just find ourselves here. Life put us in a position to make a choice, Brian. You chased your career and left us behind."

"I can admit that we made a mistake, but..."

"We? A mistake?" Lora-Beth clenched her teeth as if holding back what she really wanted to say. She closed her eyes. It wasn't them. It was him. He'd abandoned her and he knew it.

"Bad choice of words. You're right, I made a decision without speaking with you about it first. I was wrong. But I always wanted you to come with me. I'd say the mistake I made was assuming you would."

"Yeah, well… You know what they say happens when you assume."

"I was an ass. Yes. But I've regained my senses. I know exactly how I was wrong and can admit my fault. I apologize for my tunnel vision. So tell me, love, are you going to hold a grudge for one bad decision?" Brian leaned in, subconsciously getting closer to her as he spoke.

She watched him and recognized his particular brand of charm. There had been a time when all he needed to do was flash his dimples and she melted. "No grudge, but I need to be clear that things have changed. I'm not the girl who fawns over you anymore. I've moved on."

Brian eyed her, as if he were inspecting, reading her face for the truth in her words. He sat back in his seat, lifted his cup to lips, and took a long draw. "First, there was plenty of fawning on my end too. Second, so you keep telling me. "

"Number one thirteen," the person behind the counter called out.

"That's me," Lora-Beth said.

"I'll grab it."

She watched him walk up to the counter from the small table in front of the window and thought he hadn't changed a bit in the years they'd been apart. When Brian returned to the table she thanked him and started her spiel. "I know we'll see each other, we have mutual friends, and that's not an issue, but I need to be clear that—"

"Lora-Beth, stop. Don't do that. Don't hit me with the let's be clear speech. I saw you with the guy, Austin, is it? I have to be honest here. My concern is you and what it's going to take to remind you of how much you and I once meant to each other."

Lora-Beth sighed. This was what she was afraid of. "Brian, I don't need to be reminded. I know how things were with us. And I know how they ended. You made your choice. I was broken for a while, but I put myself back together and now I've moved on. I'm with Austin and I'm happy."

He raised an eyebrow and Lora-Beth recalled having seen that look on his face many times in the past. It was his way of asking, "really?" without actually saying the words. "Are you?" he settled on instead.

"Yes. Don't I look happy to you?"

He gave a sly smile. "You're as beautiful as ever, but..." he drawled, then continued, "I can't quite put my finger on it, but it seems like something is missing." Then he lifted a finger and pointed to himself. "Oh look, I've managed to put a finger on it."

Lora-Beth couldn't help but laugh. His sense of humor had been one of the many things she loved about him.

She felt soft but strong hands on hers and withdrew hers at the tingle she felt. She saw the smirk on Brian's face and knew he felt it too. It had always been this way with them. So easy, and if she were honest she missed their friendship. A part of her hoped they could figure out how to be friends.

"You should go ahead and eat while we talk. There's no need to let that Chicken Philly get cold."

"How did you… "

"Lucky guess," he answered her unfinished question. He knew her. Knew what she liked and knew that if she was at this type of place, she was here for a Philly. Lora-Beth opened the wrapper and inhaled. He always loved the way she enjoyed food.

"So, you never did get around to mentioning how it is that you ended up back here the other day," she started before taking a bite of her sandwich.

The moan she let out, he felt in his groin. He let his mind run with that thought for a second. She was right, he hadn't mentioned why or how it was that he was back in the area, purposefully. But, damn it to hell, why was he playing coy? With an air of confidence he said, "I'm back for you. You are my sole motivation for being here, Lora-Beth."

Lora-Beth tilted her head to the side, giving him a blank look, not believing he was taking a rom-com approach to answering her question. Was she supposed to believe he'd been sitting at his desk one day and realized his life just wasn't the same without her, so he'd packed up and came back with the express intent of winning back her heart?

Without so much as a call? She shook her head. "So, a promotion then?" She waited for his response before she took another bite.

Brian laughed. "Let's say an awakening, followed by an opportunity I would have been a fool to turn down." He looked at her now as she took a moment to finish what was in her mouth and compose herself to speak.

"Well, I'm happy for you. I want you to have the life you always wanted and be happy. Your career has always been the most important thing," she threw in as an afterthought as she stood and straightened her dress. He stood when she did. "I'm just going to get some water. I was going to eat this at my desk, so I didn't order a drink."

"Sit. Eat. I'll grab you one. Are you sure you want water or maybe a sweet tea?"

"Sweet tea would be great."

"I'd offer you a sip of mine but..." he trailed off.

"Here." She reached into the side of her purse and withdrew a five.

He lifted that eyebrow again and walked away, rejecting the notion that he'd accept money from her when he had offered her the drink.

By the time Brian arrived back at the table, she was nearly done with her food and had checked the time, confirming she needed to get a move on. It was a quarter to two and she needed to be back at the office and ready for a status meeting at two-thirty. One she was not yet prepared to report on. Her morning meeting had run long, which explained why it was one-thirty before she'd had a chance to even think about lunch.

"Here you go."

"Thank you."

"So this is the second time we've had lunch, what can I do to make sure there will be a third?"

"Brian."

"Lora-Beth, relax. I asked to share a meal, not your bed. What's the harm? You and I can get along well enough to sit across the table from each other."

"This was a coincidence. The last time I was caught off guard."

"And I'm trying to plan the third time because I can't count on coincidence to put us in the same place at the same time again. That would be foolish of me, now wouldn't it?"

"It's not a good idea."

"Don't tell me your man doesn't allow you to have friends."

"Are we friends?"

"We could be, if you'd open yourself to it."

Lora-Beth sighed again. "You hurt me, Brian."

"I know. I'm sorry."

"It took me enough time to get over it to not want to muddy the waters." He didn't know what to say, so he said nothing. She went on. "I don't know."

"What don't you know?"

"We were once friends, and we share a friend group, but I'm not sure whether or not you are friend-worthy these days."

He placed a hand to his chest in mock pain. "Now you're hurting me."

"Oh stop it. You're fine. I'm surprised your ego even recognizes hurt."

He flinched. "A second blow. Why are you being this way? So cold. So Toni."

They shared a laugh at their friend's expense.

"She is pretty hard on you, isn't she?"

"Just me? Don't tell me she's not like that with everyone?" He left his true question unsaid. *Is she not that way with your new man?*

"Not everyone."

"Are you saying Houston gets better treatment? Toni and I are going to have to talk the next time I'm over there."

"You know his name is Austin."

"Right."

The exes found themselves in some sort of stare down, each waiting on the other to pick up the conversation. Lora-Beth spoke, ending the silence. "I hate to cut this impromptu lunch short, but I have to run."

"Maybe we can finish this conversation over dinner, or lunch, whatever you deem is acceptable… for friends."

"I don't think so. How about we see each other when we see each other and leave it at that? I know we'll cross paths."

He didn't like the sound of that. Waiting until they happened upon each other to have a conversation was ridiculous. "Here, let me take care of this trash then I'll walk you to your car."

"I can manage on my own, I found a good spot."

"I know you can, but this time, you don't have to."

Outside he said, "So, my number hasn't changed. Should you decide you want to call, or text, you can reach me at any time."

"Why aren't you at work in the middle of the day?" she asked as an afterthought and a method of avoidance.

"I was grabbing lunch. I'm working from home and wanted to step out for some fresh air."

"So you live near here?"

"Not far. I had to run an errand on this street and just popped in when I was done. Must've been fate."

"Or you smelled good food and followed your nose."

"Maybe my nose will lead me to your place the next time you're making lasagna." When she didn't take the bait, he relented and opened the door for her.

"It was good to run into you, so if it was fate, I will admit to being grateful. I'm happy you're happy. You are happy, aren't you?"

He thought about it for a moment. "I'm content, but I can see happiness in my future."

She smiled. Brian really was a decent man. If only he'd been able to see that he could have both, his career and his life with her, before blowing things up. He hadn't and now was now. She was over him. Over them. She had been fine on her own. And now, she had a man in her life who added to her happiness and they were good together. There was nothing beyond friendship she could offer Brian. "Maybe I'll see you around."

"I hope you will. Be safe." He closed the door, stepped onto the sidewalk, and watched until she pulled away. Then he walked two spaces over, climbed into his luxury sedan and smiled, pleased with the turn his day had taken.

ص

Sitting at her desk, Lora-Beth reflected on how well her life was going. Her family was healthy, she had great friends, was a homeowner with an established career, and had a good man in her life whose touch melted her. Yes, hearth and home were great, and she couldn't be happier.

She'd spent time grieving the loss of the life she thought she was meant to have with Brian and had healed and moved on. Had there been any doubts of lingering feelings, running into him today had done its job of answering those unexplored questions. Sure, she wished him well, and could even imagine having a friendly relationship with him going forward, but her heart was both sure and full with love for Austin. They connected on a level that was beyond reason, beyond words, and for her, that said everything.

"Sorry to interrupt. You got a sec?" Sam poked his head into her office.

Startled at the sudden sound in the room, Lora-Beth shook herself out of her musing and checked the time. There was still plenty of time before her next meeting. "Yes, of course. Come in and have a seat."

"Actually, if you could meet me in Michael's office conference room in five, that would be great."

"Should I be worried?"

"You have nothing to worry about. Should be short and sweet."

Lora-Beth wasn't sure what to expect, but she had an inkling. With everything else going on in her life, as well as her busy day-to-day work life, she hadn't given much thought to this particular thing. She crossed the lobby and headed to the southwest corner of the floor, where Michael, the Director of Marketing and Brand Management sat in an oversized corner office. Reema gave her a thumbs up and cheeky smile, as if she knew what was in store. She wouldn't be surprised if Reema did know what was going on. The woman seemed to have her ear to ground for all things, so this would be no exception.

Lydia, Michael's executive assistant, greeted her with a smile. "Go on in, they're waiting for you in the conference room."

She found Michael, Sam, Noah, and Everett already seated.

"Lora-Beth. Come in, go ahead and shut the door behind you, will you? This is everyone," Michael greeted from his place at the small conference table.

She took the empty seat next to Everett and Michael wasted no time starting.

"I'm sure you've heard scuttlebutt around the office, but it's safe now to confirm that after twenty-five years with us, our good man here will be retiring at the end of the year." He reached out and patted Everett's shoulder.

Lora-Beth smiled at him and received a nod of acknowledgment in return.

"Now, with that being the case, this necessitated a change. Sam will be promoted to Everett's current position and instead of simply filling his spot, we are taking this opportunity to do a bit of restructuring. In doing so, this will create two positions and you two have been selected to fill them."

Not waiting for a reaction, Sam took over the conversation. "While we're all still under the same umbrella, marketing and public relations will now comprise two teams. Lora-Beth, you will head up the PR side of things and Noah you'll be over the marketing side."

Everett had aged well, and if it weren't for the head of gray hair and the crow's feet around his green eyes, you might not believe him to be at retirement age. The silver fox spoke, and in doing so answered the question burning in Lora-Beth's brain. "This move in no way separates the department. The aim is to allow the teams to be more productive and give the employees the opportunities to play to their strengths. I spent the past five years building a department that worked well together with a fluidity that didn't limit you as individuals and this needs to remain."

"You'll be in charge of making sure this happens," Michael started, pointing to Lora-Beth and Noah with the pointer and pinky fingers on one hand. "As Senior Principal Brand Strategists, it will not only be your responsibility to manage your teams, but work together on client projects."

Sam picked up the conversation. "Collaborative. Lora-Beth is better at getting out and meeting with the public, Noah is stronger at in-house brainstorming, and we need the best of both."

"It's what we need to take AlphaKey to the next level." Michael finished what sounded to Lora-Beth like a well-rehearsed presentation.

"Questions, comments, concerns, let's hear 'em," Sam offered.

Noah, a thin, bearded man spoke first. "Thank you for this opportunity."

"Yes, thank you. This sounds like an amazing opportunity. I'm proud to be considered."

"I'll make the announcement at the holiday party, so can we keep this between us for another day?" Michael asked. Everyone agreed. "That's all I have for you, thanks for your time."

"Thank you. Everett, again, congratulations on your retirement. You will be sorely missed around here." Lora-Beth said.

"I'm not out of here just yet. You still have time to make me one last carrot cake." He winked.

"I'll make it happen," she promised.

Back at her desk, she pulled her cell phone out and dialed Austin. He answered after the third ring, out of breath. "Hello."

"Guess who got a promotion!" she exclaimed.

"That's great, sweetie. Congratulations! I knew you would get it. How do you feel? I know you were kind of on the fence," he asked.

"It's better than I expected. As I'm told, the promotion will not pull me away from the part of the job I love most. I was worried for nothing."

"We should celebrate."

"Well, since we'll be at the holiday party when the announcement is made, I thought that would be the celebration."

"It will be a celebration, I'm sure. But it won't be yours. I will find a way to celebrate your promotion that's just for you."

"You're sweet."

"I'm so proud of you, Lora-Beth."

"Thank you."

"Your place or mine tonight?"

"Mine."

"Well if there's any hope of me being done and at your place by eight, I better get back to work. Love you."

"I love you too, Austin." *So much.*

CHAPTER THIRTY-THREE

The holiday party was held at The Rickhouse in Durham. It was a semi-formal event and Austin wore a well-fitted suit he'd purchased last week for the occasion. It had been quite a while since he'd gotten dressed up for such an occasion and wanted to make his woman proud. She wore a dress in her favorite color, deep wine red, the shade of certain leaves in the fall as she'd once described it to him, and looked fabulous in it. The dress, fitted at the top and cut in a way that displayed her fabulous shoulders and toned arms, was flowy at the bottom and broke away into splits at each thighs. If she walked just right, she gave him glimpses of the legs he adored; the thick, toned thighs that held him tight.

Heavy hors d'oeuvres and drinks were served at the cocktail-themed party and he snagged a glass of champagne and a puff of some sort from a passing server's tray. He stood, only partially involved in the conversation with Neal, Lora-Beth's coworker, and Eric, the husband of another. He watched from across the room as she talked with a few ladies.

"This town sure has changed. I remember coming to Durham when I was growing up and it was nothing like this fancy schmancy place. Are you from around here?" Eric directed a question at him, but he didn't catch most of it, since at that moment, Lora-Beth turned to face him and caught him looking at her. Of course he was looking. She was the most interesting thing in the room. Her confidence and self-assurance shined. Her presence was magnetic. She smiled and gave him a finger wave. He returned the gesture, feeling like a teenager in love.

Eric followed his gaze and offered a follow-up comment, one more likely to get a response. "I see why you're distracted. She's beautiful. Lora-Beth is a good person. I've known her for years."

Austin moved his gaze to Eric. "Oh yeah?"

"Yeah, man. She and Reema have worked together for about five years, so I've seen her around quite a bit at these things. Lora-Beth was at our wedding."

"How long have you been married?"

"October marked two years. Best decision I've ever made."

"I have fourteen years in, and marriage is no cakewalk, but I have to agree. Jennie is the best thing that ever happened to me. I know what I'm like, so sometimes, I just thank my lucky stars that she's able to put up with me," Neal added with a laugh.

Soft music played in the background as everyone milled about, socializing in groups, laughing, drinking, and nibbling. There was a consistent buzz in the room, the sound of people happy for a night out. It was obvious this group got along well. If he were to guess, he'd say there were likely a hundred people in attendance with the employees and their significant others. Austin found himself zoning out, thinking of days past. In his corporate days, he would have never attended a party like this one. He'd shied away from these types of events, finding them both stuffy and unnecessary. But he felt entirely different about being here with Lora-Beth, seeing her in this element, interacting with her coworkers, and getting glimpses of who she spent her days with. She shined even in this well-decorated room with everyone in dressy attire. Having been introduced as Austin, my significant other, instead of just Austin, caused him to puff out his chest just a little.

"Here they come. It must be speech time, then we party," Neal announced as the ladies headed their way.

Lora-Beth was stopped before she reached him and he took the opportunity to grab a glass of champagne for her. "You ready for this?" he asked, referring to the promotion announcement when she joined him and he handed her the glass.

"I'm ready, though I'm pretty sure the word is already out."

He nuzzled her and quietly asked, "Have I told you how great you look in that dress?"

She pretended to think about it for a beat. "I think you may have."

"Have I told you what it does to me when I see your thighs playing peekaboo with me when you walk?"

She blushed. "Now that, I don't think you've mentioned."

"Good evening, everyone, and thanks for giving us your Saturday night. I know it's quality date time for some of us old married folks, so I hope tonight measures up. We've had a good year at AlphaKey. I know you all appreciated it in your bonuses." He paused for the cheers his comment incited, then went on. "I want to personally thank you all for everything you do. Your hard work and dedication shows.

I'm not shy about saying, if it weren't for you, I can't imagine where I'd be. So a great deal of gratitude goes out from me and my family to you and yours. As we close out the year, we're headed for some changes. Everett McKinney has decided to retire at the end of this year. Everett has been with me since I started the company, and while some of it may be envy, it is with great sadness that I see him go."

Austin knew the man was beloved as the applause for him was loud and long, laced with catcalls. Lora-Beth smiled broadly as she applauded.

Michael went on, "I'm not going to drag this out, but Everett, sincerely, thank you. You leave big shoes to fill." Everett gave a sharp salute. "And that brings us to my next announcement. Sam Cain will be taking over Everett's position starting at the beginning of the year." Sam waved as the crowd applauded. "I'm not done yet... Two other people will be moving into new roles as well. Lora-Beth Haines and Neal Thomas have been promoted to Senior Principal Brand Strategists. More on this breakdown to come. Take a moment, congratulate them. They've worked hard and these promotions are well-earned. Now that we're done with the formal stuff, let's dance!"

Sam took the mic. "Let's eat, drink, and be merry, but let's be safe. Take a rideshare home and expense it if you need to."

Austin leaned in to whisper in Lora-Beth's ear. "Sounds like there's a story to tell there."

"I'm sure there is, but he issues that warning every year and has never shared."

Tablemates were already congratulating Lora-Beth and Neal and Austin knew the night would likely be filled with it. He'd known he was in for a night of observing, but he couldn't imagine being anywhere else. He could play the doting boyfriend and live to tell the tale. Besides, he'd been basking in Lora-Beth's greatness for months. He wasn't surprised others saw it as well.

The room filled with the sounds of Brooks and Dunn's "Boot Scootin' Boogie" and the dancefloor was suddenly filled with people. Neal and his wife looked at each other and laughed aloud as they clamored through the crowd for the perfect spot on the dancefloor.

"There they go. You won't see those two for a while," Lora-Beth informed him.

"I've never seen this dance before."

"Are you interested? This probably isn't the dress for it, but it wouldn't be the first time I've joined in on the boot scoot."

"I think I'll watch this time. Maybe on the next go 'round."

"But you will dance with me at some point, won't you?"

"I'd do just about anything with you."

"Except boot scoot?"

"If you really wanted to, I'd be swinging my feet and tipping my pretend hat."

"You're cute when you're being sweet."

"You're beautiful when you're being you."

"Lora-Beth, congratulations! Honey?" Lydia interrupted their flirting and recognized Austin from the work he sometimes did on her house. She gasped. "Oh my God! You two are so cute together. Lora-Beth, why didn't you tell me you were dating Honey for Hire?"

That sounded terrible, but Austin laughed. Lydia was not the first person to call him that and he was starting to think it was time to change the name of his business from The Honey-Do List Company.

"Lydia, I actually didn't remember that you knew *Austin*." She said his name with emphasis. "Austin, you know Lydia."

"Red Pine Road," Austin said.

Lydia took a seat next to Austin and looked over at the two of them "Good memory, Austin. Oh, I can't believe this. If you think about it, I'm responsible for bringing you two together."

Lora-Beth and Austin looked at each other, then Lydia, but didn't get a chance to respond before she went on. "Of course, that means I'd have to ultimately give the credit to my *was*band and Lord knows he's not the cause of anything good, so let's pretend I never said that. Lora-Beth, you look great. Whatever you're doing Austin…" she said pointedly. "Do more of it."

"Lora-Beth, can I borrow you for a second?" Sam interrupted. "It'll be brief. Two minutes." He held up two fingers.

Austin stood when Lora-Beth did. "Two minutes."

"Take your time, I'll be here."

"Go, I'll keep him company until you get back."

"And we'll be buffers," Reema assured as she and Eric approached.

"Can't an old woman have any fun?" Lydia teased.

Sam's two minutes had been up five minutes ago, and Lora-Beth stood idly by, counting the seconds as he, Simeon from IT, and Joan from Legal talked in her vicinity. Simeon had created an app and was looking to hire the team to test and get it out there. While they hadn't gotten the final word on whether they could take him on as a client, they seemed pretty excited about the prospect. She was happy for Simeon, and as long as it was assigned to her, she'd give him and the project her all, as she did with all her clients, but her contribution to the conversation was over. She thought it would be rude to just walk away so she waited, impatiently, for the conversation to draw to a natural close. Seriously? How much shoptalk were they going to have at a holiday party where the alcohol was free flowing?

"Alright guys, I think that's enough. Let's not get too excited, we don't have the final word just yet."

"Right, sure, of course." Simeon nodded emphatically.

"Come on, Lora-Beth, let's leave these two to it. They'll keep us here all night if we let them," Joan said, taking her by the arm and leading her away. "See you on the dancefloor."

Lora-Beth allowed herself to be whisked away. "Later, guys."

"You are positively glowing," Joan said.

"Thank you."

"What's the secret?"

She smiled at the woman. They'd never been particularly chummy, but their working relationship was warm and they shared the occasional work lunch. It wouldn't pass for friendship but they were friendly. "There's no secret, Joan. Life is good." Since Joan didn't ask any follow up questions, or offer any additional comments, Lora-Beth assumed her answer was satisfactory. "So, I'll see you on the dancefloor," she stated more than asked, as their paths to their respective tables took them in different directions.

"I'll keep an eye out for you," Joan replied with a laugh.

Instead of taking the open seat next to Austin when she reached the table, she reached her hand out to him and said, "Come on, you owe me a dance."

He took her hand in his and stood without a thought of protest.

"Have fun," Reema called after them.

Austin was eager to have her in his arms. He could be a social guy and was fine on his own while she mingled and networked, but he was here for her. She looked great in the dress and he was proud to have her on his arm. On the dance floor, he pulled her close and swayed to the music.

When he started to sing along to the Harry Connick, Jr. song, Lora-Beth closed her eyes at the smooth timbre of his voice.

"When I'm walkin'... I see you, And I'm wonderin' what it must be like to be you

You're a sunrise, you're heaven, You're the reason that God rested on day seven.

You're one fine, fine thing."

"I thought you said you couldn't sing."

"Shh. Listen. It's a great song."

"When I'm dreamin'... I love you. And I know that there is just one version of you.

Can I have you? I need you. If you tell me where you wanna go I'll lead you.

You're one fine, fine thing."

He finished the song with Harry, looking her in the eyes when he sang the words, *"So I'll loiter and linger, and I'll try to get a ring around your finger."* She smiled broadly, despite the tears stinging her eyes. She heard the words and felt his meaning behind them.

"You're right, it's a really, really good song."

"I've learned to listen to the words around me. That song, I hear it and all I see is you."

"I don't think I've ever heard this song before," she admitted.

"My mother was a fan. I still listen to his music when I'm really missing her. You think maybe she's conspiring with the universe to tell me something?"

"Probably." They laughed at the ridiculousness of their conversation.

"I'm going to kiss you now." And with that he lowered his lips and pressed them to hers in a lingering, chaste kiss.

They were able to enjoy one more slow song before the DJ changed it up and Meghan Trainor was telling them to "Dance like Yo Daddy".

"How about we sit this one out? Give my feet a break," Lora-Beth suggested.

Austin maneuvered them through the crowd with his hand at her back. "Is that your way of telling me I'm giving foot rubs tonight?"

"It wasn't, but if you're offering…"

"I'm good for it."

"Let's see if we can find the tray with the wild mushroom tartlets or the shrimp and avocado crostini."

"Hungry?"

"I feel like nibbling. I've had four glasses of champagne."

"You did say tonight would be about celebrating."

They didn't find the two items she'd mentioned but Lora-Beth and Austin grabbed Hawaiian beef skewers and brie in phyllo cups when servers floated by. She took a bite of the beef and moaned. "Taste this, honey, it's so good."

He wanted to taste her. His eyes fixated on her lips rather than the skewer suspended mid-air.

"I recognize that look. Down, boy."

Austin took a bite and chewed slowly, but didn't say anything one way or the other, he simply held her gaze and chewed, challenging her.

"You look happy," she said.

"I am. Are you?"

"If I were any happier I don't think I could stand it."

ص

"Do you want kids?"

They were lying in bed. Lora-Beth was nearly asleep and thought Austin was too until she felt his chest move with the words she'd just heard him speak.

"I always thought I'd have a family."

He kissed the top of her head. "I don't mean hypothetically. I'm asking if you could see having that with me."

Though the room was dark, she lifted her head to see his face in what little light there was. "Yes." There was no need for additional words. Her answer was yes. Absolutely. She knew he'd make a great father.

"Okay."

"Okay?"

"Yeah, okay."

"You needed that question answered before you could sleep?"

"No. But I've been meaning to ask, and since it popped into my head now, I asked now."

"Are you going to sleep now?"

"Why? Aren't you?"

"You asked a question of me, but haven't told me where you stand."

"I thought it was obvious. I want kids."

"With me?"

"With you. I want that."

"Okay."

Neither of them brought up that he'd already fathered a child. A child that had been lost in the accident that led to Janet's death as well. Lora-Beth would ask him about this one day, but not tonight. Tonight she would fall asleep in his arms, with the knowledge that he was planning a future with her and that warmed her through and through. They hadn't made love, both tired from a long evening of dancing and socializing, but she'd see to it that they changed that in the morning.

"I love you, Austin."

"And I love you, Lora-Beth. You have no idea how much."

She had an idea because she was similarly enamored with him. "I think I do."

"I intend to spend my life making sure you do."

Lora-Beth knew Austin was asleep when his hold on her loosened. She smiled into his chest, saying silent thanks before nestling in and drifting into her own comfortable sleep.

CHAPTER THIRTY-FOUR

He wasn't dreaming. Those were Lora-Beth's lips around him, her hands stroking him. He called out to her, letting her know he was awake, but he was helpless to do anything else. She took him deep and when she moaned, he felt the reverberations to his soul. He grasped her hair, halting her movements for a breath. She teased the tip, playing with the slickness of his precum. It sent shivers down his balls. He was close. Too close to have just woken up.

He rasped something that was supposed to be words. When she giggled, it sent a jolt to him and he flexed his fingers on her scalp. "Give me a second, sweetie. Damn. It's too good."

"Good morning, sleepyhead."

Austin pulled his shirt over his head and allowed her to slide his boxer briefs from his hips. He lifted her to him before he took her mouth, settling her firmly on top of him as he did. And then he was inside her, moving slowly, rolling his hips to caress spots he discovered along the way. He kissed her with the passion of a man starved, kissed her until his lungs burned and he could no longer keep up with it. He watched as Lora-Beth threw her head back, riding him, chasing her orgasm.

He rolled them so he was now on top of her and pressed to the hilt. "I want you just like this. At my mercy. Waiting for me to release you."

"Austin…" she whined, but he kissed it from her lips.

"Is that okay? Can you slow down and let me stay inside you for as long as I can stand? Do you think you have it in you? Can you wait?" he whispered into her skin as he stroked her. He pinched her nipple between his thumb and forefinger and she whimpered.

"I feel that, every time I'm inside you and I tweak your nipples, or bite them, you contract."

"Yes."

He took her lips again, moving just a smidge faster as he kissed her. "You want that now, don't you? You want to feel my teeth on you?"

"Yes, Austin, please."

"So you can't wait?" he teased.

"I just need you to take the edge off, then we can ride it out, slow and sweet."

He chuckled and placed kisses on her face. "Open your eyes."

She complied and held his gaze as he moved inside of her. Lora-Beth took her nipple between her fingers and pulled. She'd wanted a quickie to start her Sunday, but Austin had a different idea. She loved the way he held her eyes, made love to her body and her mind. Austin seemed to know what she liked and she'd discovered much about herself since being intimate with him. He removed her fingers.

"Austin, I'm close. Please, I'm so close."

"I know." Of course he knew. Austin knew her body, knew what she felt and sounded like when she was close. He could stay on the edge if he wanted, but he wouldn't tease her too much this morning. He increased his pace, rotating his hips just so to hit the spot deep within her that he'd learned caused her leg to shake. He stayed there, rubbing that tender spot and holding her eyes. He pinched her nipple at the same time he said, "Come."

Lora-Beth's body responded to the command like a well-trained soldier. Her legs trembled and she cried out with the force of her release. Her eyes closed involuntarily as she threw her head back and keened. Austin watched, felt her coming apart beneath him, and the strength of her orgasm sparked his own. He stroked hard and deep, burying his face in the crook of her neck and growling her name with his release. She held firm to him, wrapping her arms and legs around him, calling out his name over and over. She was coming again. Lora-Beth couldn't stand it. She mewed, in shock that she was having another orgasm so close on the heels of the monster from which she had yet to recover. Austin closed his lips around her nipple and sucked earnestly as he stroked her through her second release. When her body went lax and he collapsed on top of her.

He kissed her nose before rolling them to their sides facing each other. Her body shuddered with an aftershock and she buried her face in his chest and planted a kiss there. "Jesus, Austin."

"You are incredible."

"We need to get my truck," Austin said several hours later as they dressed. They'd found sleep again and it was now nearly noon.

"Where are we going again?"

"Tree shopping."

"I told you I have a tree."

"And I told you, we're getting a real tree."

"What do you have against artificial Christmas trees?"

"Nothing, but I prefer real trees. It's what we always had growing up and I want us to have that. Now, are you going to argue or are you going to go tree shopping and start a new tradition with your man?"

"What do you think?"

"I think maybe a bit of both."

"Okay, you got me there, but are you going to feed me first? I'm starved."

"I feel like grits this morning. There's this place near the house, so we'll stop there."

"Why didn't you tell me you wanted grits? I could have made us some."

"Lora-Beth, I wanted to do something nice for you, instead of you having to cook. Why are you stalling?"

"I'm not stalling." Austin was laying across the bed and Lora-Beth sat on the edge of it to pull on her boots.

"Then what would you call it?"

"Well, it's Sunday, it is already noon, I'm just trying to get a feel for our day."

"Okay?"

"It's Sunday," she repeated.

"I'm aware."

"Usually on Sundays you disappear for a few hours."

"I don't disappear. You know where I am." When he received no response, he commanded, "Look at me." Lora-Beth turned to face him and he assessed her face. He wasn't sure what he saw there so he asked, "What kind of conversation are we having right now?"

"A regular one."

"Okay. Is it a problem for you that I go out there?"

"No, that's not what I'm saying."

"Tell me what you're thinking. No filter, just say what's on your mind."

"It was just a question."

"It wasn't just a question." Austin used his finger to lift her chin so he could see her face. "Hey, give me your eyes." When she gave them to him, he told her, "I went yesterday afternoon while you were out running around. I had our day planned and made it work."

"I didn't know that."

"Level with me. What's happening right now?"

"I don't know. I'm not bothered, it's just something felt weird. I guess I'm just used to a certain rhythm and wasn't sure what to make of it being out of sync. I don't know."

He studied her for a moment, sensing her conflict, trying to find the understanding of what she was ineffectually communicating. He was coming up short. "Lora-Beth, you gotta help me out here. Am I screwing this up?"

"No, of course not. I didn't like the idea that I was keeping you from something I know means so much to you. I don't want you to think I'm asking you to forget about that part of your life."

"What about what you mean to me? How about we work on what we're building and let me figure out how to manage my time so nothing stands in the way of that? I could never forget what I lost. I'll live with it forever. But can you trust me to work out a balance? And I'll promise to let you know if I'm struggling with that."

"Okay. I'll stay out of it."

This wasn't going well at all. He took her hand and brought her over to sit on the couch. "That's not what I'm asking. You can talk to me about whatever you're feeling, but I don't want you to worry about it. You've never had a problem talking to me, there's no reason to start now." She gave him a faint smile. "Now, tell me, honestly, for now, would you rather I found a different day? Do you want to come with me? There is no wrong answer."

"No, no. None of that is necessary. I know that has nothing to do with me. I wouldn't want to intrude."

"First, you can be involved in everything I do. I don't want to keep any part of me separate from you. Second, I may not need to visit weekly forever, but I still need that now. Can you be okay with that?"

Lora-Beth nodded and gave him a sad smile.

"I know you visited her… "

Her eyes jerked to his in shock. "You knew? Why didn't you say anything?"

He shrugged. "I figured if you wanted to talk about it, you'd bring it up. I trusted you and supported whatever reason you had for going."

"I had never given it much thought, but I saw how sad it made you when you talked about her friends not visiting and the idea that she could hear what was happening around her. I guess I didn't want her to be lonely."

When her eyes grew misty, Austin threw his arm over her shoulder and squeezed. "You're too sweet, but no tears."

"Anyone in my position would have done the same."

"We both know that's not true. But it's who you are. Your heart is the size of Texas," Austin said.

"Maybe I did it for you."

"If that were the case, you wouldn't have kept it from me."

"I know how much you love her. I don't ever want you to feel like I'm trying to replace her in your heart."

He sighed. They really were doing this. "If I'm honest, it's something that I struggled with from the moment we met. I felt guilty about being drawn to you. It ate me up for a while. I was fighting myself against the chemistry between us, and at the same time, I couldn't stay away. I was drawn to you. I talked with my dad about it actually. He helped me realize that no matter how much I love you, or what our lives end up being, it will never erase the love I had for Janet and that time in my life, and that's okay. Meeting you made me face an issue I hadn't realized had been eating away at me, about how my dad moved on after my mama died. It's not easy and it's not something I take lightly, but I've realized that it is simple. I loved Janet. That love for her will always be inside me, but that doesn't mean I can't love you and devote all I have to making sure you know that."

He kissed the tears on her cheeks. "Come on, I said no tears."

"I can't help it."

"Did I tell you he planted roses at my mom's grave?"

"No, you didn't."

"Eighteen years, a second wife and two kids later, and he found a way to fit in doing something for her. Loving her hasn't gotten in the way of what he has now."

"Sounds like you and him are in a better place."

"Yeah. Once I got some stuff off my chest, and I realized I had the wrong idea of it, we've been able to talk. We're working on our relationship. The kids help. My brother and sister are now keeping tabs on me. I'm letting them." He smiled.

"Austin, that's great."

"Yeah, eventually I want us to go down for a visit. I promised I'd make an effort to be more present in their lives."

"I'd love it."

"But today I want to take you to breakfast and pick out a Christmas tree. Can we do that? Did you get what you needed or do we need to talk more about our feelings?" he teased.

She kissed his lips and lingered. "I got what I needed."

"What about this one?" Lora-Beth exclaimed. This was the third giant tree she'd pointed out.

Austin laughed at her enthusiasm. "I think we need to stick to a tree that is less than ten feet tall considering your living room has nine foot ceilings."

"Killjoy!"

"I practically had to drag you out here, now you want to take home the White House Christmas tree."

She bumped him with her hip. "Exaggerate much?" She hurried to another, smaller tree. "Okay, how about this one?"

He laughed and led her down a row of trees. "Come on. Let's see if we can find something between Charlie Brown's Christmas tree and one fit for Times Square."

"Should we get two? One for your house and one for mine?"

"If you think we need two, we'll get two."

"I have to warn you, none of my ornaments match."

"Well, I have no ornaments so there's that."

"Guess we'll have to make a Target run."

"How did I know you were going to say that?"

"You only think you know me. I'm actually quite the enigma."

"You're an enigma? With your feelings all over your face?" He laughed aloud. "Sweetie, you're an open book."

"Oooh, this one! This is the one!" she exclaimed, releasing his hand to embrace the tree she'd deemed to be the one. "Come, let's take a picture."

He joined her near the tree and smiled broadly for her phone. "Aww, you're so handsome. Tag this one."

"You don't tag it, you just take it."

"We can't carry it around with us, we still need to find another one. Wait here so no one claims it. I'll go ask the guy."

He laughed at her exuberance. "You're so cute. No one is going to take our tree. What about this guy here? He looks good."

She assessed it quickly, "Okay, but that one is going up at your place."

CHAPTER THIRTY-FIVE

Lora-Beth was inside working on Sunday dinner and Austin asked Chris to come over and help him put up lights. In addition to trimmings for the tree and lights for the exterior of the house, she'd insisted on two lighted reindeer for the front yard, but he'd drawn the line at the inflatable Santa they'd come across, even though it had been adorable the way her eyes lit up at the sight of it. He wondered if they'd be the house in the neighborhood with yard decorations for every holiday. Just thinking of it made him wish her house had a garage. With the addition of all these items, and the ones he envisioned would appear in the future, they'd need the extra storage space. When they came down, he'd store them at his place for now, he decided.

"Thanks for helping me. I thought this would be quick and easy. I should have known she'd want a Winter Wonderland."

"Judging by the smile you've been sporting lately, I'd say you wouldn't have it any other way."

"Guess I'm transparent."

"Lately. There was a time when no one knew what the hell you were thinking, you were so closed off. We should all be so lucky. Shit, does she have any sisters?"

"She does, but she's not available. And she doesn't live here."

"What about friends?"

"She has those too, but I can't speak on that."

"Hopefully I can snag an invite for whatever she's cooking. It sure smells good."

Austin laughed at his friend. "That's the only reason your greedy ass agreed to help."

Lora-Beth was talking with her sister as she mixed diced potatoes, boiled eggs, chopped celery and onion, sweet pickle relish, mustard, and good ol' Duke's mayonnaise in a bowl. She sprinkled in her chosen seasonings, a pinch of sugar, and a dash of vinegar, and mixed some more.

"Tricey, are you sure you can't come home for Christmas?" She spoke loud enough so her voice could be heard over the phone clipped to the top of her apron.

"I'm sure. We were just there less than a month ago, and we're spending Christmas with Damon's family this year. You know that's how it goes. One for one."

"Couldn't you make an exception this time? Austin and I are going to be in Asheville for three days and it would be so good if you were there. The four of us had such a good time together."

"LB, I can't. Why don't you plan to bring him out here after the new year?"

Lora-Beth placed her hand at her hip. "You know he works for himself. He can't just take off whenever he wants."

"Oh, I forgot."

"I wish you would reconsider moving back this way. I miss you so much."

"I miss you guys too, but you know it's not as easy as you make it out to be."

"Fine. I guess I'll get used to seeing you once a year and when we have children, they won't know each other. It's cool."

"Don't do this to me, sissy. I get enough of it from Mom."

"Don't do what? Speak the truth?" Lora-Beth covered the bowl, placed it in the fridge, and pulled out the carton of whipping cream and set it on the counter. She opened the oven door to check the progress of the bone-in ham. Satisfied with the look of it, she lifted the lid on the pot of greens and stirred. "I'm sorry that your family wanting you close is a bad thing."

"You're going to make me cry. Are you trying to make me cry?"

"The thought of our children not knowing each other makes me want to cry." She poured the cream into a bowl, whipping it with a metal whisk.

"We don't have children!" Tricey exclaimed.

"But we will one day."

"Then we have time to decide on this."

"We always think we have time," Lora-Beth said ominously.

"What does that mean?"

"Nothing. I just wish you didn't live so far away. I'm being selfish. I want you here, close to me. I want us to be a part of each other's lives."

"We are a part of each other's lives. You're my sister, so we'll always be a part of each other's lives. Distance doesn't change that."

"It changes it," she said quietly. "But I understand. Your life is there. My life is here."

"Is there something going on that you're not mentioning?" her sister questioned. She was caught off guard by Lora-Beth's insistence. They often spoke on living closer, but never had she pressed the way she was today.

"No. Can't I want my family close? Growing up we always talked about how it would be when we were older, our kids growing up together, our husbands being friends, and I still want that."

"Are you pregnant?"

"Of course I'm not pregnant. You know I would've led with that."

"Are you getting married?"

"I think you and I both would say we've found *The One*, are you going to argue that?" Her sister was silent, so Lora-Beth went on. "So, it's not as much of a reach as you're making it out to be. No, I'm not getting married, but we both are settling down, right? I just want us to do that as together as possible."

Austin stood in the foyer listening. He hadn't meant to eavesdrop but he'd entered the house to flip the switch to power the external lights and froze in place when her sister asked Lora-Beth if she was pregnant. If she were, he wouldn't have wanted to find out this way. He decided he'd let himself be seen and not pretend he hadn't inadvertently overheard her conversation. He walked to the entry of the kitchen and cleared his throat.

Lora-Beth faced him and smiled. "All done?"

"What?" Tricey asked.

"Not you, sissy. I'm talking to Austin. Say hello."

"Hey, bro," she called out.

"Hey, Tricey."

"Call me back when you're done, LB," Tricey said.

"K. Love you."

"I love you too, Mom Jr."

Lora-Beth clicked off and Austin was suddenly in her space, pulling her flush to his body. He kissed her softly, then nuzzled her neck. "How much of that did you hear?" she asked.

"Some. Why are you giving your sister a guilt trip?"

"I'm not."

"Making her feel bad about not knowing our non-existent children? Are you sure?"

She laughed. "They won't always be non-existent. You practically asked me to have your children last night."

"Is that what I did?"

"Yes, it is. And I agreed."

He lifted her onto the counter and stepped between her legs. "So does that explain this morning's freak out? I scared you?"

"What? What freak out? There was no freak out this morning, Austin."

"There wasn't?" he questioned playfully, raising his eyebrow as he peered into her face.

"What we had this morning was a discussion."

"Got it. So then the guilt trip on your sister isn't part two of that freak out?" She nodded. "And there will be no call to Toni *not*-freaking out either?"

"Look at me. Take a good look. Do you see it?" She used her index finger to point to her face in a counterclockwise motion for emphasis. "There is no freak out happening here. Stop saying that. I'm fine."

"So then, I shouldn't tell Chris he can't stay for dinner because my woman is in the middle of a meltdown?"

She swatted his shoulder. "You're not funny. Of course Chris can stay for dinner. The more the merrier. I was going to call Toni to see if they wanted to come over as well."

"Not to freak out though?" he teased.

"I was not going to call Toni to freak out because I am not freaking out!"

He kissed the tip of her nose. "Okay, I'll drop it, but you're cute when you're flustered."

"I'm not flustered."

"Call your sister back. You owe her an apology for not freaking out on her."

"I'll call her later."

"Sweetie, call her. She didn't deserve that guilt trip."

She scrunched her nose. "Fine."

"You're good to stay for dinner," Austin told Chris when he returned outside. "I forgot to ask what else was cooking but I know you eat pork so you won't mind that there's ham in the oven."

"She's cooking some kind of greens to go with that ham, I know that for sure. My mouth is already watering."

"She's a fantastic cook, so your mouth will thank you."

"Lucky bastard."

ص

Toni looked up from the puzzle she and MJ were working on when the doorbell chimed. "I wonder who that is," she said to herself, then asked the toddler, "Are you expecting anybody?" He paid no attention to his mother as he worked to make the wrong piece fit. "Keep trying, I'll be right back. Let me see who's at the door."

She reached the door and looked out to see who was on the other side, then flung the door open. "Brian, were we expecting you? Marcus is at the gym."

"I just spoke with him. He's on his way. We were going to watch a little basketball. I hope it's okay that I'm a tad early."

"It's fine. Come on in. MJ and I are doing a puzzle." She turned to walk back into the living room, but he touched her elbow.

"Toni, there's something I wanted to say to you." She looked at him, but didn't respond. "I'm sorry."

"Why are you apologizing to me?"

"Because it's clear that what happened with me and Lora-Beth changed your opinion of me."

"I won't argue that point."

"I never meant to hurt her or you. I know it did and I'm sorry for that. It was the wrong decision, but how is it that she and I are able to be on better terms than you and me?"

"You're not on good terms with LB. She's tolerating you, because she's too nice for her own good."

"We are. We're friends. At least we're trying to be. If I have my way, eventually we'll find our way back to each other."

"That. That right there is why." She walked away then and plopped on the couch, immediately picking up a piece of the puzzle and snapping it in place.

Brian sighed and smoothed his hand down his face before following her route. He ruffled the hair on MJ's head and greeted the boy warmly. "Hey, MJ."

"Hey." MJ replied absently.

He took a seat in the chair opposite Toni and sighed once again. "I love her."

"She's moved on."

"I miss her."

"Of course you do. And you have terrible timing. She missed you too. She waited for two years. And then she moved on."

"I have terrible timing and shitty decision making skills."

"Do you not see my son sitting here?"

"Sorry. I made a bad decision, but I didn't cheat on her, I didn't disrespect her or string her along. I took a job to further my career. I wanted her to come with me. I accepted her decision when she didn't. I'm not the bad guy you're making me out to be."

"Men really are dense. You didn't choose her. You let her know she was an option. She made the right decision letting you go without her."

"So you're telling me, if it were Marcus, you would've let him go without you?"

"I'm telling you Marcus wouldn't make the decision to go without me."

He nodded slowly. "And it means nothing to you that I'm back now, fighting for her, because I realize leaving was the worst decision I've ever made."

Toni studied him for a moment before answering, "No. It doesn't. I'm not saying this to hurt you, but she's happy. There's a light shining in her that I hadn't seen in years. He gives her that. I would never discredit what you had with her, but what they have is different. The kind of happiness she has right now, she deserves it. If you really loved her, you'd let her have it. You wouldn't interfere with that."

"I can't do that."

"Then you don't really love her and this is about your ego."

The sound of the opening garage could be heard in the room and Toni breathed a sigh of relief that Marcus was home. When the sound of her cell phone pierced the silence, she scoffed at the irony of Lora-Beth's call coming through now. She lifted the phone to her ear. "Hey, LB." She eyed Brian warily as she got up to leave the room, not wanting her conversation to be overheard. She greeted Marcus at the back door and pointed to the living room where she'd left Brian and MJ.

"Hey, girl. Ham is in the oven and greens are on the stove. Are you up for it?"

Toni groaned. "Greens, you say? Umm, yes, I'm up for it, but it might just be me and MJ."

"Why, where's Marcus?"

"He's here, but he has company."

"Bring 'em. The more the merrier." She repeated her earlier sentiment.

"It's Brian." There was a silence on the line, and if Toni knew Lora-Beth, she was considering extending the invitation to him as well. "No."

"What do you mean no?"

"No, LB. You're not inviting Brian over for Sunday dinner."

"It's fine. I'll see if Austin minds."

"He does. I do. You should too."

"We're trying to see if we can be friends. What's the harm?"

"About that. Since when did you and Brian decide you were going to try to be friends anyway? Friends or not, SpongeBob Square Idiot is no longer welcome to Sunday dinner at your house."

She laughed at her friend's sense of humor. "Really, Toni? Hold on, let me see what Austin thinks," she replied with a chuckle.

"Lora-Beth, do not ask that man what you think you want to ask him. There is no room for him at the Krusty Krab."

"Just hold on a second. He's still outside putting up lights and seriously, you need to watch something other than cartoons."

"Sometimes I wonder what is wrong with you. Really, I do," Toni mused. Then she had an idea. "How about I agree to bring them some leftovers?"

"Let's call that Plan B," she said into the phone, then called out, "Austin, can you come here for a second?" He looked at her from his position on the ladder at the corner of the house. She couldn't see Chris and assumed he'd already rounded the corner. "I would come to you, but I'm not wearing any shoes."

"What's up?" he asked when he was within two steps of her.

"I just invited Toni and Marcus over for dinner, but Brian is over there. Do you mind if he comes along?"

"Brian?"

"Yes."

"Are you good with that?" He searched her face.

"I think it'll be fine, unless you're—"

He shrugged and placed a kiss on her forehead. "If you're good with it, then I'm good with it."

"Are you sure? It won't be awkward?"

"Remember when I told you I'm not worried about that dude?" She nodded. "I'm still not worried about that dude. If he wants to come over here and see what he missed out on, that's on him. He'll be the odd man out, not me."

"Big dick energy. I knew I liked him, Love this for you!" Toni cheered into her ear.

"I can hear you," Austin said, amused. "Is that all?"

"That's all."

"Did you mention your freakou—"

Lora-Beth cut him off. "Off you go."

He laughed. "Kiss me before you send me back on the ladder in high winds and forty degree weather."

She pressed her lips to his before saying, "Toni is having an adverse effect on you."

On the other end of the line, Toni beamed at the interaction between Lora-Beth and Austin, happy for her friend.

"You heard him. He's good with it. So if Brian wants to torture himself, he can come too."

"I'll pass along the message." She said the words, and she would, but she'd take care to make the invitation sounds as unappealing as a trip to a gastroenterologist. She understood being evolved, moving on, and all that other crap, but she saw no reason to invite trouble into your life. She considered it her duty as Lora-Beth's best friend to protect her, even from her own good intentions.

The woman was incorrigible, Marcus thought as he took the exit toward Lora-Beth's and looked at her from the driver's seat. "Are you going to pout because you didn't get your way? What is that teaching our son?"

"MJ can't see me. And I'm not pouting anyway. I'm sulking." MJ sang along to the movie playing on the screen in front of him, not noticing the quiet conversation his parents were engaged in.

"Right. Because, there's a difference."

"You knew I was trying to get you guys not to come. What exactly do you call what you were doing back there?"

"I'm trying to go eat. Come on, baby, you know that's none of our business. They're both our friends. We shouldn't take sides."

She looked at him with a grimace. "Seriously, Marcus?"

"Seriously, Toni."

"And how is that taking sides anyway? I want my girl to be happy and it just so happens he's no longer a part of what makes her happy. I'm obviously still his friend." She rolled her eyes.

"I love you, and you know I'm on your side, but you may be a little blinded to your own preferences in this situation."

Toni folded her arms over her chest and leaned her back to the window and faced him. "And you're not?"

"I'm staying out of it, where I belong, because *I* haven't lost perspective."

"Whatever. Just don't encourage him," she huffed.

"Yes, dear."

"Titi car!" MJ called from the back seat when they pulled into Lora-Beth's driveway.

"Yes, let's go see Titi."

"Can I help with anything?" Austin asked, coming up beside Lora-Beth as she sat at the table, staring down at her phone.

"You can show Chris to the bathroom and you both can wash your hands."

"Chris knows where the bathroom is."

"He does and he's heading there now," Chris chimed in.

"Did you make me anything sweet?" Austin asked her softly.

"Am I not sweet enough for you?"

He hummed low in his throat. "You know you are."

She giggled. "Behave. We're having store-bought cream cheese pound cake with strawberries and fresh whipped cream."

"Sounds amazing. So when our guests leave, and I hope they don't linger, we'll trim the tree and I'll tell you why this particular part of the Christmas season is important to me."

"I look forward to hearing it and sharing it with you."

He moved to go wash his hands. "Oh, I was supposed to ask, this sad sap wants to know if you have any single friends," he said as he passed Chris in the doorway.

"I may have a couple. Maybe we'll host the next game night and you can meet some of my friends."

"I say the sooner the better."

There was a knock at the door, then Toni's voice filled the room. "Titi! We're here."

"Finally," Chris muttered.

Though Lora-Beth hadn't lived in this house when she'd been his, Brian didn't need directions to her place. Just a couple weeks ago, he'd picked up Thai food and came out hoping to surprise her with an impromptu dinner of her favorites. But when he'd slowed to turn into her driveway, he saw that she and a man were heading out. He now knew that man was Austin. He'd continued down the street as if he were just passing by. He didn't mention this to Marcus when he'd insisted, "Just follow me."

He pulled onto Lora-Beth's street and slowed to a crawl. He wasn't trying to win her over, he just needed to be present. That was all. He had no ulterior motive. She'd extended an invitation to Sunday dinner, as a friend, and he'd accepted, as a friendly gesture. Period. *Then why am I nervous?* There were already three cars in the driveway and Marcus had pulled in behind Lora-Beth's. Brian pulled his car to stop at the curb and moved the gear shift into park, already feeling like a fifth wheel.

"Here we go," he said to no one before opening the door and stepping out.

Toni, Marcus, and MJ were already walking through the door so he picked up the pace to close the gap between them as Lora-Beth's excited voice exclaimed, "Hey, MJ!"

Austin appeared in the kitchen and greeted Toni first, folding her into a brief embrace before shaking the hands of both Marcus and Brian. Hellos and what's ups were exchanged as Lora-Beth stood to the side, slicing the ham.

"I'll help Lora-Beth dish up everything; you guys can have a seat at the table," Toni said decidedly. Lora-Beth had already set out serving bowls and Toni started with the greens.

"I'm on drink duty, so what'll everyone have?" Austin asked.

"You know I want some of that sweet tea, brother," Chris said.

"Same," Marcus answered.

"Whatever you got is fine," Brian said.

"Toni, what'll you have?" Austin asked.

"Tea for me too, and my baby has his cup so he doesn't need anything."

"Your house is beautiful. Lora-Beth, what I've seen of it anyway," Brian complimented.

"Thanks, Brian. I can credit Austin for some of what you see here."

"Don't be modest. I had little to do with what you see here. She tells me what she wants and I do my best to give it to her."

"Smart man," Marcus called from the table.

Brian eyed them closely. Things between them seemed comfortable. It was clear to him that Austin was at home in her house, in her kitchen no less.

The table was set family-style and everyone served themselves from the bowls of food, just the way Lora-Beth liked it. The round table had only six chairs, so they'd pulled another chair over for Brian. The table in the dining room was larger, more formal, but this was just a regular Sunday dinner between friends. There was no need to use that space for this occasion.

Conversation flowed smoothly, after only a few moments of silence. She thought it helped that Chris didn't seem to know who Brian was and the man had unknowingly done his part to smooth over any awkwardness. Austin sat to her right and Toni to her left. The ladies shared personal conversation as the men's conversation turned to sports. Austin showed no signs of being uncomfortable with Brian's presence at the meal and she felt good in her decision.

Austin leaned her way and said in a quiet tone, "Dinner was fantastic as usual, thank you." He placed a soft kiss on her cheek.

"I second that. I don't know when I last had a true soul food Sunday dinner. Girl, those greens, mmm. Thank you for having me," Chris chimed in.

"You're welcome anytime."

Austin ribbed his friend. "You are not welcome anytime. Don't tell him that. You don't know what you're asking for with this guy."

"Ignore him. There's usually enough to share." Lora-Beth directed her comment to Chris.

"Um, you must be planning to start cooking larger portions. I'm with Austin, I didn't cosign this," Toni chimed in. "We're already sharing with Austin, now you gotta share with Chris too?"

"Baby, you know we don't live here, right?" Marcus asked.

"Titi, want more meat," MJ said.

"Please," Toni and Marcus said in unison, correcting their son's manners. MJ looked to his parents in turn as if to ask, *please what?*

"Of course you can, sweetheart."

Then Toni went on, "See, my baby already didn't have enough. Sorry, but Brian and Chris, y'all might need to find somewhere to eat Sunday dinners," Toni joked.

"Toni, why are you this way?" Lora-Beth asked.

"You know I'm just teasing."

"How did I get dragged into this? I'm just sitting here, watching it all go down, and still I'm disinvited to a future meal I haven't yet been invited to," Brian protested.

"I don't have to be present, but I'm thinking Austin can start bringing enough leftovers to share," Chris tried.

"How about we let Lora-Beth decide who has dinner at Lora-Beth's house?"

"Other than Austin, she means. This conversation is about you all," Austin clarified, throwing his arm around her chair, gesturing to the table at large with the other hand. "My seat at the table is secure, right?"

Lora-Beth leaned closer to his side. "Yes, you're safe and MJ is safe."

"Well, since MJ can't drive, obviously that means I'm safe, so it looks like we're right back where we started," Toni stated matter of factly.

Marcus tapped her shoulder. "You remember you have a husband, don't you?"

"Oh, baby, relax. Where I go, you go, you know that. LB knows we're a package deal. With every Toni, you get a side of Marcus and little MJ for dessert."

"On that note, who's up for something sweet?" Lora-Beth asked.

Brian spent most of the evening observing. Memories, vivid and agonizing, of countless mornings spent around tables, sharing meals with Lora-Beth played through his mind. The sweet nothings he took for granted. He could admit to staring at her longingly. And sure, he'd noticed Austin noticing him looking at Lora-Beth a couple of times, but it wasn't as if he could avoid looking at her. Her presence commanded attention. And why had Austin been looking at him every time he looked up anyway? And what was with this guy constantly having his hands on her, or his lips, or whispering something in her ear? Sharing inside jokes with the rest of them sitting right there at the table. Didn't he know that was rude? A bitter taste suddenly flooded his mouth. He reached for his glass and took a long sip hoping to counteract the sour taste settling in his stomach.

She looked happy. Bittersweet torture when her eyes met his and he saw no longing there. Nothing for him. He broke contact when Austin threw his arm around her chair. A lump formed in his throat. The weight of regret sat heavy in his gut as he sat as an outsider in a life that should've been his. Dread gripped him. He'd lost her and had no one to blame but himself.

"Okay, you cooked, so I think I can handle the dishes." Austin said.

"I can help with that," Marcus offered.

"That's sweet of you two, but no thanks. I'll handle it."

"And I'll help. I know how she likes to put away leftovers," Toni added.

"Marcus, weren't you and Brian planning to watch basketball or football or something?" Lora-Beth added.

"Come on, men. I'll turn on the game in the living room. I know what it sounds like to be dismissed," Austin said ruefully.

"No one is dismissing you."

"But you are saying we'll be in the way," Austin supplied.

She held her forefinger and thumb in the air and drew them together. "Maybe a little." She laughed.

He kissed the tip of her nose. "Okay," he said, then asked the men, "Anyone want a beer?"

"Yep," Chris said.

"Me too," MJ added. The men erupted in laughter.

"LB, did you hear my baby? Girl, he wants a beer."

Brian met Lora-Beth's eyes as he walked toward the sink with his plate. "Dinner was delicious. Thank you for the invite. But I think I'm gonna head out. I don't want to overstay my welcome."

"Don't be silly. No need to rush."

"Your home is nice. Very you." He leaned down and kissed her cheek. "But seriously, I'm gonna run."

Several pairs of eyes floated between them. "Austin, Chris, good to meet you. Marcus, let me holla at you on my way out."

ص

Austin was excited to share this with her. Janet's family didn't celebrate Christmas so he hadn't celebrated in years. He hooked his phone up to Lora-Beth's speakers and set it to Christmas music. They pulled out her Christmas decorations and the bags of stuff they'd purchased earlier and were set to trim and decorate the tree.

"Okay, I'm ready."

He held up the gardening shears. "First, we trim and shape the tree."

"I meant I was ready for the story," Lora-Beth said.

Austin met her eyes with an amused smile, "This is how I'm telling the story."

"Oh, sorry. Continue."

"We'd go out as a family to pick the tree, usually the Saturday after Thanksgiving. My dad would always let Mama and me decide on the tree, or at least he let us think that. We'd have hot apple cider and sing Christmas carols in the truck."

"Are you going to sing today?"

He grinned. "Probably. Mama and I would sit back and direct, telling my dad what pieces needed to be trimmed, anything that was dead, or messed with the symmetry." He trimmed a few pieces.

"Like this?" Lora-Beth pointed to a wayward piece.

He snipped it. "Yeah, like that," he said before continuing his retelling of Christmas at the Watts'. "We'd sing along to whatever Christmas song was on the radio, and get the tree just so, before we started adding ornaments she'd collected over the years." He stood back and looked at the tree, then asked, "What do you think? Pretty good?"

She stepped to the opposite side of the room and assessed, "Looks good to me."

Austin picked up the few pieces he'd trimmed and placed them in the box he set aside for that purpose. He took Lora-Beth by the hand and brought her to sit on the couch with him. He could hear Bing Crosby in the background singing pa-rum pum pum pum. He used to enjoy singing and acting that one out with his mom. They'd use their fingers as drumsticks and tap out the beat on the coffee table or mantle. "After Dad hung the lights, we'd start with the ornaments and Mama had her favorites, they went on first. She'd tell me where and I'd put them on, and my dad would if I couldn't reach. Then we'd take turns filling in the gaps with the other pieces. And we'd sing and laugh. Occasionally she'd recall the memory of when she'd gotten a particular piece, what year, if my Dad had given it to her, or if I'd made it, it was a whole thing for her, and for me. She loved Christmastime."

"It all sounds so sweet."

"When the tree was done, we'd sit in front of the fireplace and have hot chocolate, and they'd ask what I wanted to see under the tree most and if I thought I'd made Santa's nice list. My parents didn't give many gifts; Mama had a rule about not spoiling me. I was given a want, a need, something to read, and something from Santa. But what was most special to me was Christmas Eve. We each got one Christmas Eve gift that was a free-for-all. We would spend the day with family, everyone gathered at my Aunt Ida's house for Christmas Eve dinner. Her house was like yours, always full of people, food, laughter, and love." He smiled fondly at the memory.

"When we got home, the three of us would exchange our Christmas Eve gifts with each other and it was always so exciting because each parent took me separately to shop for the other's gift. I was more excited to see their reactions to the gifts I'd chosen for them than I was for my own, because I tried my best to pay attention and select a gift that, to my mind, was perfect."

"That sounds really precious."

"After she died, my dad and I didn't continue those Christmas traditions that had been so special to me. I resented him for it and I've only now realized why. He avoided it because it hurt him to continue them without her. I haven't been excited about Christmastime in a very long time, but this year I am. I'm excited to share this with you, to bring back moments like this from my childhood that I'd buried."

"I'm happy you want to share this with me. It means so much."

"I only had one Christmas with Janet before the accident and her family focused more on religion, not so much the commercialization of the holiday, so it wasn't a part of our life."

He took a moment to gather his thoughts. "What we had was good. I was happy. But it's not the same as what I have with you.

"I don't mean to steamroll you. If I'm overwhelming you, tell me, but I'm finding it difficult to tamp down my excitement about life with you. I find myself looking forward to every day, every event, thinking of how we're going to spend it. I look at you and I see five, fifteen, twenty years from now."

"Austin," she whimpered as tears tumbled from her eyelids.

He wiped her face with the pads of his thumbs. "I know my words overwhelm you. You're still getting used to them." She shook her head emphatically and he went on, "But I need to say them. I don't know why, but I need to get them out. I think I'll credit you for that." He smiled at her and gave her a gentle kiss. "You mean more to me than I thought was possible a year ago. I couldn't see a life beyond what I was existing through and I was resigned to live my life that way. And then I walked in here on an ordinary day and my whole world changed."

She made no effort to stop the tears now, she just let them fall freely.

"I'm not in a hurry, but I want you to know where I am."

He patted his chest, over his heart. "It hits me here, that I can make you speechless. Can I expect tears every time I open up?" She buried her head in the crook of his neck and held on tightly.

Lora-Beth giggled. "I love you so much."

He pulled her into his lap and took her mouth. "I know you do. I love you too."

When she dropped her head onto his shoulder and sighed, he held her to him and ran his hand down her back. "Can we decorate the tree now or do you need another minute?"

"I need another minute."

"You got it."

CHAPTER THIRTY-SIX

It was race day and Lora-Beth was excited to participate in this year's Chapel Hill Christmas City Classic. Though it was her first time participating, the city she called home had been hosting the race for fifteen years. She'd cheered Toni on from the sidelines last year and felt a twinge of envy at the sea of runners, excited and decked out in holiday-themed costumes.

She wasn't nervous, running six miles was no longer a big deal. Still, she was up way earlier than she needed to be. Maybe she'd missed Austin's presence in bed beside her and that roused her from sleep. Austin had gotten up early and went to pick up a carb heavy breakfast from her favorite bagel shop, The Bagel Bar. Maybe she was just excited.

"Eat."

She took another bite of her fresh egg bagel, with thinly sliced avocado and provolone on top, and chewed. "Thanks again for this, it's perfect."

"Are you anxious about the race? You shouldn't be. You did seven miles two days ago, easy."

"Not anxious, but I'm excited. Maybe a race day jitter or two," she admitted. "I've never run an official race."

"No wonder you're so dressed up," he mused.

She'd laid out her running attire the night before, complete with red and white striped tights and a red, green, and white running tutu, because apparently running tutus were a thing. She'd ordered the matching outfits for herself and Toni from Etsy and couldn't have been more pleased when they'd arrived.

"Are you really wearing that?"

"What? Don't I look cute? Call me LB the Elf."

"You look… cute. Even if, a tad deranged."

"You love it!"

Her phone rang, interrupting their banter. It was Toni. She'd known the call was coming. They were an hour and a half out from run time.

"Good morning, Elf Toni!" she answered cheerily.

"Good morning, LB the Elf."

"I just told Austin to call me that. Didn't I?"

"You did."

"Are we carpooling? You know parking is going to be crazy. We can swing by and pick you two up."

"Do you want to take one car?" she asked Austin, who gave her a thumbs up by way of response.

"Yes to carpooling.."

"Okay, we'll be there in about forty-five minutes. We're just finishing breakfast. I still need to get MJ dressed, then we can head that way. What time are you guys getting on the road for Asheville?"

"Not until four or five. We have a little quality time planned before we get on the road."

"Quality time, huh?"

"Toni."

"Okay, okay. See you in a bit."

"We'll be ready."

"Did you sit your camera out like we talked about? I want to get some good pictures for you."

"Yep, it's on the table in the foyer."

"Good. How are you feeling? Are you ready for this? It's not too bad out. Low forties but will warm up a bit."

"I'm ready."

The official start time for the half marathon and 10K was nine-fifteen a.m. The 5K started at nine thirty-five a.m. There were over fifteen hundred runners in total. Her hands were cold at the start and she wished she'd thought to wear gloves, but luckily, they weren't standing very long before the gun went off. The first mile of the run was filled with supporters and volunteers, all dressed for the occasion as well, wearing Santa or elf hats and ugly Christmas sweaters. To Lora-Beth's eyes, it was wonderful, festive, and exciting. For a moment, she wished Austin had decided to join them.

She was surprised to see Santa, Mrs. Claus, and several elves at the water station about midway through the race. She and Toni didn't chat much during the run, but occasionally, they shared a laugh, complaint, or anecdote.

With one mile to go, Toni asked, "What do you have left in the tank? Ready to kick it up a notch and finish strong?"

"I have it in me. Let's go."

"Way to go, Lora-Beth! Woo hoo!"

"Yeah, Toni!"

"Yay, Mommy!" She heard from the sidelines as they neared the finish. She looked over and saw Austin had the camera up, capturing the moment.

She did it! Bib number ten forty-three crossed the finish line at fifty-eight minutes and twenty-one seconds. She'd made her goal of running a sub one hour 10K. Lora-Beth and Toni embraced in triumph before jogging over to their men.

Austin cheered as Lora-Beth approached and crossed the finish line. She looked so happy, he couldn't help but match her smile.

"Good job, sweetie! You did it, fifty-eight minutes!" He lifted her from her feet and spun her around. He planted kisses on her sweaty face. "I'm so proud of you."

"I did it! Thank you!"

"It was all you. I'm happy to be here to see it."

There were plenty of Christmas goodies and fresh fruit to nosh on at the end of the race, but Lora-Beth didn't want any part of it. She was loving the feel of the crowd, the excitement of the runners as well as the supporters.

"You would have loved it! You have to do it with us next year."

He laughed with her. "Okay."

"Marcus, can you take our picture? Honey, give the camera to Marcus."

"You guys should have worn ugly Christmas sweaters," Toni said.

"That's where I draw the line," Marcus added. "You can pull off this insane look, even make it look cute, but I'm not about to be walking around looking crazy."

Lora-Beth looked at Austin but he wasn't going for it either. "Don't get any ideas."

Photos were snapped and a kind passerby offered to take a few of the five of them. They didn't place high enough to qualify for any medals, but Lora-Beth didn't need a medal to solidify this race for her. She loved everything about it and wondered why she'd never joined one before now.

As they walked to the car, Lora-Beth flipped through the shots and tilted the screen to Austin proclaiming, "This one and this one, I'm going to have framed." It was one of her and Toni crossing the finish line and one of the five of them. "Thank you for taking these."

For his part, Austin simply loved seeing her happy. Now that he had it, he didn't want to think about not being a part of everything she shared with him.

"Why aren't you more excited?" She directed her question to Toni.

"I'm excited, but it's not my first race."

"Trust me, she was plenty excited the first few times. Don't let this calm she's projecting fool you, LB," Marcus said.

"I think right now I'm happier to see how excited you are and honestly, I love you two together. So if I'm quiet, it's because I'm observing. You're always happy, but I've never seen you this way. Austin, I'm glad we found you."

"Well, Toni, I'm glad to have been found."

ص

"So, are you ready for your one Christmas Eve gift?" Austin asked when she entered the bedroom naked and freshly showered. He was laying across the bed, watching her.

"You're doing a good job tamping down your excitement."

"Am I?"

Her eyes shined with amusement. "Not at all. It's cute how excited you are."

"Not sure how I feel about being called cute." He smiled. The man was all smiles lately. He often thought how much of an effect her smiling face and happy disposition had on him.

"I said *it's* cute, not you're cute, but you are a very handsome man."

He sat up on the edge of the bed and called her over. "Come here. Let me help you with your back."

She handed him the jar of mango citrus body butter. He loved the smell of this on her skin. He scooped some of the cream onto his fingers and rubbed his hands together. Lora-Beth moved her wet hair over her shoulder to rest in front. Austin pressed a kiss to one shoulder then the other. "You have such beautiful skin." He placed his hands on her back and smoothed in large circles, kneading her muscles with slight pressure.

"Thank you."

"How do you feel?"

"Happy."

"Can you elaborate?"

"I'm trying to calm my still strumming excitement from the race. I'm excited to see the gift you got me and looking forward to spending Christmas with you and my family."

Austin dipped his finger in the butter once more and smoothed it down her arms and sides. "I'm looking forward to those things too."

"Are you excited to see what I got you?"

"I am because I know I'm going to love it."

"No pressure," she teased.

He smoothed his large hands over her stomach and up between the valley of her breasts. She moaned and leaned her head on his shoulder behind her. He ran his tongue up her neck and took both breasts in his hands. "I love your breasts. The way they respond to my touch. The way you respond when I touch them."

Lora-Beth's hands came up and rested on top of his. "I love your hands, your mouth. I love how tender you are with me at times."

"I treasure you." He laid her down and moved over her on the bed. Resting his weight on his elbows, he looked down at her face. Her eyes met his and she took his face between her hands and pulled his lips to meet hers.

"That is not where this was going," he said against her lips.

"I think you need to change those plans."

Austin kissed every bit of skin his lips could reach before Lora-Beth begged him for more. When he found her core, she was drenched. "Fuck," he murmured. He dipped a finger inside before he buried his face in her sweetness. He lapped at her, laving attention on her clit but taking care not to take her there too soon. He slid a finger into her up to the knuckle and stroked her slowly, then added a second finger. He groaned when she shuddered and tightened around him. He flicked at her clit, stroking her just so, and Lora-Beth came in a flourish, gripping the comforter as she gripped his fingers. He stroked her through it, lapping at her, taking everything she gave.

Austin looked down on her as she fought to return to the here and now. Her eyes opened and found his eyes on her, full of love and adoration. He was fully dressed and she was bare to him in every sense of the word. He placed a kiss between her breasts before divesting himself of his clothing and joining them.

Austin lodged himself to the hilt on his first stroke, her orgasm making his entry easy. Lora-Beth wrapped her legs around him and groaned with pleasure. It was incongruous, the way he took her sometimes. His powerful strokes seemed unmatched to his gentle kisses and tender words. This odd combination had her near the edge again. She'd had him inside her for less than two minutes and was on the verge of another orgasm. "I'm going to come again."

He growled before he kissed her and quickened his pace. He broke free and watched her orgasm unfold on her face as he felt it around his body, the way she gripped him from inside and clung to him with her arms and legs. When she came down, he kissed her forehead and whispered, "On your knees." He pulled out and slid off the bed.

Oh God. He wasn't done with her yet. The race may not have worn her out, but it seemed Austin was determined to. He folded over her and slid in slowly, knowing she was hypersensitive from two rapid-fire releases, but he needed to be inside her for as long as he could. They were heading to her parents' and it would be days before he could have her again. He held her hips as he moved slowly within her, placed kisses up her back, and settled at the base of her neck.

She looked back at him over her shoulder and he lost it for a second, as he stroked inside, full tilt. She whimpered and groaned his name. Before he knew it, she was begging him to keep it right there. He placed his thumb in her mouth for her to suck, then placed it on her spot. She came apart and he chased her when she fell onto her stomach on the bed as his orgasm took hold of him.

The animalistic sound he let out with his release drove her crazy. She loved knowing he held nothing back with her.

Whatever he felt, he let it out, let go, and felt it. "Was that my gift?" He laughed and she felt it inside her.

"You are my gift. I don't know what I did to deserve you." He kissed her temple and started lifting off of her.

She groaned in protest, bending her knees and locking her legs over his in an effort to keep them combined. "Not yet."

He chuckled. "I'm smothering you."

"You're not. I like your weight on me."

He rolled them to their sides, wrapped her tightly in his arms, and let out a contented sigh. "You have to take another shower. I love the smell of us on you, but I don't think your folks will appreciate it as much as I do."

"I don't think I have it in me at the moment."

"We'll take as long as you need."

ص

"Can I go first?" Austin asked. She nodded and he pulled the gold box from beneath the tree and handed it to her. She shook it and eyed him curiously. "Well, open it."

She wasted no time undoing the ribbon securing the box. She lifted the lid and peered inside and gasped. "Is this my kitchen?" She lifted the mockup from the box and noticed there were two others. She looked at him wide eyed, not fully understanding.

"These are the three mockups I came up with for your skylight. I started working on the plans and realized with your new skylight, you'd benefit from a new island. And since I knew you wanted to revamp your kitchen anyway, I factored in new cabinets. Well, you can see."

"Austin, are you serious?"

"I have my favorite of the three and I won't tell you which, but whatever you decide, I have a crew that will get started on the skylight right after the first of the year, weather permitting, and we can start looking for cabinetry when we're back from Asheville."

She was speechless, so he went on. "My crew and I will do most of the work, but as I said, I've contracted out the skylight."

"Austin, this is too much. I can't let you do this."

"You can, and you will. Please. It's what I do. Besides, you wouldn't refuse a gift on our first Christmas together, would you?"

"But I didn't have this in the budget right now."

"It's not your budget. It's a gift."

"No, Austin, I —"

He took her chin in his hand and searched her eyes. "It's not. Look, do you love this house?"

"You know I do."

"Do you plan on staying in this house?"

"Yes."

"Do you plan on me being in this house with you? At least until we've outgrown it because we have too many kids?"

She nodded vigorously.

"Then what are we talking about?"

Lora-Beth launched herself into his arms and his outburst of teary laughter filled the room. She placed kisses all over his face. She was so happy. Not just because of the gift. The gift was overly gracious, but the sentiment warmed her to her core. "I absolutely love you."

"I love you too."

"Your gift is going to make my gift look really lame."

"No gift from you could ever be lame." She sat up and looked at the mockups again. Her eyes fixed on the one with light oak cabinets and two-tier island. He liked that one best as well, and if he knew his woman, the more seating in the house, the better.

Lora-Beth set her gift on the coffee table. She reached down and retrieved the box she'd wrapped in navy blue and silver paper and labeled Amante.

Austin looked at it. "Um, I think you gave me the wrong one."

"No. That's yours. I didn't write your name on it, just in case you were a peeker. This means lover."

"Is that what I am? Your lover?"

"Among other things."

Satisfied with that answer, he opened the box to reveal another box. He should have known to expect something like this. When he reached the box that contained his actual gift, he lifted the tickets from it and smiled. She'd remembered.

"So, these aren't the actual tickets. I made these and had them printed. But, since you've never gone, I'm taking you on a weekend trip to DC for a tour of the National Building Museum and a DC Twilight Tour."

For a man who was into the art of architecture, engineering, and design telling stories, this was better than a trip to Disney for a kid. He was touched. He pulled her to him and kissed her. His emotions were getting the best of him.

"You've completely captured the essence of Christmas Eve. This is exactly something my mother would have done."

She beamed under his praise. "Really?"

"Thank you for being willing to allow me to have a little of her here with us."

"Austin! You're going to make me cry again."

"Who knew you were such a crybaby?" he teased. "These are happy tears, I hope."

She brushed a gentle kiss on his lips. "Definitely happy tears."

Chapter Thirty-Seven

Living and loving life was what Lora-Beth had been doing the past several months with Austin. Life was good. Really good. The days were getting longer and the weather was changing. Spring was definitely in the air. Today was Sunday and she'd just awakened to an empty bed. This was unusual since they spent most nights together at either her place or his. And they had this night too. Still, when she realized his arm wasn't around her and she couldn't feel his heat on her body, she sat up with a start.

Austin smiled to himself when he noticed her rousing, searching for his presence. "I'm here," he assured her softly.

"Hey. Why aren't you in bed? What's wrong?"

"Nothing's wrong. I was watching you sleep. Waiting."

"Why didn't you wake me?"

When she moved to get out of bed, he stayed her with a raised hand. "No. Don't get up."

Lora-Beth reached her hand out to him and he rose to his feet. She lifted the covers for him to climb back in bed with her. When he did, she found her spot on his chest and snuggled in, throwing her leg over his and draping her arm over his abdomen. "You're so beautiful, Lora-Beth. Inside and out."

"You're sweet this morning."

"Do you know what today is?"

"Sunday?"

"Yes. Sunday. But more specifically, it's one year since I knocked on your door and you, frantically, in your wet socks, welcomed me like I was an old friend."

"Was that only a year ago? Feels like I've known you much longer."

"From the moment I heard your voice on the phone, something in me recognized something in you. And when I saw your face, your gorgeous face, and radiant smile, and your warm disposition, you grabbed a hold of me and you haven't let go since."

Lora-Beth hadn't realized Austin felt the instant connection as she had on that day. She tried to lift her head to look at him, to share her sentiments, but he held her there, wrapped in his embrace.

"Just listen. I have all these thoughts running through my head and if you're looking at me I may lose them." She placed a kiss on his chest, right where his heart was. "I was a shell of a man, but every time you looked at me, it was obvious that you saw beyond what I was portraying for the world. You saw me when I wasn't even sure I was still in there."

She could feel his heart racing in his chest. As much as she wanted to, she didn't interrupt.

"I didn't think I could have this kind of happiness. I didn't know this kind of raw vulnerability existed. Every part of me is open to you. Every part of me loves you."

"Austin."

"Your face is the first thing my eyes want to see in the mornings and the last thing they want to see at night. My skin longs to feel your skin. My ears listen for your voice, my heart is drawn to your heart." He chuckled at himself. "I love you so goddamned much I'm waxing poetic."

She giggled too, and when she lifted her head this time, he didn't stop her. She looked up at him and saw a bright smile and eyes filled with tears. He kissed the tip of her nose.

"I may never be able to give to you as much as your presence in my life has given me, but I promise I will spend all my days trying and praying that you'll never get tired of me trying."

"I could never tire of you loving me."

"I want to marry you. This isn't me asking, this is—"

She cut him off. "Yes."

"Yes? But I haven't—"

"When you do, the answer will be yes." She straddled him and kissed him thoroughly.

"I wanted to get you a gift. Something to mark this day. I thought about it for weeks. I wanted it to be special. But I honestly don't know what could be special enough to represent the day you shined your light on me. I have something, but I'm not sure now that you've said yes to my proposal when it comes. Kinda feels like my gift won't measure up to the moment."

"Austin, I'm sure I'll love it. So far, you're a great gift giver."

"So you want to open it now then?"

"Yes! You know I do."

"You have to let me up so I can go get it."

Lora-Beth rolled over and sat up on the bed, tucking her feet under her. Austin leaned down, reached under the bed, produced a box, and handed it to her silently.

She shook the box, then ripped it open to reveal a notecard which read: *This isn't your gift.*

She couldn't help but join him in his laughter.

"I'm sorry, that was a decoy."

"Meanie."

"You're cute when you pout." He gave her a chaste kiss before getting up from the bed. "I'll go grab it."

Moments later he called out to her from the door of the hall and she jumped at the sound of his voice. She raced to the door and went in search of him. She found the pantry door open and called out to him before walking over.

"In here," he called back.

Lora-Beth walked to the pantry door and found Austin there, on one knee, velvet box in hand, presenting himself and the ring to her.

She couldn't believe this was really happening. "Austin."

"So I've asked your dad, and you've already said yes, so this is just a formality. You can't take it back."

She rushed to him and met him on her knees. "Yes, yes, yes."

He removed the ring and slipped it on her finger.

"It's gorgeous!"

"This is my mother's ring. My father gave it to me when we visited them last month."

"Now it's mine."

"Now it's yours. I'm yours for as long as you'll have me."

"Forever sounds good to me. Wait, you asked my dad?"

"And your mom. What kind of man do you think I am?"
"The perfect one for me."

Late that year, on the eve of Christmas Eve, Austin Watts stood in front of the big Christmas tree that topped the Christmas decorations in the hall, watching Lora-Beth walk to him on the arm of her dad and fought to hold back his tears. The intimate ceremony had only their families and closest friends. Joyce and David were in attendance. Chris, Marcus, Rob, his brother Alex, and MJ stood at Austin's side. Toni, Tricey, her cousin Chantal, and his sister Erica stood on the other. Rob's two year old daughter served as flower girl, sprinkling soft pink and white lisianthus petals in Lora-Beth's path.

His bride was stunning and he could hardly wait to make their union official. He felt a hand on his shoulder.

"Breathe," Chris teased.

Austin took a deep breath and let it out just as Lora-Beth and her dad stopped in front of him.

"Who gives this woman to be wed with this man?" the minister asked.

"She gives herself, with blessings from her mother and me," Art answered, full of pride.

Lora-Beth could admit to most of the day being a blur. It had all seemed surreal. Like she was watching it rather than living it, but she was fully present now and listening to the minister speak on marriage as she prepared to make her vows to Austin.

"This ceremony will not create a relationship that does not already exist between you. It is a symbol of what you have found in each other," the minister said. He went on. "It is a symbol of the promise to grow together as individuals and as partners. The love between you joins you now as one in the eyes of God and all your friends and family." He looked at the audience and continued. "Austin and Lora-Beth have chosen to share their own vows. Austin..."

"Lora-Beth, meeting you was like walking into a house and knowing I was home. Everything in me recognizes that you are my home and your love is my sustenance. You are light. Your love is the warmth of the morning sun on my face and the moonlight that brightens the dark sky." She touched his face then and he turned and kissed her palm.

"I want to be able to explain the depth of my love for you; but I know that will take me a lifetime. So today I vow to spend the rest of my days proving through my actions that I know what a privilege it is that you chose me.

"On this day, I promise to stand by your side and face the world; to step in front of you when necessary and take your back when the situation calls for it.

"I promise to seek your counsel when I am in need and give mine when asked.

"I promise to be your taste tester and guinea pig; and to never bring you fake ice cream." Everyone chuckled at that one.

"It is my privilege to love you, Lora-Beth, and I promise to love you to the best of my ability, to respect and treasure you and strive to give you the best of myself.

"I promise to choose you, and us, always. Everything that I have, and everything that I am, is yours."

Lora-Beth took her turn. "Austin, you are so easy to love. Somehow, you ended up at my door and brought your calm to my chaos, and I saw you. You spoke and my eyes went to yours and calm came over me. I knew at that moment, my life had changed. That it wasn't by chance, but by some divine intervention, is the most powerful and humbling way I can describe it. You fill me with joy. I love the very thought of you.

"Today, I promise to show you every day how much I love you. I promise to encourage you to follow your dreams and to share mine with you. I promise to never ask you to be anyone other than your true self.

"I promise to challenge you and accept your challenges, to be your biggest fan and partner in crime and games.

"I vow to love you faithfully through good times and bad.

"I promise to build a family with you in a home that is filled with compassion, patience, laughter, and love.

"Austin, in your hands, I place my hand to hold, my heart to keep, and our future to build."

THE END

ACKNOWLEDGMENTS

Bringing *Shadows and Sunshine* into the light has been a journey, one that started several years ago with the first rough draft tucked away, waiting for the right time. This year, I finally decided it was time to "get it out of drafts" and share it with the world.

My deep gratitude to J.L. Seegars and Natasha Bishop for hosting the Pens and Pages romance writer's retreat 2024! It was just what I needed to reignite my passion and get the ball rolling. To my fellow retreat goers being in that space with you was simply wonderful! I walked away inspired. And to those of you in The Smut Peddler Collective who I've leaned on in the months following–Shakerra, Stephanie, Sanetra, and Adrienne–the sessions, your feedback, and unwavering encouragement, all of it is priceless. Thank you. I'm happy we're in this together. I can't wait to also celebrate your upcoming releases!

Melissa, thank you for always showing up; for always supporting me. Ain't no sister like the one I got! Period. You've been listening to me talk randomly about the books I'm writing since forever, and finally, you get to see this one come to life. Let's book a trip to celebrate :)

Ma, my love for books started with you. Watching you read made me fall in love with the written word. Thank you for planting that seed. This one's for us.

A. Noelle Smith is an indie contemporary romance author constructing narratives rooted in love, and its many manifestations. *Shadows and Sunshine* is her debut novel. Her storytelling mirrors the richness and complexity of life itself.

Her journey began early when she discovered her love of reading and later, her true passion: crafting stories where everyday people revel in the depth and beauty of soul touching love.

The Carolina Girl writes from her home in Raleigh, NC.

Visit her online at anoellesmith.com
Instagram:@a.noellesmithwrites
TikTok: @a.noellesmithwrites